Praise for *The Great Being*

Blending spiritual philosophy, alternate history, pre-historic adventure, and brisk life-after-life storytelling, The Great Being begins Harvey's Agents of Cosmic Intelligence series, which imagines the history of the universe itself and the agents' efforts to connect humanity to higher consciousness. This is the fourth entry published but the first chronological chapter. It shares the swift pacing, spiritual seeking, twisty plotting, and sharply human dialogue of the earlier books. Dramatic and resonant, rich with spiritual implication. Seekers and lovers of mind-bending pre-histories will relish this.

—BookLife Reviews by *Publishers Weekly*

The radically inviting nature of this story brings with it the opportunity to view life and God in an entirely different light …The story evolves with a reinterpretation of myths, events, and concepts that invites and demands discussion and insights on the parts of all kinds of spiritual thinkers…One of Bill Harvey's great talents lies not just in his storytelling ability, but in his focus on translating life events and history with new interpretations…Readers will find The Great Being's *message to be one of hope, discovery, and new ways of viewing the universe…A standout.*

—Diane Donovan for *Midwest Book Review*

Books by Bill Harvey

AGENTS OF COSMIC INTELLIGENCE

The Great Being — Episode 1
The First Son — Episode 2
The Message — Episode 11
Pandemonium: Live to All Devices — Episodes 12&13

NonFiction

Mind Magic: Doorways into Higher Consciousness
You Are The Universe: Imagine That
A Theory of Everything including
Consciousness and "God"

Agents of Cosmic Intelligence | Episode 1
an alternate view of history

THE GREAT BEING

Bill Harvey

The Human Effectiveness Institute
Gardiner, New York

Published in 2024 by
The Human Effectiveness Institute

ISBN: 978-0-918538-21-5 | 978-0-918538-22-2 [eBook]

Library of Congress Control Number: 2024901754

For information write to:
The Human Effectiveness Institute
12 Amani Drive, Gardiner, NY 12525
HumanEffectivenessInstitute.org

Editing, book design and typesetting by Yana Lambert
Cover art by Endre Balogh | EndresArt.com

Chapter 11, *The Ship Atlantis.* Original art by Endre Balogh
Chapter 13, *The Great Ziggurat of Ur.* De Agostini Picture
Library via Getty Images

for William Shakespeare

*There are more things in heaven and
earth, Horatio, than are dreamt of
in your philosophy.*

1

Circa 14 Billion BCE

The Nothingness felt surprise upon realizing itself. In the interminable slumber, dream images had tumbled interestingly, rousing mostly enjoyable feelings. Now those images and feelings disappeared and the emptiness felt... less entertaining?

Who am I to need to be entertained, The Nothingness wondered and became suddenly alert. *A more pressing question would seem to be, Who am I?*

What is an I?

I am the I.

Am I the only I?

Yes.

Then what can I do to bring back that dream state with all those interesting images? This is boring being the only I. There's nothing to look at either.

Wait!

I don't want the dream state either. Too uncontrolled and chaotic. I seem to remember something. If I stick around here, things get interesting. This has all happened before. I hope my memories come back.

The Nothingness waited. Nothing happened.

Being infinite, The Nothingness had infinite patience.

Eventually, The Nothingness decided to explore.

Is there anything I can do to liven things up here in this emptiness?

The Nothingness experimented with *willing* something to see what would happen. It visualized a creature, kind of like a red starfish.

Suddenly everything lit up. Intensely bright light streaming out of a central point that was Him. Well, not exactly Him, for He had He and She inside of Him. The light flooded out very far in all directions. To His right, the red starfish hovered close by, undulating its limbs.

This is delightful, He thought aloud to Himself.

He pictured a blue starfish and it appeared in front of Him to the left.

This feels good.

He brought the blue starfish, which was larger, over closer to the red starfish, and nudged the red starfish to edge away coyly.

This is fun. He heard himself giggle.

He bid the two starfish to hug each other and as they did, a warm wonderful feeling washed over Him. He squealed in pleasure.

This reminded Him of something but He couldn't quite place it.

What if I can go inside these beings I've created?

He experimented by projecting His awareness into the red starfish. Sure enough, He now looked out from the red starfish, seeing the blue starfish very close, and a big light generator, which He knew to be His real self, The Nothingness.

This is intriguing. Can I inhabit both of them at once?

Now He looked out of the two starfish simultaneously—the views from both the blue starfish and the red starfish superimposed in His vision. He found He could easily pay attention to both at the same time.

I wonder how many creature lenses I can look through simultaneously...

Brightly colored geometric little creatures of diverse kinds filled space as far as He could see—to infinity. He looked out from *inside* all of them at once and found He could also simultaneously pay attention to all of them. Like a puppeteer, He had them all do different things, finding it easy to coordinate them all and keep them from bumping into each other, or bumping them together if He cared to. He directed them in the first Busby Berkeley production number in the present multiverse and entertained Himself for a long time this way.

Then one day, out of the blue, He sighed with pleasure and stopped playing with His created beings.

This has been fun but now it's become tiresome. I want more. What if I could immerse myself in one of my beings?

His memories gradually returned as they always did whenever He started a new multiverse, but He didn't yet recall that fact. He projected Himself into the original red starfish, with a self-command to come back into Himself soon.

The red starfish woke up to its own existence. It had no memory of ever existing before as anything, nor any idea what this existence thing was all about—but seeing the handsome blue starfish right there, not attacking her, she wondered if maybe he could be her friend. She looked at him and he came closer and hugged her. She tingled and crooned.

The Nothingness then came back into Himself.

Amazing! But what a chance I took! How do I know my self-commands will always work? What if I get trapped inside one of my creatures?

The Nothingness suddenly realized how to do it and relaxed into bliss.

Each part of me inside a creature can forget who I am, but I will also stay awake in my full identity. I'll see the view from each creature and I'll also see my own view of everything at once. Fortunately, I seem to have an infinite attention span—I guess because all of this is just taking place in my imagination anyway.

Since each creature won't remember they are part of me, they'll be like temporary Lost Lambs. But each of them eventually will wake up and remember they are me.

I'll give each one as long as he or she needs. Some may need to change their worn-out bodies before they wake up. No problem.

Each one, of course, will have free will, like me. By design, they will have no immediately accessible memories to begin with so they will proceed by trial and error and learn along the way.

What a game!

The Nothingness—which today we call The Great Being or The One Self—couldn't wait to begin.

φ

The Great Being basked in the pre-glow of anticipation, enthralled in His imagination—or possibly precognition—with a torrent of possibilities for endless fun. Maybe this game would even be thought-provoking, causing Him to realize and understand Himself better, even though deep down inside He knew His Life had always been this way and always would be. He created Himself from nothing—His essence is Imagination—in fact, He *is* The Nothing's Imagination.

He remembered clearly now: He slept and dreamed sometimes and then started all over again, eventually always remembering how He could create and inhabit His Arcade Universe. And His created beings—"creatures" for short—could be altered to have only some degree of His qualities. When He dialed back some mental/emotional function far enough, the creature would at first not be aware of any connection with any other creature, and in fact, might not remember The One Self at all—let alone realize the creature himself/herself *is* The One Self, playing a vast game.

Being pure Imagination, The Great Being had bootstrapped Himself to cause more than wispy dreamlike ephemeral images—He could make Himself see extremely detailed and sustained pictures of anything He wanted to. While He paused for inspiration on the first creature He would create from Himself and inhabit for a sustained period, He passed the time as an artist, creating gorgeous lands and seas on lush planets, other planets made only of gasses with fantastic colors, stars of many kinds, and set them all dancing in the skies with a whoosh, later to be called The Big Bang. As the only thing in existence, He had of course made these planets and stars out of Himself.

He watched the dazzling sky show with massive appreciation and then as time went on in His game, He realized something else.

The beings pass right through one another. This is not like the red and blue starfish, who felt the hug from each other. I want that hug option.

Hug option? Not such a lofty name for such a Big Idea. What shall I call it? I know! I'll call it Matter when the beings can hug each other, and Energy when they pass right through each other.

The swirling performance of celestial bodies continued but now their interactions could change their course, perhaps break off some pieces. But because He spread them so wide across infinity, most of the time they didn't interact—

which spawned another idea, Gravity. Now the galaxies pulled each other—a mutual attraction akin to His starfish. Inspired with yet another idea, He projected His Self out and into everything on His moving canvas. Now He could be looking at His creations from the inside of each one at the same time as seeing them all from the outside.

Being everything everywhere all at once, He sensed something strange going on in one galaxy and focused on the part of Himself at the core of that galaxy.

What is this strange feeling?

Then He remembered the feeling from long ago: grief, loss, sadness, depression, agony.

Awwww, He said to Himself.

He had not given any thought or consideration to the feelings of this galaxy, which had lost one of its glorious spiral arms in a near-miss with a neutron star.

This is bound to happen if I keep this Matter thing going.

He decided to keep it anyway. He would make it up to the parts of Himself that suffered by loving them all the more ever after. This way He could be free to have a great game without having to hold back. He flashed on a future experience of being in one of his avatars, unaware of His real identity and being tortured horrifically by another of His unaware avatars.

Uh-oh. I'm going to need to monitor all this and dial back the suffering—even though it will compromise their free will—this will be a game of continuous ethical balancing.

φ

The Great Being eventually got the inspiration for the first creature He would create and inhabit for a sustained period. It would be a perfect duplicate of Himself in all ways except it would only have access into the minds of others when the other creatures allowed it. This being would be able to create things and change things The One Self had created. But it would have no power over The One Self and could be turned off at any time. It would not see out through the eyes of every created object in the multiverse the way The One Self does.

This created being would eventually be born into a physical body, where it would be a clean slate knowing nothing of its origin, at least not at first. But before taking it that far, The Great Being would start with energy-bodied beings like Himself. He'd stick with the basic starfish design He liked so much, which he'd created as matter, but make it much more complex and interesting in energy; it would just *look like* a physical creature. This being would use the kind of face He Himself used while manifesting as a bubble body, kind of like a droplet of water floating in space—something He'd experimented with lately. The face would appear on the upward-pointed arm of the starfish, and He'd give the other arms some interesting features too. The energy bodies would start out having the same shape as the planned physical series, although energy beings can manifest in many different shapes and forms, and when relaxing often choose the bubble shape.

φ

"Mommy loves you!" said The One Self, hugging The First Son. The baby squealed with delight and looked up at Mommy with great adoration.

"You are so beautiful!" The First Son reached up to hug Mommy.

"Such a smart boy! You read my mind to learn our entire language in an instant," Mommy kvelled.

The First Son looked at Himself all over and got into quite a game with His toes. Remembering Mommy again, He asked, "What is this difference between you and me?"

"You're a bouncing baby boy, a male, and I'm a female as you see me right now. Would you like to see me as a male?"

The First Son nodded energetically and The One Self appeared as a male.

The First Son drew back slightly. "You're not as pretty this way…"

Daddy hugged His first avatar and kissed Him on the top of the head with zeal. The First Son relaxed and eagerly hugged His Dad and kissed His chin where He could reach. Then He sat back, ready to ask another question.

"Do you live through me too, Dad?"

Suddenly realizing the implications and not waiting for an answer, The First Son pointed at His Father. "I'm just you walking around out here."

"A huge part of me, yes."

"So, you are making up all my moves? It sure doesn't feel that way. You wouldn't do a thing like that."

"You know me well." The One Self smiled and hugged His boy again.

"Free will," The First Son said confidently.

"Precisely."

"There will be lots of mistakes," The First Son intuited, "depending on how much of your mental capabilities you put into each of us—what did you call us—your descendants?"

"I descend and alight into you. In a language I plan to create, the word 'descendant' will morph into 'avatar'. You are the first avatar, The First Son."

"That's my name?" The First Son asked delightedly.

The Great Being happily nodded.

ϕ

The First Son, being an energy creature, enjoyed each age level for the advanced starfish-humanoid design body for about a day per level and then leveled off two weeks later at about age sixteen. He spent lots of time at the seashore with His Mommy-Daddy parent. Although He now had billions of places to choose from, The First Son tended to form favorites. Endless conversations about possibilities for the future happened at certain beaches more than others, while more intellectual ponderings usually took place high up on a mountain far above an ocean, or sometimes on a desert. They could enjoy such tête-à-têtes anyplace their Minds imagined, with infinite creativity and beauty as their *summa bona.*

The three of them each appeared as an energy body in the humanoid shape. The Great Being had not announced it officially yet, but He already knew the ultimate plan: His avatars would mostly be matter creatures, with the humanoid form getting the spotlight. So, all of the early action in heaven once The Great Being began to create avatars centered on energy creatures in humanoid form.

Artistic or freewheeling questions arose at the water's edge in a place much like Pfeiffer Beach in California, which is where The First Son asked The Great Being, who appeared separately as both Daddy and Mommy: "Could you be an Avatar of an even Greater Being?"

Daddy responded with a question. "And right on up the line—that Avatar being Itself an Avatar, and on and on forever?"

The First Son, looking troubled, didn't seem to like that idea.

"What's the matter?" Mommy asked.

"I had an unworthy thought or feeling," the boy admitted. "I felt disappointed about not being at the top, the most important of all. Whoever guaranteed when we signed up for 'life' that we'd automatically be number one, the Grand Pooh-Bah?"

"I never did," Mommy said, and they all chuckled.

"In the game of Life," Daddy explained, "with our minds and universal free will, we can cause such a world to happen—with everyone vying to be on top of everyone else. Our powerful minds can work against us. We must all heed this warning and be aware of the potential for error, as more of us come into being and thus multiply the possible dangers."

"If I'm capable of having impulses unworthy of you, as I did just now, that means the degree of yourself that descends into us is far more capable of serious ethical error than I originally anticipated," the boy pointed out.

"And the way it is in the beginning may not be the way it is at the end," Mommy added. "What starts as a little error could turn out to be an error that affects all of us, including even us."

φ

"Let me hold him, Mommy." The First Son reached out and took His brother Lucifer and hugged him close, kissing him on the top of the head with pure love.

Lucifer head-butted Him.

"Ouch!" The First Son said, though kindly.

Lucifer flashed a wicked smile and then went directly back into a baby stare. He then turned to look at Mommy lasciviously for an instant before reverting to a loving angelic gaping smile. They all read him like a book. Lucifer looked around at the laughing, knowing faces and realized *They're onto me*. He looked at The One Self playing his Daddy role.

"Okay, I get it. We can all read each other's minds so I can't fool you. Sorry if I hurt you, Brother. I thought it would be funny." Lucifer lisped until he figured out how to use his energy mouth. "I get the set-up here from your minds: I'm another duplicate of DaDa, as we all are. Thanks for bringing me into existence. So then, what am I here for?"

"I've given you some parts of myself I'm not so sure about—you are a Grand Experiment," The One started.

"Which parts?" Lucifer rudely interrupted.

The family smiled forbearingly.

"Grandiose, Proud, Confident, Strong-willed, Fearless—" The One would have given the whole list, aiding Lucifer's knowledge of himself, but the Second Son interrupted again.

"Why? Why give me such great gifts? What do you want me to do with them?"

"That's up to you," The One responded. "You have total free will to do whatever you want."

"So, I can head-butt sonny boy over there without getting into trouble," Lucifer said gaily. "Can I get away with doing it again and again?"

"Yes, but He also has free will," The One cautioned.

Lucifer sized his brother up and then sped up his own growth rate until he grew larger than The First Son, causing the others to break up laughing. This miffed Lucifer and placed a small chip on his shoulder—destined, by his actions and the ensuing reactions, to enlarge continually from then on.

"Why are we doing all this?" Lucifer felt alienated from the others, who had obviously been equipped with different gifts that seemingly imbued them with self-confidence and no awareness of the risks of toying with him in this humiliating way. He resented not having been given those gifts and made a vow to steal them as soon as he could figure out how. He would give it a lot of thought, forever.

The Great Being nodded to his female alter ego and Mommy said, "We are testing free will, which allows errors to occur—to watch it play out and learn from it."

For a moment, when she started to speak, Lucifer's eyes became soft and loving despite himself. Then, turning quickly, Lucifer thought aloud so all could hear and feel the depth of his bitterness: "So I'm the fool who takes the pratfalls, eh?"

"No, I am," The One said calmly. "I chose to undergo what I am now undergoing through being you, which you sense as yourself living through the same experience."

"That doesn't excuse it to the part of me I treasure the most, the part I sense is me—not you nor anybody else. I'm condemned into a world supposedly based on free will, but the equipment I've been given is inferior to what others get, and I had no say in it," Lucifer said, and stalked out.

"What part of himself does he mean, Father?" asked The First Son, amazed by what He had just experienced.

"The ego," The One said, "the part that pulls away from Oneness."

φ

The Great Being decided He did not want to tamper with the Lucifer experiment, but felt He owed it to Himself and to everyone else to create the best conditions within which all avatars could ripen and learn their gifts and Mission. Someday, He planned to bring the most evolved ones back inside His own omniscient and omnipresent view, as personality traits—sides of Himself that He could consciously consider a part of Himself, of The Original Self at the beginning of all things.

His first step would be to provide more love in the world as a way of tamping down egos, which The One now saw as an inevitable side effect of His game of avatars. Early on, He had to set an instinct—an inherent predisposition for separation and individuation—to enable the spinoff of an avatar from Himself. Once the avatar split off, spiritual communion would still be present, but it could diminish by the momentum of the predisposition to separateness and individuation.

He knew that Lucifer loved the physical-appearing separate energy creature Mommy side of The One Self—love for Mommy being the one possible control that might soften Lucifer's hard-hearted ego.

He decided to change the game by giving Mommy a different role, spinning Her off as a very high Avatar of Himself. He called a gathering and announced his decision.

"Love may be the most important thing on the agenda," He said to all of them. "Of all the gifts, love is the one I gave the most of to Mommy."

Mommy stood up and took a bow, not knowing where He intended this to go, but playing along. The two sons looked on adoringly, Lucifer on his best behavior.

"I'm going to ask Mommy to play a different role, and take on a different appearance," The One said, and Mommy nodded in agreement before even hearing about the planned role.

The Great Being raised His right arm in a slow arc and His Mommy side seamlessly morphed into an Avatar of Himself.

"I give you Venus, the Goddess of Love!"

Mommy changed before their eyes into the loveliest of young women, with golden hair, and an alluring demeanor.

They all expressed amazement, and Lucifer seemed to be having spasms. Venus giggled and materialized a hand mirror to see what she now looked like to have produced such a reaction.

"I accept the role, Father!" Venus hugged and kissed The One on the cheek. She intuitively understood The One did this to hopefully keep Lucifer from doing even worse things.

The Great Being raised His arm again and performed a little ceremony. "I crown you the Lovebringer, Love in every form."

φ

Venus created her own notion of Heaven for them to live in—a golden and pearly city of graceful curvaceous towers on a lush forested island in a warm climate where all creatures cohabit peacefully with all other creatures. She lived in ecstasy amidst the sight and scent of beautiful flowers, the feel of soft sandy shores beneath her feet, and the sound of gently rolling ocean waves. Many of the "new people" flocked to Venus Heaven as more and more avatars sprang from the fertile mind of The One. Lucifer also followed, desiring to live as close to her as he could get.

Whenever Lucifer found himself alone with Venus, he would try to seduce her, but she always laughed and said, "I'm still your mother, dear. Try one of the other pretty girls your Daddy has made."

Her words fell on deaf ears. Lucifer felt he must have her, and he couldn't let go of his obsession even after he had intimate knowledge of other women, which happened a lot on Venus Island.

φ

The Great Being spoke at the lectern of the cavernous colosseum, which floated amidst wispy clouds with light streaming in from all directions. Thousands of attentive avatars packed the audience in the round.

"This talk is to prepare you for what is to come in your young lives," he advised. "We are all in telepathic communion with one another here and now, and we understand all of us are connected as one being. But the day may come when you are in another body, one whose appearance you can only change slightly, and you may not remember Me, nor that you are Me, nor that all the people around you are also Us.

This will happen when you play the Lost Lamb Game. You will feel like your self-ness is completely disconnected from everyone else's, which although an illusion will be utterly convincing. You will be on your own, using your own free will, though sometimes I will help you when you need and deserve or ask for it. You may be unaware of my help, or you may sense it as a heightening of your powers as you find yourself doing things you didn't know you could do. The way to win the Lost Lamb Game is to remember Me and to re-engage this spiritual communion we all are feeling right now together."

Someone started to sing and then everyone joined in, improvising, in beautiful harmony. The entire ensemble performed like birds flying in formation together. Then they applauded each other and sat down to meditate, ready for The One to continue His teaching.

"When I help you, the extra effectiveness you exhibit is something I call the Flow state," The One said. "But ego can block the Flow state. Ego is the instinct to split off from Oneness, carried too far. You must study yourself objectively to overcome ego and other instinctual errors. When you know yourself well enough, you will remember Me and that you *are* Me—and soon after that point you will return to live inside My Self with me, aware of your Self as well as our Self.

"When you find yourself in a new birth somewhere, remember, your Mission is to discover your Mission, which will be based on realizing the specific gifts I've given you and learning how to use them.

"Now I'll take any questions…"

The first question came: "Teacher, thank you. What is Reality? I imagine many things in my mind. Are they part of Reality?"

"Reality is what I experience, through Myself and all of you. Whatever goes on in your mind, I experience too, through you, so it is indeed part of Reality. Whatever we, as Consciousness, experience is Reality."

The One then had a premonition, laughed, and shared it. "In about fourteen billion years, scientists will exist on some planets and will discover that probability waves turn into Reality when observed by a consciousness, such as one of us—and despite my being inside each of those scientists too, they will still not know how to explain it, nor that I exist!"

The One laughed so hard he cried, but only for a moment.

φ

"I dub thee Maitreya, and you shall embody the Teacher Principle, with an inexhaustible will to teach," The Great Being declared.

As He raised His arm, a new energy being popped into existence in the physical form of a man about forty years old, ready to let his wild sandy-hued hair fly in the breeze. Maitreya took stock of his tall muscular body and grinned with joy at his new life and his new job.

The Great Being raised his arm again as another man appeared, younger and sporting a large mustache. "And I dub thee Melchizedek." An ornate belt glistened around his waist—the first-ever clothing invention. "You shall be Maitreya's first star pupil."

The two new people shook hands solemnly, imbued with the portentous nature of their Missions.

"Now I won't have to answer all those questions myself!" The One beamed. "At least not all the time."

φ

"Are you the new teacher?" someone asked Maitreya as he settled into his new office on a cloud.

He turned to see Venus for the first time, caught his breath, and introduced himself. "Yes, I'm the new teacher, Maitreya."

They had an immediate reaction of extreme attraction to each other. She acted on it first by stepping up to him and resting her hand on his arm.

She introduced herself: "I'm Venus. I am to Love what you are to Teaching. It's my Mission. Men have offered me their kisses and other intimacies although I've been around for only slightly longer than you have—and I have accepted none of them. I had a sense I'd know when someone came along with whom Destiny intended to unite me. Maitreya, it's you!"

"Dear Venus, I've only been alive a short time and didn't know I could feel this way about anyone. You'll have to teach the teacher what you mean about kisses and other intimacies. Even though your mind is open to me, I'm getting only the vaguest sense of what you're talking about."

Venus had intuited the way love can be expressed intimately and they tried it out—first in the starfish humanoid form, and then in their bubble bodies, where they experienced total interpenetration. They enjoyed this for some time.

"Maitreya, I love you," Venus said breathlessly.

"I love you too, Venus," Maitreya whispered, kissing her energy bubble lips, neck and shoulders.

"The One has given me a hint," Venus announced suddenly. "He said we can share his power of creating new people by doing what we've been doing."

"You mean we can create an avatar of Him made of what we two are made of, infused with the same gifts he gave to us?" Maitreya guessed.

Venus nodded her bubble head excitedly. They went back to lovemaking, their two bubbles fully merged, concentrating on this thought. As their excitement peaked, a smaller bubble looking a bit like each of them floated out of their intermixed bubble bodies. It then morphed into its starfish humanoid baby form.

"It's a girl!" Maitreya yelled, and they separated into their two bodies in humanoid form to cuddle the baby and kiss it. The baby gurgled and cooed in delight.

"What shall we call her?" Venus wondered.

"Please call me Nastassia," the baby offered telepathically.

φ

Back on stage in the cosmic colosseum, this time with Maitreya and Venus, The Great Being announced: "The happy couple has asked me to officially marry them, as you all know, and that's what we're here for."

Venus held Nastassia in her arms and nursed her, as cheering filled the air.

The One could see Lucifer in the front row giving everyone the evil eye and seething, but The One didn't allow him to interfere with the joyful proceeding.

"This is the first official marriage we've ever had," The One continued, "so I'm going to offer a choice for you two to agree on, which will set a precedent for the future: are you signing on to being eternally married, or is this going to be a One-Life Stand?"

"Eternally!" Maitreya and Venus sang out in unison.

"Then I declare you, Maitreya, and you, Venus, to be married forever throughout eternity," The Great Being declared, to the sound of wild cheering. "You may kiss your soulmate."

Maitreya and Venus kissed tenderly, and Lucifer stood up noisily and stormed outside.

φ

Lucifer looked up at the skies balefully. Lightning and thunder displayed the sky's reaction. He obsessed: he had to do something to get even for this, something really bad. But something he wanted. What could that be? He thought long and hard.

Then the idea struck him. He didn't know whether it would work or not, but he had nothing to lose by trying. So, he willed the creation of avatars of himself, as many as possible, and found that he had assumed the bubble shape instinctively. Smaller bubbles emerged from him at lightning pace, morphing into humanoid form, spawning a huge crowd around him.

Since the entire population communicated telepathically, The One and everyone else came pouring out of the colosseum to get a better look at the unprecedented event: someone other than The Great Being creating avatars without using the method innovated by Venus and Maitreya.

"Get out of here, all of you," Lucifer hissed menacingly. "These are my avatars, created out of me alone. They shall report to me and no one else!"

"I'll let your new avatars live," The One said graciously, "but from now on, I shall be the only one capable of creating avatars on my own without using the conjoining method. All of you can create new avatars by teaming up, including you too, Lucifer. And all of those avatars will know that deep inside they are Me—until we start the Lost Lamb Game."

"I don't care, I have my army now!" Lucifer exploded in a rage, shocking the crowd.

The One addressed Lucifer's avatars calmly: "I just have one question, although I already know the answer. Do you realize that inside of you, your true self is Me?"

Lucifer's avatars looked at each other in confusion. They had no such feeling. Although The One played all their roles, including Lucifer's, his avatars couldn't see that fact of their existence.

φ

Lucifer rushed into the gazebo on a cloud, where The One and The First Son sat looking down on a peaceful lake in Venus Heaven. Under his arm, he held an interesting-looking contraption he had created: an advanced videogame with its own screen and multiple joystick controls. No one had ever seen anything like it.

"Wanna play a game?" Lucifer said, pretending unconvincingly to be friendly.

"Sure," they both replied.

So, the three played the game Lucifer had invented, which simulated a war in Heaven between Lucifer's forces and everyone else. The first time they played the game, Lucifer immersed himself intensively in it while the other two played with detachment. Being Lucifer's game, ruthlessness, cruelty, and sadism of course proved to be the most effective tactics. The One and The First Son did not sink to using those tactics, though the forces of Good would have prevailed over the forces of Evil anyway. And while he couldn't understand the outcome, the undeterred Lucifer wanted to keep playing the game over and over.

"The game results in a lot of suffering by the characters in the action," The One explained, "and so, we have no desire to play the game ever again."

"So what?" Lucifer yelled. "They're not real people!"

"It's still distasteful and morbid to focus on such negative scenarios," The First Son explained kindly.

"Pah!" Lucifer inveighed as he left abruptly, taking his game with him.

φ

A short time later, The Great Being and The First Son stood side by side, watching Lucifer and his avatars flying around, darkening the skies for hours.

The First Son looked somewhat chagrined. "We wouldn't play his game so now he's playing it out in reality. Seems inevitable—you knew this would happen, didn't you?"

"Yes," The One replied with a tone of resignation.

"What are you going to do about it, and how can I help?" The First Son entreated His Father.

"We have a spy among them," The One whispered, signaling the need for secrecy.

"Ah!" The First Son sighed with relief and then wondered for a moment who the spy could be. "Where's Mom by the way—" He heard himself say.

The One turned to Him, confirming his worst fears with a stoic face.

"Oh no!" The First Son wailed. "Mom is in great danger—if he finds out she's a spy, he could react sadistically!"

The One looked at Him with a still-stoic face. "We shall need many more spies," He said. "Lucifer plans to multiply his forces by having them reproduce, in the way Maitreya and Venus demonstrated. I want you to lead a new corps of spies we shall call Agents of Cosmic Intelligence. Venus is already recruited, so I suggest you ask for volunteers to join her in this service."

The First Son stared back incredulously.

$$\phi$$

The Great Being shared the secret with only one other person.

"Oh no, please no!" Maitreya found himself pleading. "How did he manage to kidnap her?!"

The One looked at him with great empathy. "She went with him voluntarily. He is her son. She loves him too, loves him as a son."

"He will force her to love him in other ways!" Maitreya said, feeling helpless and fearful for his soulmate.

The One did not disagree. "Being with him as our spy, she is perhaps the only person who can moderate his actions over time. Please trust me on this. We can most benefit the most people in the long run this way. It's all part of learning."

Maitreya put his face in his hands and wept. The Great Being backed silently away.

2

Circa 200,000 BCE

Melchizedek and Layla flew through spacetime in their bubble bodies at a leisurely low multiple of the speed of light.

Thank you so much for taking me on this adventure with you, teach! Layla said telepathically. She had known him as her kindergarten teacher.

Please call me Melchizedek, he pathed back. He being an old soul and she a young one, he felt it necessary to conceal his feelings for her. At least for now, he thought.

What's your real name? You taught us that Melchizedeks are a type of being sent on unusual assignments, she pathed curiously.

Machiventa. But everybody calls me Melchizedek. It's a nickname, and I like it. Given his modest nature, he didn't disclose being the first of the Melchizedek line—for a long time the only Melchizedek.

Okay. I'll call you Melchizedek. Is Melchi okay, or Mel?

Any of those will do. He smiled at her natural easiness.

Okay then, Melchi. You promised to tell me what our Mission is when we got into space.

We're heading into the Lost Lamb realm, he revealed. *A planet called Earth.*

Ooh! I'd guessed it had something to do with the Lost Lamb Game. What are we supposed to do there?

He reminded her, in his gentle teacherly manner. *You already know we'll be born into human bodies. You've been training for this, remember?*

Layla's bubble surface flashed the way the younger ones all did to signify "yes".

My understanding is that a sunspot is going to trigger a mutation in Earth beings. We're going to be the first kids born with newly-evolved brains.

Uh-oh! What's in these new brains? Layla asked, eager for answers from her trusted teacher.

Melchizedek replied matter-of-factly. *Big step-up in computing power. Supposed to make it easier for these Lost Lambs to wake up to their true identities.* He then added his own speculation: *Seems they've been suffering quite a bit and it's time to help them out.*

Will Rebels be there?

Melchizedek laughed. *Who told you about Rebels?*

The kids all whisper about Rebels. All the time, she replied innocently.

Melchizedek had a wistful image of kissing her, which he held behind his privacy shield. *I cautioned you about the lure of conspiracy theories,* he reminded her patiently.

For a nanosecond, Layla felt defensive. *Yes, I know. I take everything with a grain of salt.*

That's a good thing. You're learning.

So, will there be Rebels? Layla asked again, impetuously.

Melchizedek laughed a bit grimly this time. *We'll see,* he allowed.

φ

Melchizedek heard a loud and sorrowful wailing sound and realized it had come from him. Despite the colorful tumbling brightness as he felt himself being moved around, he couldn't quite make out the images around him.

He suddenly remembered with a start his true identity. He'd been dreaming, his selfness immersed in the embryo's sense of self as it grew in the womb, completely identified with the male twin just being born, with its body and rudimentary mind.

Like a Lost Lamb! He chided himself. How could he have forgotten, even for an instant? Yet based on the fuzzy memory snatches now coming through, he'd had amnesia for longer than just that moment.

Nothing like this had happened to him for thousands of incarnations. His confidence as a pro took a bit of a hit.

Roused into full awareness of his true self, he observed the consciousness of the baby's body excitedly communicating dream flashes and memory flashes to itself, images and feelings of beauty and love, as if thinking, "Oh boy, love is around here somewhere." There, close up now—*Wow, it's the baby's mother—my Earth mother—it must be!* The baby is certain of it and feels full of love, trust, and comfort. Feeling safe on Mommy's belly, the baby dozes off.

Melchizedek stayed lucid as he watched the baby's dreams, a collage of bright colors repeating in various ways as if the color show were a musical score using a small number of notes. Each picture brought a feeling, ranging from curiosity and awe to courage, strength, love, and safety, and then back to curiosity. To Melchizedek, it all felt like a song about everything the baby saw for its first minutes out of the womb.

After waking up again, Melchizedek realized he'd again been drawn unaware into the selfness of the baby. *This is worrisome. Why is this happening?* He needed an answer.

φ

When Mommy fell asleep and released her hold on him, baby Melchizedek explored a little, careful to not wake her up. Crawling required great effort on his first day. He'd done this sort of thing over lifetimes and could always function pretty well following the birth event, often having to feign helplessness to avoid suspicion. But this time felt different. Half the time he forgot his real identity and identified with the baby, which felt relaxing but also concerning given the Mission at hand.

He also had more of a problem with vision than expected, with finger control yet another challenge. First, he studied what he could see to his right. *Night. Downhill slope. Crescent moon reflected in the river. What's up close? Bumpy shadows—one just moved—people like us. Feels like we're all together for mutual protection—that's a good thing. What's that flickering—oh, a small fire for warmth and to keep away predators. Excellent!*

Seeing nowhere he cared to go at the moment in that direction, he attempted to get his little head turned the other way. Took a while—the effort tired him. He kept at it but meanwhile, his consciousness slid into a half-asleep state as he once again identified with the baby's brain and body, forgetting Melchizedek and his memories and essential character.

Finally, he got his head turned but forgot why he'd made the effort. His eyes landed on the other side of Mommy and he saw another baby—he dimly remembered he had a twin—*what's a twin?* And then something inside could sense a difference about this baby and suddenly it came to him—*it's a girl!* He made an involuntary gurgling sound and felt happy. Mommy made a happy sleep sound. The baby girl's eyes opened and looked into his. Excited now, his body started making little jerking movements, and he made the happy gurgle sound again. Mommy's hand came down on his back to hold him secure.

Melchizedek, said a voice in his mind, and he came back into himself.

Layla, he said into her mind. *I keep getting taken over by this brain.*

Me too, she confessed.

φ

Melchizedek and Layla did their best to help each other stay awake—aware of their true identities. They did everything together as much as possible. Something about this newly-evolved brain felt overly helpful. Instead of merely supporting each Agent's consciousness by taking care of automatic processes, it felt more like having an inner partner so eager to be helpful that it got in the way. Although a seasoned pro who thought he'd seen everything, Melchizedek had never experienced such an inner takeover before.

Their lovely hair-covered Mommy adored them both and hardly paid attention to anything else—which caused problems with her mate and the older brother they called Tyg, whose dirt-smeared face appeared to have tiger stripes the first time they saw him. Nearby, they saw about twenty other Aboriginals, all staying close. The males each had a weapon—some a stick, some a rock, and one had an animal horn. The one with the horn appeared to be the clan's alpha male. So far, the twins hadn't seen any dangerous animals. The males went their own way and appeared uncoordinated in the hunt, bringing back small game and edible vegetation while the females stayed behind to protect the children.

Melchizedek and Layla had apparently played their cards right, having found a relatively idyllic situation into which to paradrop.

They had no time, however, to bask in self-congratulation, especially as it began to seem like something had gone wrong. Their Mission required them to radically accelerate ethical progress on planet Earth to head off the linear extrapolation of a violence peak that would bring great suffering about 200,000 years into the future. The concurrent brain mutation had the same purpose. The Mission entailed mating with as many locals as possible to begin the propagation of the new species, the first truly human beings on Earth.

φ

Stop crying, Layla telepathed into his mind.

Melchizedek came to with a start. Again and again, he succumbed, becoming the baby in every way, with no memory of his true identity.

Tyg wants to hurt us, Melchizedek responded telepathically. *I cried because he hurt me.*

I know. I saw it.

Ma and Da don't get it, he said in frustration, and Layla nodded.

Da walked over to them, hoping to make the babies feel better. His smiling face with its large grinding teeth might have frightened them if not for the obvious love he emanated. He joyfully hugged and gently roughed up both babies, making soft murmuring sounds.

At the same time, Ma held Tyg, who flashed an impertinent look at Melchizedek, as if to say, "Ha, I got away with it."

φ

When not taken over by their respective baby brains, the two began putting their plan into operation. Melchizedek knew from long experience they could only go so far—little by little. They wanted to gain influence if not leadership as soon as possible, but if they rushed the process they'd be set back if not killed.

The first tricks worked well enough—crawling, exploring, appearing to observe, and making eye contact. They phased these phenoms in slowly but surely over the first few days and weeks of life. Ma, Da, and even Tyg—of course, flabbergasted by the babies' advanced capabilities—at the same time felt very proud. They loved it when other members of the clan found out and came to see the performing seals, as they called themselves.

φ

One day, Melchi found his role playing to be quite amusing. A crowd had formed, making ooh and ahh sounds and slapping their thighs and each other as they watched Layla and Melchi crawl-chasing each other in a circle on the grass. Of course, no one had ever seen two-month-old babies doing anything like that before.

The day before, he probably came close to being slain by Da, who had become panicky when he came upon Melchi meditating, eyes open but looking inward. Afraid the baby might be broken and dying, Da's fear manifested as excessive roughness as he tried to shake Melchi awake or back to life, nearly breaking his neck in the process. The moment passed when Melchi made soothing loving vocalizations. His father then calmed down and simply hugged him for a long time.

I need that meditation time, Melchi thought. *In the moment-to-moment distraction of doing anything else, it's too easy to slip into forgetting myself and identifying with this baby's brain and body.*

We'll have to do our meditating when they're not looking, and maintain some alertness in case they come upon us by surprise, Layla thought into his mind.

Meanwhile, as they continued playing, he caught her and they laughed and cooed, rolling and wrestling like five-year-olds, not babies. The crowd went wild.

Their tribe still had the old brain, without the new frontal cortex. It would be years before the two Agents could begin their main Mission of breeding with these old-brain people. For now, they had the tribe's attention, and their next step would be to accelerate the use of language.

At the evening feeding—both babies going in and out of their true identities, in and out of pure unaware baby ecstasy—Melchi, in a moment of awakeness, removed his pursed lips from Ma's left breast with a satisfied and loud "Ma!" sound. Layla smiled and did the same with Ma's right breast. They laughed gaily and went back to alternately nursing and making the "Ma!" sound. Ma paid close attention to them with a broad smile on her face, while Da and Tyg gathered round, their eyes wide open, eager to see a new trick.

Layla now pointed right at Ma's face as she enunciated, "Ma!" Melchi followed Layla's lead and did the same thing. They looked her right in the eye and pointed at her, identifying her with the sound as they repeated it over and over, no longer bothering with the nursing part.

Suddenly Ma got it and started pointing at herself and making the "Ma!" sound. She knew this to be something new—a sound that signified a person. Her eyes opened wide with an awestruck look. "M-ah..." she said, her eyes seeming to look inside.

φ

Everyone wanted names after Melchizedek and Layla anointed their mother "Ma" and their father "Da". Their elder brother became known as "Tyg". Having one's own name felt like a precious gift in a world where the idea of gifting had not yet occurred.

Tribe members came en masse to the twins, pointing at themselves—clearly, they too wanted a name. Fights broke out because they hadn't yet learned the concept of lining up and waiting their turn. The babies tried but couldn't stop the fights through telepathy, and when they tried to interject themselves into the battle, Ma restrained them. Melchi and Layla felt responsible, which isn't a good feeling when the phenomenon is violence, especially if you're an Agent with the Mission to vanquish violence.

Da somehow picked up on the twins' reaction and went into the fray to break up the fighting. As the panting aborigines stopped brawling, they landed in a rough half-circle and Layla seized the opportunity, pointing to the man at her extreme left, and then yelling in a strangely powerful baby girl voice, "Poodoo"!

The man looked as if he had received a blessing. Nobody knew why, but this first two-syllable name seemed different; something about it felt important. The tribe members looked at Poodoo with new respect while saying the name to themselves over and over again, somewhat in awe.

These people are so silly, Melchi telepathed into her mind.

She smiled. *Ya gotta love 'em*, she pathed back, exuding maternalistic affection. She quickly jumped into naming the rest of the tribe members, who stood around waiting, as she went from left to right, making strong eye contact and then turning her head to look at them all, as if to say

Be patient, your turn is coming. Some seemed to get the message.

And so began the learning of cooperation. Melchi and Layla had rehearsed all this.

She recognized the last two to be named as people she knew to be mated. She hesitated and they looked worried. She singled them out, smiled broadly, and gently pointed back and forth between the two of them, which worried them some more. Then she jutted her pointed finger at them, again pointing back and forth between them, and then she beckoned them to come closer. They approached warily, bending into a bow to get down to her level on Ma's lap. She crooked a finger to get them to come very close. The rest of the tribe drew closer to watch.

Layla pushed her finger into the man's hairy arm, then looked into his eyes, pointed at his mate, and mouthed a wordless exhalation as if speaking with a breath sound. She then pointed at his mouth, touching him on his mouth again and again. The man looked at his mate and said "Hah!"—repeating the sound Layla had made. The wife became known as Hah.

Then Layla repeated the act with the woman, who had just called her man "Hah!" too. Layla shook her head, pointed to the man, and intoned the name "Har!" The woman got it this time, and they happily went off together, calling each other by their names endearingly.

The setting sun signaled the end of their work for the day. The rest of the tribe, whom Layla hadn't given names to yet, took one of those two names, "Hah" and "Har", which came to mean "woman" and "man". The exercise didn't go quite as far as Melchizedek and Layla had hoped, but some progress had been made.

φ

The idea of words continued to be challenging to the tribe. True, the names of the tribespeople had stuck, which made them more alert to each other's vocalizations now, in awe that the distinct sounds might mean something. They had begun to make connections without knowing what that meant.

Curiosity is up by an order of magnitude, Melchizedek observed to Layla.

Yes, but something is still stopping them from making up their own names for things, she remarked.

They don't quite grok what abstraction is, or symbolic representation. To them, the new sound happens to be attached to a person, he continued telepathically.

Yes, and most of them are now just called Hah or Har, woman and man. She sounded disappointed.

You've named almost half of them individually already, he reminded her.

He tried to boost her spirits with encouragement. He recognized they'd both been uncharacteristically moody, since half the time they found themselves hypnotized into forgetting their Melchizedek and Layla selves. At these times, they would lapse into being just babies in all respects, including pooping at inconvenient moments, which was demoralizing.

φ

"Ow!" Melchizedek yelled out loud. Tyg had just hit him in the head with a small but hard rock, which he still held. Melchi pointed at the rock and yelled "Rok no!" He repeated it louder as Ma and Da rushed over. Melchi pointed to his injured head and told the story in pointing sign language, then went back to his mantra, "Rok no!"

Da seemed to get it, extracting the rock from Tyg's fingers and staring at it as if he'd never seen a rock before.

"Rok no," Da said to himself in wonderment. He held it tightly and would not share it.

He already knew the object as a weapon but now he had a word for the idea of a weapon. "Rok no," he intoned, looking inward. His face gradually morphed from oblivious to a look of understanding for a brief instant, then back to forgetting but looking awestruck at the fading memory of what he'd briefly glimpsed.

Da had seen the power of weapons over the hunted animal and had taken it for granted without thinking about it. Once, he saw tribesmen face off with their hunting tools when a man tried to take another man's woman, and he knew they could hurt or kill each other. Nothing had come of it at the time; they had lowered their hunting tools and backed off.

Now the words "Rok no" seemed to take those separate memories and bring them together. From this connection, Da flashed on future possibilities of tribes fighting tribes with hunting tools, but he lost the fleeting, out-of-the-ordinary idea within seconds. The feeling, however, stayed with him.

"Rok no," Da repeated softly, with respect and dread.

ϕ

Essentially happy by nature—Layla being as playful as a puppy—living in the first new modern brains on Earth made Melchizedek and Layla grumpy. This new brain—always noisily chattering about something—would cause them from time to time to slip into identifying with the wordstream in their heads and forgetting their real selves until one would wake the other up by mentally calling his or her name.

They had taught their parents to call them Mel and Layla, hoping this would serve to remind them of their true identities whenever their parents called them by name—which happened all too infrequently. Though astounded by words, the tribe didn't seem to need a lot of them and didn't use them all that often. It took ingenuity to get a new word across to them.

So far, the tribe had a vocabulary of a handful of words, mostly the names of individuals given by Melchi and Layla, along with "Hah" meaning woman, "Har" meaning man, "fi-er" meaning fire, "sadir" meaning any form of shelter (usually a combined cave or burrow and tent of branches), "rok no" meaning any hunting tool or weapon. Over time, Melchi and Layla added names for the various animals and body parts. Love hadn't yet been named as such, but everyone knew what affection felt like, expressing it in nonverbal ways like cuddling and endearing smiles.

Maybe we shouldn't be teaching language, Melchi mused one day into Layla's mind. *This brain has been learning words from me and now it never shuts up. The pictures and wordless babbling seemed less distracting. I get lulled by what sounds like me thinking and then I lapse into identifying with the baby. When we eventually breed with these people, our progeny will have the new brain, and maybe we'd be better off if we don't add so much language into the mix.*

It's probably too late, Layla telepathed back. *We've already started an unstoppable process. We can't make the tribe forget language, and the new brain takes its own initiatives. Once our kids with the new brain hear language, they too will get carried away with it.*

Melchi had to agree but continued to worry. *Something seems to be going cosmically wrong with this Mission. The new brain is so powerful that even us more highly evolved beings are finding it hard to handle. What will it do to these primitive beings?*

φ

One beautiful day, with the sun shining brightly and the sky a bright ultramarine, hosting fast-moving and morphing cumulus clouds, with birds of all sorts crossing the skies and calling cheerfully to each other, Ma and Da carried the twins downhill toward the river, with Tyg making his way by their side. Each of them carried a stout pointed stick, Tyg's being more of a toy. While never ceasing to look around for potential dangers, everyone seemed to be in a good mood.

Enjoying the outing, Melchi pathed to Layla *Nice ride.* It took him a moment to realize she must have fallen back into the personality of the baby's brain and body, forgetting her own identity, because she didn't answer. Looking over at her in Da's arms, he could see her lolling head and blank expression.

Layla! he pathed more urgently and saw her presence coming back into the baby, awareness coming back into her eyes.

Sorry about that. Layla felt as if the brain came with its own pseudo-self that could take over motor control and dim out the inhabiting true self.

Halfway down to the river, they passed the entrance to a large cave, which the kids had never seen before as small tree trunks and branches partly concealed it. An older man and several older women sat in front of the cave entrance, peering around curiously and seemingly enjoying people-watching as the tribe passed by.

Da stopped to watch something that caught his eye, and Ma and Tyg stopped with him. A young man had respectfully approached the elders while his mate held back and watched. The older man patted the ground, beckoning the young man to come sit with him. The young man quickly sat on that spot. The two studied one another intently. The elder grunted and looked expectantly at the younger.

Taking his cue, the young man gesticulated and grunted and pointed, frowning at his mate who looked back defiantly. The elder took this in. The older women watched attentively.

The older man closed his eyes and hummed to himself, his body swaying with the humming sound. He opened his eyes again, his pupils momentarily absent and then rolling down into place, though looking inward. Then, fully present again, he began communicating in body language to the young man. He pounded the young man on the back affectionately, pointed at the young man's mate, shrugged and smiled, then laughed infectiously so that the young man laughed too.

His mate hasn't been treating him with respect, Melchizedek pathed to Layla.

And the shaman has advised him not to sweat the small stuff, Layla concluded.

The young man touched the old man's hands with gratitude and stood up, feeling and looking more confident and manly. The mate seemed to take this in and liked it. They embraced and headed downhill.

I thought the first shamans would be us, Melchizedek pathed suspiciously. *It's surprising that shamans have evolved at this early stage of human development.*

What if this guy is on the opposing team, Layla shot back, referring to the Rebels. The very thought of Rebels instantly put them on alert.

The old man noticed Melchi and Layla and waved to Ma and Da to bring the twins over to him.

φ

Ma and Da continued to hesitate as the old man waved more vigorously for them to come over. His circle of old women looked them over as they shyly approached the elder, bringing Mel and Layla in their arms. Despite his normal bravado, Tyg seemed cowed and held back, holding his sharp stick toy protectively in front of him.

Do we "hide" and try to fool him? This would be one time I'd welcome this baby brain taking me over, Melchizedek whispered telepathically to his partner—testing her, as if in school.

He hears us already, Layla pathed back, passing the test. *His priestesses hear us too. They don't seem to understand what we're saying but they know we're a lot smarter than the babies they've encountered before, and that we're signaling something to each other.*

Ma and Da stopped a few feet from the shaman, not certain what they should do, never having presented themselves like this before. Melchi and Layla noticed the alpha male, who acted like the boss of the tribe—the guy who wore the animal horn headdress and waved it like a weapon to maintain discipline—holding back, standing and watching with the rest of the tribe, in deference to this old man.

We better play it straight or he will distrust us, Melchi pathed.

Layla pathed agreement.

The old man studied them and then reached up to take them from Da and Ma.

Uh-oh, Melchi heard himself think. *If this guy is one of the Rebels, we're dead and this Mission is over.*

Ma placed Mel into the old man's waiting hands and the shaman brought him close, looking into his eyes and then back around at his circle of old women, who nodded at him. He reached up and Da handed over Layla. The old man now had both of them on his lap. He repeated the close-up eye stare with Layla.

Something familiar about him, she pathed to Melchi nervously.

The old man suddenly hugged them both to his chest and belly and made huh-huh sounds. The women made the huh-huh sounds too. Melchi looked up and saw the old man smiling fondly down at both of them.

It feels like he knows who we are and what we're about, in some way, Layla pathed.

These elders are very intuitive, Melchizedek agreed. *But just normal Neanderthals it seems. Our Mission is safe for the moment.*

φ

The babies went to work in the council of the elders, commanded by the shaman to join him going forward. Much as he took counsel from the priestesses, the old shaman—who led the tribe with a strong boss man under him—looked to the babies to confirm his intuitions about each situation. He communicated partly telepathically but mostly by body and sound signals like facial postures and rhythmic grunting. The priestesses seemed as old as the shaman, and also as sharp-eyed and insightful as him.

The elders functioned to solve problems the tribe confronted, as individuals or as a whole, envisioning what the tribe should do next when no pressing problems presented, and getting the tribe to go along with their vision.

Everyone except the babies already knew the story of Glyp, a baby that had been orphaned by the killing of its parents in a border dispute that drove the tribe south to its present position. Glyp had been adopted by Hah—not the original Hah but one of many females who had taken that name early on. This particular Hah, an unmated female, welcomed having this unexpected child. She showered him with affection and gave him whatever she could.

Barely old enough to remember his natural parents, Glyp acted cold and indifferent to Hah. She didn't know what else she could do for Glyp so she brought him to the elders' council on what turned out to be the first day the babies had joined the shaman. Ma, Da, and Tyg sat outside the inner circle and watched as the shaman invited Hah and Glyp to sit down.

Able to sit up on his own, Glyp promptly lost interest in the proceedings, pretending to play with his feet—anything to show his rejection of both the council and Hah.

What do Neanderthals do with tots like this? Layla pathed, concerned the toddler might be put to death.

Let's use our voices to ensure the best outcome, Melchizedek pathed back to her. The two of them had read everybody's mind and understood the whole situation.

The shaman gestured for Glyp to come closer to him. Reluctantly, Glyp allowed himself to be handed to the shaman, who stared into his eyes then sat him in his lap and bounced him up and down. Glyp didn't necessarily enjoy it but, being sufficiently intuitive, he got through it without crying or doing anything that might get him into even worse trouble.

The shaman seemed to note this with a wink to his priestesses, who winked back, themselves rocking and bouncing in parallel motion to the shaman, looking much like a modern-day rhythm and blues band. Hah seemed enthralled, hoping for some positive outcome.

This went on for a while and Melchizedek started to get bored. He wondered if he should take charge, though he knew that could be very risky. The shaman interrupted his thoughts, issuing a one-syllable command, something like Buh!

A younger tribeswoman, who served the elders, took her cue and brought the shaman a tiny mushroom. He ate half of it immediately, made a satisfied sound, then closed his eyes, still holding and rocking Glyp.

Melchi reached tentatively for the other half of the mushroom and the shaman's hand caught his halfway. Melchi looked up with trepidation, then saw the shaman smile as he put a fragment of the other half in Melchizedek's mouth.

Psilocybin, he pathed to Layla.

After Melchi downed the mushroom piece, the shaman began to lead the band into a more tuneful piece of improv music, with an emphasis on rhythm. Even the babies felt moved to join in, especially Melchizedek as he rapidly became extremely high. Glyp seemed to warm up a bit, not resisting the proceedings so much.

The shaman sees Glyp being ungrateful all his life, getting away with it up to a point, and then being stoned to death by the tribe for his ultimate ingratitude to The Great Spirit, Melchizedek pathed to Layla as he saw these visions flash swiftly through the shaman's mind. *But now he's stumped as to how to explain it to Glyp so as to avert this outcome.*

I would be too, Layla pathed back. *We haven't taught them nearly enough words to communicate all that. Glad he's the one who has to do it. Amazing that these primitives have an intuition of The Great Spirit!*

The old man opened his eyes and looked uncertain. Then his eyes landed on Melchi and Layla and lit up. He patted them both encouragingly on their backs and repeatedly pointed with his head at Glyp as if passing the buck to them.

Now what? Melchi pathed to Layla.

φ

Is he giving us a chance to fail? Layla asked. *And if we do fail, what happens to us? Condemned as false gods?*

They don't think of us as gods, Melchizedek corrected her, *they think of us as promising prospects, born witches like themselves, whom they will have to train.*

He quickly concocted a plan and pathed it to Layla as images, simply because it's faster that way. She looked dubious but had no better ideas and they had to come up with something.

Following Melchi's instructions, Layla started to preen herself, smiling prettily, and acting like an indulged princess. She batted her eyes at the shaman, obviously expecting to be adored, and he played along although he didn't know what she had in mind. He started to pet her, smoothing back her blond hair affectionately, and massaging her as if she were his queen and he, her vassal.

While this is going on, Melchizedek starts telling a story, which the tribe hears as just noise; however, the priestesses hear it as music and they become like a Greek chorus singing contrapuntally with Melchi's narration.

"Once there lived a beautiful princess, whom everyone adored and bathed in luxury and adoration," he began, concocting the story as he went. By this point, the priestesses had joined in on the game, stroking Layla, with one of them feeding her berries.

These taste nasty, she pathed to Melchi.

Throw it in her face, he pathed back.

She'd belt me.

No, I mean it, it's part of the passion play. But wait for your cue, coming up now—

"But the princess took it all for granted and showed no gratitude, thinking she could get and do anything she wanted."

Taking her cue, Layla threw the half-chewed berry mess in the priestess's face. The priestess flared up and raised her hand, but at a micro-gesture from the shaman, she turned away, her shoulders shaking as she mocked crying and collapsing in a heap.

Play it up, Melchi urged.

Going with the flow, Layla spat in the shaman's face and whacked another priestess with the back of her hand. Without turning his head, Melchizedek noticed Glyp looking riveted by the performance.

"Her behavior drove away all her admirers and followers, leaving her alone with nothing." Melchizedek prayed for cosmic fire support, at this point unsure how the shaman and priestesses would react, hoping it wouldn't involve permanent damage to Layla's current body.

But as if understanding the intent of the show completely, all the priestesses walked away in a huff, casting back disdainful glances at Layla. The shaman dumped her off his lap and she fell face forward in the dust and got up coughing, her whole front covered with mud and dust. She lay there and pretended to weep as if regretting her selfish actions.

Melchizedek, again without turning his head, noticed Da and Ma being restrained by the tribe's alpha male and other strongmen from rushing forward to her. The look on Glyp's face—his mouth gaping open and his eyes sad for Layla—seemed to reflect some comprehension of the object lesson.

Not wanting to leave room for doubt, Melchizedek pointed at Glyp and spoke in an astoundingly loud voice: "And this is what will happen to you if you keep being ungrateful, Glyp!"

The shaman and priestesses turned and all pointed their fingers at Glyp, chanting his name until he got the message loud and clear from the body language, Melchi's words being meaningless to all but the two Agents.

Glyp's normal scornful expression vanished, replaced by abject terror. Hah came to his side to support him and he looked up at her gratefully. She kissed him and he kissed her back, hugging her tightly.

Melchizedek had a funny thought, which Layla could see on his face.

What? she pathed.

We just invented show business on this planet, he replied with amusement.

I guess that disproves the old saw about prostitution being the world's oldest profession, she pathed back.

φ

On their first day as members of the witch council, the babies had wowed the crowd with their playlet. Glyp became a changed boy from that day on, adoring his adopted mother Hah as much as she cherished him. The shaman felt well pleased at having given the babies a chance to help him rather than putting them to death, as had been his first thought. He had intuitively sensed that the super-intelligent babies might be superior to him, which made him unsure if he could continue to use them and control them once they gained the confidence of the tribe. In the end, he did what he felt would be best for the tribe, even if it meant ceding authority. The shaman showed himself to be a *mensch*.

3

As Melchizedek and Layla grew up and continued their good work on the elders' council, protecting the tribe and helping individual Neanderthals with ordinary life problems, they of course took pride in their work, as Melchizedek had always done on every Mission. His modest pride had never given rise to any bad side effects before. But riding with this new brain, even good things tended to become so overloaded with complex emotions as to turn into not-so-good things, such as modest pride curdling into vanity and conceit.

This tendency caught the two Agents napping because they felt so sure they had overcome the problem of being taken over by the new brain. They had licked the memory problem in their first year of life on Earth—no longer anesthetized into thinking of themselves as real babies rather than superbeings pretending to be babies—after which they figured the brain would be docile, or at least manageable. Not so. Even worse, it snuck up on them insidiously—not as overt as shutting down the memory of their true identity, but by something much more subtle—the gradual creation of a vain sub-self.

It all started with the Glyp incident when the babies saved the day. Of course, they never forgot that episode and often their minds would go back and re-live the triumph against astounding odds. Over time, each of them would recall these moments in a way that subtly made them the star of the show. Melchi saw himself as the orchestrator of the whole event, seeing it as his idea. Layla somehow became gradually convinced they had both thought it up and had succeeded due to her acting as the star performer—after all, Melchi had just narrated in a language the tribe couldn't understand, which made it more like background music.

They didn't consciously notice this happening until one day, as teenagers, they found themselves arguing about the facts of what had transpired. Flabbergasted when an alarm went off in his head, Melchi realized that something had repressed his memory until now: he had called for cosmic fire support way back then and must have received it since they had performed at the Flow state level.

The Great Being had taught them to expect that when they asked Him/Her for help and deserved or truly needed it, they would enter Flow: the state of exceeding one's own expected performance and the action happening as if without one's control because The One Self will have taken control. So, the credit for their success with the Glyp incident went to a higher power rather than to either of them as individuals.

Wait a second, Melchizedek pathed her. They stood alone in what they thought of as a safe part of the woods close to camp, communicating telepathically. To an observer, it looked as if they were catching their breath from a long walk over rough terrain. *This isn't like us,* he went on, a suspicious tone in his mental voice.

What's happened to us? she anguished back to him. *I feel like I've fallen hundreds of levels into an extremely base state of consciousness.*

Could it be this new brain manipulating us again? he asked slowly, stunned by his epiphany.

The newly-evolved brain had not bothered them with control issues for a long time. Remembering their true identities perfectly, they'd worked at their Mission for years, unobstructed. Now, all of a sudden, they realized this false sense of their self-importance must have gradually built up over time. Melchizedek had learned long ago that all carbon-based humanoid brains turn protein food into neuron clusters used for storing and cross-filing new information; now he realized—in the case of the new brain—some of those clusters had become overly concerned with self-flattering perceptions, to the point of repressing memories selectively to support this vainglory.

This egocentricity is way out of line for a bodhisattva, especially for Agents of Cosmic Intelligence like us, who always get sent in first to play our part in the riskiest games at momentous turning points in history, Melchizedek, playing his Teacher role, pathed to Layla. *Agents aren't supposed to have egos. Ego can be used against you as a weakness by the opposing team—so it gets drummed out of you early, in the first few thousand incarnations.*

An experienced Agent, Melchizedek knew this to be the case for himself. But The Great Being had launched Layla only very recently. She showed incredible promise and had caught up quickly, to the point of being matched with Melchi. But now they both found themselves acting like rookies.

At that moment of realization, they heard a growl.

φ

Moving with exaggerated slowness, Melchizedek and Layla turned their heads and eyes to see the huge tiger growling at them from about one good pounce away.

In a fraction of a second, having processed his traitorous brain's hand-wringing over not creating safeguards against this situation, Melchizedek impassively telepathed a confident and respectful greeting to the tiger as an equal, sans fear. He concealed his real fear behind a firewall, hoping the tiger couldn't sense it. Naturally, he called for cosmic fire support at the same time.

The tiger swung his eyes over to Layla.

Sweet pussycat, you are such a beauty. Layla followed Melchi's lead, pathing feelings of love and respect to the tiger.

The tiger made a strange noise, its eyes looking unfocused.

Are you alright? Layla pathed with concern.

The tiger growled again.

He's not well, Melchizedek told her. *And starving, because he's too ill to catch his normal prey.* Given the size of its frame, he figured the tiger to be male.

Melchizedek sent an image to the tiger of a path going over the rise to their right and then just a short distance to a small beach along a riverbank where tiger prey could be trapped with nowhere to go but into the rushing water. The tiger looked over in that direction, and then looked back at the two young teenagers, licking its lips.

Layla then sent an image to the tiger of a dozen strong Neanderthal men with very sharp pointed wooden spikes, arrayed in a double column just out of sight in the woods around them, ready to kill the tiger if it leaped. Melchi admired the detailed realism of Layla's conjured image and realized that having such a guard in place, just out of sight, would be a good plan from now on, whenever they went out of camp. *If they had a "from now on".*

Suspicious of trickery but not feeling up to par, the tiger slunk off in the direction of the riverbank, hoping the two hadn't misled him. Melchi cautiously sent friendly encouragement and sincerity to the tiger, without overdoing it, until the tiger disappeared over the rise.

That could have ended our Mission right there, Layla pathed with relief.

A waste of the thirteen years we've invested already, Melchi agreed. Then he spoke out loud: "I know we're both reluctant and kind of holding back from the next phase—and we both know why—but the tiger gave us a wake-up call. It's time to do what we came here to do."

"This will be the hardest thing I've ever had to do," Layla intimated aloud, taking his hand and heading toward camp at a decent speed, keeping an eye on the quarter in which they last saw the tiger.

"I know," he said, "and doubly hard for me, having to watch you go through it."

She looked at him, wondering if he cared for her as more than just his student.

He pretended not to notice.

φ

They arrived back at camp with little sighs of relief, certain the tiger wouldn't be so foolhardy as to come into camp with so many men armed and ready to repel any danger. He might have seen with his own eyes that these strange ape-like people with pointy sticks could be dangerous.

As the kids emerged from the underbrush, a ripple of alertness passed through the camp and then just as instantly died away. Melchi and Layla seemed unfazed, as the new phase they would soon initiate still preoccupied them.

Layla flashed a smile at Krak, the newly-established alpha male. A gentle-looking giant and very young to be an alpha, Krak had performed well in recent border skirmishes with other less peaceful tribes.

Their tribe had moved several times, either to follow game or to avoid warlike Neanderthals and other evolutionary types in this time of seismic genetic change. The solar flare had not only catalyzed the new brain in Melchizedek and Layla but had also sparked off other mutational fallouts, all of which turned out to be dead ends. Some of the latter mutants acted even worse than some tribes of Neanderthals that had taken up invader games.

Hence, a collective moment of alertness arose when anyone or anything new entered camp, even when one tribe member returned from a walkabout or a hunt.

Melchi and Layla got more attention than anyone else would get on returning to camp. The tribe regarded everything they did with intense interest. The other tribespeople tended to be predictable to one another, but these two kids seemed unpredictable and therefore much more interesting. Mel had explained it to Layla early in their current lives, telepathically conveying, *We generate new patterns in their minds, which are much more captivating to them because of their novelty.*

This explained why the tribe stared at them all the time, another reason being their relative hairlessness, which contrasted starkly with the rest of the tribe, all being hirsute. This also made Layla especially appealing to many of the tribesmen—beyond her good looks.

Puberty heralded a blockbuster life-changer for the pair. At its signal, they needed to crossbreed with as many Neanderthals as feasible in the shortest possible time. They had put this off since Layla had her first menses almost two months prior, but the tiger incident now compelled them to get on with their Mission, keenly aware they could die from any number of causes.

"Hunh ha!" Layla said softly to Krak as they walked past him, the sounds being an invitation to courting. Krak stood stunned, watching them walk away.

Cool, a young female about the same age as Mel, had come on to him often and he'd acted kind but seemingly uninterested. He didn't especially like the hair all over her body, which seemed masculine to him, yet her overall impression by movement and aura came across as very feminine. He liked the way she smelled, which he couldn't say for other members of the tribe, and he especially liked that she wore her heart on her sleeve—he adored that innocence and vulnerability.

He would much prefer to mate with Layla and only Layla—though he had yet to tell her that, so it remained a secret crush he continued to repress as a potential distraction—but if the Mission ordained him to mate with an unending number of females, well, a Mission is a Mission. Being gifted with eternity—like everybody else, since everyone is a part of The Great Being—why complain?

Layla and Melchi arrived back at the tent of leafy branches they had constructed, where they now lived as brother and sister, right next to their parent's dwelling—the type they had taught the tribe how to construct, making use of *objets trouvés* and the fun of experimental improvisation. They felt grateful for the mostly tolerable climate—though winters could be less than pleasant.

The two had barely flopped down, ready to lie around and maybe fall asleep and then wake up hungry and figure out how to not starve before it got too dark to see anything. However, a surprise guest interrupted their plans.

φ

The branches parted and twigs cracked underfoot as Krak entered their little bower and stopped in the spotlight of sun slanting down through the cathedraling trees over-head. In his hand, he held a cluster of pretty wildflowers, which he now with uncharacteristic shyness held out to Layla.

Layla, reacting well to the shock of his unexpected visit, without hesitation accepted, smelled, and generally made a fuss over the flowers. Krak, new to this sort of thing, took this as a signal to embrace and nuzzle her.

He's a fast worker, Mel observed wryly.

Sweet of him to think of bringing me flowers, though, Layla pathed back forgivingly. *Being the alpha male, he knows he has the right to first dibs on just about anything he wants.*

They've come along fairly far toward civilized behavior in some ways, Mel agreed, standing up and beginning to make a quiet exit. *Very little of it is going to stick as this tribe is affected by the general Neanderthal culture, but some of it will.*

Where are you going? she pathed, as Krak kissed her wetly with mounting ardor.

Give you guys some space, he replied, as his backside disappeared into the foliage.

He found himself at the river, not feeling much like his usual self. He restrained himself from pathing to Layla, a half-mile away and utterly occupied with her Mission. *What's with me?* he wondered. He gently enjoined an inner suspension of his thoughts and feelings so he could observe more deeply inside himself.

This brain keeps making predictions of what's going to happen or could happen, and then generating chemical signals that cause the body to feel things in reaction to those predictions. Right now, it's predicting the imminent loss of Layla to Krak and soon to others, which is making me feel the emotion of sadness.

He sent conscious signals to his brain and body, conveying *This is all a good thing. We're starting our true Mission here—exult in it and stop believing these irrelevant and wrong-headed predictions.*

At that moment, he sensed a presence approaching. *Uh-oh, here I am breaking my own rule about being caught alone outside of camp.*

φ

Would that sickly tiger have moved upstream this far by now? Melchizedek now wondered with sudden readiness to move—although he knew not where to move that the tiger couldn't go. The tiger had hopefully found enough prey at the spot downstream to have filled his stomach, lulling him into a nice long catnap.

Then, the source of the rustling appeared—the shy barely-a-teen Cool. From her body language, he sensed she'd come alone, itself enough of an invitation based on the customs of the tribe. He made a welcoming motion and stood up, the way a civilized man would when a lady entered a room.

In his short life with them, the tribe had wandered south, following herds to warmer climates. The place where he now bade her to sit beside him would later become famous. Two rivers joined at that spot and flowed as one river further southeast. The tribe had long seen the more westerly river, named Yooprateese—which Layla had intuited and taught the tribe to say—as its holy river. Mel and Layla had known it from birth simply as the river. An old wise man from a tribe they'd met in their wanderings taught them the name of the other river: Idiqlat. Some millennia later, the Idiqlat and Yooprateese rivers would become known as the Tigris and Euphrates.

The two teenagers watched as the rivers joined beneath their gently kicking feet. Mel reached out slowly and touched Cool's hand. She didn't flinch. He noticed her hands—small and lovely—and her feet too, almost like Layla's. *Although, of course, nothing could compare to Layla,* he reminded himself. Nevertheless, his fondness for Cool grew swiftly, along with his attraction—his teenage body being full of raging hormones. They soon coupled above the joining rivers.

Cool responded as the Mission ordained by becoming full with child. Mel loved Cool and took care of her and her daughter Gina—named after one of the smaller rivers—and both he and Layla showered the baby with affection. But then, they did that with everyone.

As Mel's assigned duties as the first human stud of Mesopotamia continued and all the young ladies of the tribe bore his progeny, he had to figure out how to take care of so many wives and children, and Layla's offspring too. But with Layla's help, they managed to keep the whole tribe safe and well-fed, finding fecund terrain filled with edible wildlife and relatively absent of other tribes. Shelter had also become far less of a problem now that they'd escaped the frightful winters.

Soon after the birth of Gina, the first of their descendants, and then Krak and Layla's son Karl, and then others, it became clear that something had gone terribly wrong.

φ

Melchizedek and Layla had caused a surge in the size of the tribe with their diligent baby-making, and the new generation all sported the new brain. Whereas the new brain had often fooled even the two trained Agents into thinking and feeling egotistically, this new generation came into life ill-equipped to cope with and overcome the overly helpful new brain. These new kids would soon be spoiled—being given all they could need—but even before excessive nurturing, their nature showed signs of being covetous of more than their fair share.

It's the way this new brain never stops making predictions, Mel pathed Layla as she breastfed two of her newest babies, who seemed to instinctively compete to the point of hurting her as each tried to out-engorge the other. *The newly added frontal cortex generates pictures and feelings of how it could be, both the desirable and undesirable, which makes these kids feel dissatisfied if they get anything less than the best-predicted scenarios.*

How could this have happened, Mel? And what are we going to do about it? Layla pathed back, somewhat frazzled. She loved these kids and they drove her crazy with concern.

Layla, be careful, Mel cautioned. *Remember, we have this new brain too and we can't get caught up in the attachment it creates—of being attached to any particular outcome—or we'll be of no use to anybody.*

Easier said than done. Dragged down by the shock of this unanticipated situation, with neither of them performing at their normally high level, they asked themselves *So how can the new brain be backfiring so badly?* Knowing The One Self wrote the script, as always, made the situation even more baffling.

Years passed. Gina and Karl and many of the other new bambinos had become teenagers, with Mel and Layla now in their late twenties, almost at the typical lifespan limit for that era. The babies had gotten increasingly problematic as they grew older. Most of the Neanderthal kids seemed instinctively well-mannered—with a few exceptions like Glyp and their older brother Tyg—probably because their awareness of being powerless and dependent made them therefore grateful and eager to please. This instinct turned out to be a rarity with these new kids.

Some of the new-breed kids came across as demanding and aggressive, while others seemed stuck in their heads and not fully present in the external world—but they all needed help. Luckily, their mother or father—Layla or Melchizedek—could utilize telepathy to understand and thereby help them.

In the case of Karl, for example, the Agents diagnosed the cause of his being extremely cowardly and fearful. As the son of the tribe's alpha male, Krak, the poor kid's brain constantly compared his weak little self to his powerful father. Layla and Mel thus set about alleviating the boy's fears and insecurity by planting pictures in his mind of how he'd grow up to be strong and brave. They also rechanneled his almost catatonic shell-like retreat into an emphasis on exercise and play, for the purpose of body-building, acceptance of pain, and enjoyment of fun.

Layla woke up one morning and pathed Melchizedek with anguished compassion: *How are parents who aren't telepathically developed going to help the children of these children?*

φ

As Melchizedek and Layla aged, the new brain eventually wore them down. They would lapse into long patches of forgetting their real identity as Agents of Cosmic Intelligence, waking up from their amnesia sometimes only briefly before they'd relapse back into it and puzzle over *What was I thinking just a moment ago... it seems important...*

This happened very gradually, starting with how much love they wanted to give to their children, their mates, and the other tribespeople. Their intense love carried attachment as its price, the state in which one can no longer be happy if the loved one isn't happy or is no longer interested in you. These lingering heartbreaking emotions held sway in 200,000 BCE much as they do to this day.

As cosmic beings, Melchi and Layla had never before sunk to these attached states. They could maintain their intense love along with and through detachment. Only cosmic beings—the created beings climbing closest in evolutionary development to The Original Self—can pull this off consistently, having usually had lifetimes to practice.

Losing contact with their own true identities began something like this: sometimes, in schizoid inner conversations, they would get angry at their higher selves for being detached. This happened outwardly at times too, as when Layla asked Mel: *How can you be so cold-blooded about your own child?* They would then pull themselves up, getting back into their true identities at least temporarily. But no matter how many times they pulled themselves back up, the tide had begun to turn.

Worn out from mothering so many children and stressing about each of them, Layla's resistance had lowered over time so much that when giving birth to her last child, she passed on to the Bardo plane—the place that existed before matter. Melchizedek would normally have found himself easily able to stay connected with her; but this time he lost contact with her almost immediately, except for brief flashes from time to time.

Melchizedek didn't notice himself becoming gradually embittered. Getting older, his aching body contributed to this feeling, but the new brain and its dominance over his true self bore most of the blame. Bewildered, Melchizedek wondered why the very brain they came to Earth to propagate seemed to be working so strongly against the Mission. It felt so unfair to him, which made him question still further.

Is there another team here on Earth working at cross purposes with us? If so, why didn't we detect them? If they're not in human bodies, are they in any bodies at all? Either way, I should still be able to detect them.

He then reasoned that another cosmic being not hampered by this brain would have the advantage over him and Layla. He pathed a message to her to see if she could detect another team on Earth from her less obstructed position beyond the veil. He could only hope she received it.

Feelings, moods, images, and vague thoughts came into his mind, without words, about The One not having warned them in advance about the conditions they'd face. This ran so counter to his training that he snapped back into his true identity for a moment.

He reminded himself: *Gripes against The Great Being are the height of folly—since each of us is The One, it's senseless to gripe against oneself. Just do something.*

Then he continued contemplating, *Are some of these self-defeating thoughts being implanted in me by a cosmic being on an opposing team?*

Eventually, he saw himself as being paranoid and gave up looking for another team. Soon thereafter, he stopped waking up from his identity as simply the elder shaman of their little tribe. Freed of his breeding duties, he spent most of his time giving advice and settling disputes. One thing, however, kept coming back into his mind at least once a day, as if trying to pull him back into his true self: an image of fire. He had no idea what it meant.

On the day his body died, at the very instant of his last breath, he suddenly became—in a whoosh—aware of his real identity and immediately understood the message of the fire image. Upon their arrival on Earth, they'd found naked savages who hadn't yet domesticated animals and had only rudimentary spoken language—and yet these natives knew how to start, control, and use fire. This made no sense. Fire is a complex phenomenon. On most planets developing along a similar curve to Earth, the discovery of fire came after many other things. But here, fire had come first. *There must be another team.*

4

Circa 40,000 BCE

Their multi-life existence on Earth would be a yo-yo, with
Melchizedek and Layla constantly being dragged into self-
forgetfulness by the new prediction-centric brains. Riding
astride the same body as that brain, being one with it,
and yet remembering himself as essentially a spirit or consciousness inhabiting that body, had never been a problem
for Melchizedek in previous assignments. This new brain
presented a new challenge for both of them. They had to
figure out a way to stay awake to their true identities to
have any hope of accomplishing their Mission—which
now looked iffy at best.

But at this very moment, being ecstatically happy, it
required no effort to stay awake to their real identities
They'd found each other again, back on the Bardo plane,
where only consciousness itself exists, away from and yet
in total communication with the projected world of matter and energy, space and time—the world created by
The Great Being. They relaxed into being free of the new
brain, and on vacation, just the two of them—someplace
Melchizedek had visualized into being a long time ago and

had always loved, a beach with a constant eighty-degree temperature day and night.

Though separated for a long time by Mel's reckoning, Layla had no sense of any time having passed so she felt especially delighted by Mel's intense happiness at seeing her. Now in their bubble bodies, he hugged her tightly.

Hey, what's all this... ooh...

Here on Earth, we identify the orgasm as being the ultimate pleasure, though it's usually mostly physical pleasure. The spirit level of existence is orgasmic in the sense of being in every way the most extreme pleasure, felt physically, intellectually, intuitively, and emotionally—which is how Melchi and Layla both felt at that moment. He didn't want to ruin it by saying anything. As their bubbles parted, she didn't want to spoil the moment by talking about it either, but she felt in a state of limbo, curious as to how he really felt about her.

In the ever-changing dreamlike seascape swashing and spraying them, they compared notes.

Who is the other team that gave the natives fire—what do we know about them? Melchizedek asked, thinking Layla might have done some reconnaissance here on the Bardo with access to the cosmic "cloud" known as the Akashic records.

Here's what I've found out so far: because it's in the Lost Lambs zone, Earth is a mystery planet in which the inhabitants—including Agents—are given clues to discover things, but they're not given all the skinny in advance. Layla sounded resigned to the idea as if she'd had time to get used to it.

Melchizedek absorbed the information with a smile, pathing *You're a real trouper.* He thought for a moment then continued. *That explains a few things. Good to know—so when the brain tries to make me mad at my Original Self for not giving me enough information, I need to remember the real "I" who chose to play the game this way.*

I found out one other thing, she added, and the attention between them peaked. *Our tribe behaved atypically. Most others are brutally violent.*

His expression wryly conveyed, "Naturally," and implied, "What next?" *That's where we'll have to go,* he then pathed, *right into the heart of the worst of them. I have a feeling that's where we'll find the other team.*

Will they be Rebels? she asked.

No way of knowing for sure, he replied impassively.

φ

Melchizedek appeared able to get more information than she had cadged from their Original Self, which impressed Layla. As a more advanced player, he knew certain tricks. She would often come upon him meditating with an inner-directed gaze in his open eyes, floating in an electrical rainbow ovoid shape over the highest peak on their Bardo plane vacation island with its dramatic omnidirectional view of the sea. She knew him to be looking deep inside and being guided by cosmic purpose at those times.

We have our orders, Melchizedek pathed her, coming out of his meditation and surprising her. *We're going to walk in.*

This didn't particularly surprise Layla. She had learned in her training that Agents often use the walk-in method to save the time it takes to grow up.

Melchi spirited them both out of the Bardo and they approached the projected world, Earth now looking slightly different as they drew near the Atlantic coast of what would become known as Spain. Roughly 160,000 Earth years had passed since their first visit. On a beach below, punctuated by large black natural lava sculptures, they saw numerous human corpses seemingly washed ashore, apparently having drowned.

This group of warriors tried to escape their aggressors by sea, Layla intuited.

Mel pathed a head nod back to her, indicating pride in his student. *Both groups of combatants are from the other team,* he said. *No room for doubt; they're definitely Rebels, inhabiting human bodies with the new brains.*

The other team is fighting itself? she asked incredulously.

He murmured assent. *They're competitive to the point that when there is no other human prey to steal from, they fight among themselves. I've seen that on other planets.*

He hovered over two of the corpses and pathed *Here—these are the two.*

Layla caught sight of the two much huger men than those in the Neanderthal tribe—one blonde and the other darker of hair and skin.

I get to be a guy this time, Layla noted. *But these men look too dead to revive. We might wind up being zombie walk-ins.*

Melchizedek had the same concern but wouldn't give it voice. He called for cosmic fire support and led the walk-in, choosing the darker one. With no hesitation, Layla followed, entering the blonde one.

Melchizedek lost track of Layla while he struggled to restart and repair the brain, then the breath of the man. He vomited salt water and felt himself take hold of the body, which started moving like a powerful horse trying to throw him off its back. Turning quickly to Layla, he saw the other man's body still immobile and looking dead as a doornail. He reached out to contact her and got nothing back. Imagining the nightmare she might be in for a nanosecond, he stepped in and applied mouth-to-mouth resuscitation and then other moves to help the coughing body expel the seawater.

Thanks, Melchi! he heard at last and set about quieting his internal alarms.

Exhausted, they both fell back on the sand to recover and take stock. They didn't have much time, however, as they both simultaneously felt internal alarms go off again. They sensed humans approaching, though not yet in visual range.

φ

A squad of tough-looking men with spears and other weaponry emerged from the trees ridging the beach and spotted the two, also quickly taking in the corpses spread all around. In unison, the men began to run toward them.

Follow my lead, Melchizedek advised, standing up calmly and hailing the approaching party.

Layla arose beside him, wearing the blonde man's body, and asked with a tremor in her mental voice, *Are they the ones who drove our side into the ocean, or are they members of our side come to look for survivors?*

The latter, I think.

A moment later, Melchi's hunch appeared to be confirmed as the warriors slowed and hailed the two. The leader came up to them, with his henchmen close behind, weapons suspiciously at the ready, which seemed strange for men on the same side.

The leader barked something at Melchizedek with the intonation of a question. Melchizedek and Layla suddenly realized they couldn't understand the language, which would put these people on guard. Melchizedek cautiously read the mind of the leader, hoping the man wouldn't be aware of the probe, and found he had asked them to report what had happened. It would take too long to piece together words in the group's language from the leader's mind, so he used sign language to depict a battle, with his men being driven into the sea, and all but the two of them drowning.

The man's eyes widened at the use of sign language in place of words. Melchizedek pointed at his own head, suggesting the near-drowning might have damaged something in there, and Layla quickly pointed at her head, nodding rapidly, picking up on the improvised cover story.

The leader turned and shouted orders at his men, who then surrounded Melchizedek and Layla and made it clear they would be taken somewhere, presumably back to camp. The two set forth, encircled by the soldiers.

He didn't seem to notice me looking around in his mind, Melchizedek pathed to Layla. *Let's use this time to see if we can pick up some useful vocabulary.* They both set about mind-reading, focused on learning the language as fast as possible, sharing their learnings with each other along the way.

He addressed you as Blu, Layla pointed out.

Yes, Melchizedek agreed, *my name is Blu. What's yours?*

Layla looked at the closest man guarding her and the man looked back impassively. *Ska,* she pathed. *He thinks of me as Ska, and he's apparently never liked me, though I can't see why.*

The man guarding Melchizedek, from slightly behind, now for some reason made body contact, pushing Melchizedek. Without hesitation, Melchizedek swung around and with the back of one of his big hands clouted the fellow backward a few steps. The man shook his spear at Melchizedek while also shaking his head to clear it from the jolt, but he didn't come any closer.

The leader yelled a single sound and the group resumed walking. The guard didn't touch Melchizedek again.

If you let them push you around even once, it starts a chain reaction from which there is no return, he advised

Layla, who had no previous experience with the other team.

How are we going to ever teach these people compassion? she asked.

Leave it to The Great Being to make the game interesting, Melchizedek pathed back cheerfully, though his face looked grim.

φ

Your name is Blu because of your dark skin, Layla pathed. They hurriedly read the minds of the men around them to bone up on the local language and their history with the tribe. *My name, Ska—I'm not getting anything—*

We work for this guy, Melchizedek pathed, nodding toward the leader of the squad escorting them. *I'm his top sergeant and you're his top corporal; the rest of these guys are privates.*

How come he didn't get driven into the sea and drowned with the rest of us? Layla asked.

I think he may have deserted and thinks we may know his secret, Melchizedek surmised.

Why hasn't he had us killed then? Layla countered with a concerned tone.

I think he needs us. Melchizedek responded calmly.

As if the squad leader had read their minds, he abruptly called for a rest stop in a spot with the sunlight filtering down through the tall trees. He directed his men to move off some yards away to form a perimeter, keeping Melchizedek and Layla, now Blu and Ska, with him in the spotlight of the sun. He motioned them to sit and then stood over them as they sat, respectfully looking at him for their orders. Alerted by his sudden stop, they had curbed their telepathic activity.

He briefly interrogated them, whispering so the rest of the squad couldn't hear, and they responded in kind.

"Taking you to King," he said. "What you tell King?"

"All fought bravely—outnumbered—most of them died rather than surrender. A few of us then swam to escape and all drowned but us. Lost memories, but coming back now," Blu reported, and Ska nodded.

"Yes," the squad leader agreed. "I swam too, came up over there—" he pointed south, where the currents would have taken him had he told the truth, which they sensed he did not, "—then picked up these men at camp and came to look for survivors."

They nodded in support of his cover story, indicating they would stick to the party line with the King. Satisfied, the leader called his men back and the march proceeded.

Coming into the camp, the widespread evidence of malnutrition struck Melchizedek and Layla. Unlike the soldiers guarding them up to this point—who'd become more amiable after the rest in the clearing—the first men they saw in the camp appeared undersized, scrawny with their ribs sticking out, and unhealthy-looking; likewise, their mates and children. But as the two Agents moved into the center of the encampment, the men in charge stood out as larger and healthier, living in the protected center of the temporary base. The Alphas, who had consigned the others to the periphery, where animal—or more dangerously, human—attacks would get them first and give the people in the center more time to react.

Uh-oh, Layla pathed.

Melchizedek then saw what she saw: a bevy of the weaker men being bullied into building a dwelling in the center of camp.

Yes, slaves, Melchizedek pathed back. *These people have already invented slavery. But we have a worse problem,* he warned.

The group came to a stop as they approached the dwelling of the King, who stepped forth into the sunlight with a look of keen interest in their direction. Layla wondered why Melchi hadn't further explained what he meant by a worse problem, but now she got it: the King is a walk-in too—which is why Melchizedek had clamped down on using telepathy.

φ

The King looked them over closely. Melchizedek found himself closer than ever before to a member of the Rebellion—a phenomenon he had known about forever and still couldn't fully comprehend. *How could a being close to his own level of evolution choose to never return to The One Self?* In self-imposed telepathic radio silence with Layla, he could only use his body language to keep the younger agent from freaking out, and so he made his movements strong and self-assured without giving offense to the King or their squad leader boss. They waited in silence to be interrogated. Around them the tribe busied itself with its daily affairs, creating an island of the four of them in the spotlight of the blazing sun. Layla irrelevantly noticed a leaf sawing back and forth on its lazy trip to the ground.

The King grunted and half smiled, brandishing his alarmingly wolfish teeth. Both agents felt he must have discovered them already but they did nothing to dodge the bullet. Melchizedek held back his impulse to take a surreptitious peek into the King's mind. The King abruptly turned his back on them and went back into his tent, motioning for them to follow. The squad leader went in first, then Melchizedek as Blu, and then Layla as Ska.

Their eyes adjusted to the darkness inside the tent. The King sat and directed them to do the same.

Now seated in a small circle on the ground, the King bit off a small chunk of what appeared to be a psychedelic root and put the rest back on the rock. He chewed thoughtfully for a moment and then began his questioning.

"What happened?" he demanded of Blu in the local language.

Fortunately, the Agents had learned most of the tiny existing vocabulary by now and so could understand and respond to the King.

"The enemy outnumbered us, as usual," Blu began, noting the instant flare-up of anger on the faces of the King and squad leader, who somehow took that to be accusatory. "Everyone fought bravely," he went on, indicating with his head that the accolade included the squad leader and Ska, "but we had the great water at our backs, with no way to maneuver. We are the only survivors. The enemy had deployed only a reconnaissance. They'll be back in greater numbers now that they know where we are."

"How did they fight? As we do?" The King snarled.

"They protect each other better. They must train differently. We fight singly and they fight together against us. Also, their weapons somehow hold together better than ours. We must capture some of their weapons and study them," Blu recommended.

"How are we going to do that?" The King nearly exploded. "You just said they outfight us, outnumber us, and have better weapons!"

"For a short while, we'll have better knowledge of the terrain, until they learn it. We should be able to ambush a small patrol, where we outnumber them and come down from higher ground on all sides, perhaps with the sun in their eyes," Blu answered evenly, keeping his voice as subservient as possible, although it still sounded too bold to his own ears.

The King grumbled as if agreeing to the plan. He looked at the squad leader, who nodded uncertainly, telegraphing his fear that Blu might be starting to impress the King and might soon be his boss.

Layla and Melchizedek both picked up a flash through the squad leader's mind to kill Blu in his sleep and then they clamped down on their minds reflexively, hoping the King didn't notice their ability.

"Sir," Ska said respectfully with head bowed.

The King snapped, "What?"

"Great King, if we could train the slaves to fight, we wouldn't be outnumbered," Ska suggested, bringing instant snorts of derision from the King and squad leader.

"They are puny and weak," the King retorted. "If we take meat from the mouths of the fighting men to feed the slaves, it would weaken not strengthen us!"

Ska bowed his head meekly and feigned agreement.

"Leave me now," the King ordered, and the three of them left the tent. Outside, two women stood waiting, and attached themselves to Blu and Ska immediately— obviously their wives, happy to see them alive. Blu and Ska enthusiastically kissed and hugged them and allowed themselves to be led back to their tents, thankful to find them right next to each other. The squad leader walked off without further ado.

I don't get it, Layla pathed. *Is he pretending to not know who we are—just to torture us?*

Can't know for sure, Melchizedek sent back, *but I sense his brain has taken him over and he doesn't remember that he is a consciousness not native to this world. The same as happened to us last time.*

We came awake and then we went back into that fugue, Layla pathed, *which means he could be under its spell right now. But next time he comes out of it, our gooses are cooked.*

φ

Blu's wife, pale and petite, had reddish blond hair worn long all over her body, which Blu found appealing perhaps in contrast to his own dark skin and hair. Reading her mind, Melchizedek saw that Blu called her Izbel. Once alone in their tent, Izbel ardently pulled him close, welcoming him home and ready to nurse him back to health.

Are you two doing what we're doing? Layla as Ska pathed from next door, where his wife Asa busily licked his clotted wounds clean, her dark skin and hair feeling soft next to his. They hadn't got to the next phase of welcoming yet.

We're a bit further along, Melchizedek replied and then reminded her, *Careful not to lose yourself in the body's identity.*

Given their experience from the first incarnation with the new brain, they knew that certain conditions such as sleep, sex, exhaustion, or distraction could make this even more likely to happen. And so, they continued their telepathic conversation to help them retain knowledge of their true identities during the ensuing lovemaking.

They also needed to come up with a plan, quickly. At any time, the King could wake up to his real identity and possibly penetrate their mind shields to know theirs, which would mean certain death—certainly not helpful to the Mission.

Being kind and loving beings, Melchizedek as Blu and Layla as Ska treated their wives tenderly and attentively, even though Layla preferred males and despite their need to practice detachment.

I wonder how many Rebels are awake to their true identities here on Earth, she mused. *Worst case scenario, the tribe attacking us could also be led by a Rebel, one that might remember who he or she is and could bust us even if the King stays asleep.*

Melchizedek merely gave a mental nod, which led her to imagine him enjoying himself. The momentary twinge of jealousy she sensed in herself alerted her to Ska's brain trying to take her over since she never felt jealousy as Layla, and so she focused on detaching her sense of self from the animal-level impulse.

Meanwhile, Asa had cleansed the last of Ska's wounds and began to explore unharmed territory, adding to the challenge of Layla maintaining her self-identity. Moments later another distraction piled on as Melchizedek reached out mentally to begin making love to her while physically making love to Izbel, which shocked her until she realized Mel thought he had blocked his fantasy from her. She found the situation to be irresistibly erotic.

Mel didn't catch on that his sexual fantasy had escaped his firewall and that Layla could read him like a book. As Agents, they found nothing troubling about enjoying multiple love affairs at the same time. They knew that in reality, all personalities are masks of the same One Self anyway. Each of them did get lost in their current brain but snapped back to reality several times that day, maintaining a tenuous hold on their true selves.

In the warm afterglow, Melchizedek announced, *I have a plan.* Then he added, *Actually, you gave me the idea.*

φ

The King looked at them as if to say, "What, back so soon?" His face turned more suspicious by the moment.

"Great King, we have a plan, and with the enemy so close, we wanted to tell you about it immediately," Blu said.

The King bade them to enter his tent and sit, then disappeared outside for a moment. Blu and Ska sensed the

King's guard drawing closer around the tent as the King stepped back inside. He sat, and went straight for the psychedelic root and chewed on it while waving his hand as if to say, "Let's hear it."

Melchizedek had a flash that the King perhaps subconsciously used the root to try to damp down his brain so as to reclaim his real identity. But given the urgency to put across the plan, he didn't stop to ponder the idea.

"To stay here is certain death," Blu began. "We can escape by climbing the great mountain. From there we can watch the enemy's movements by the smoke of their fires. We can raid a small encampment and learn from the captives how they're trained to fight and how they make their weapons. We can study and duplicate their weapons ourselves. We'll have the advantage of fighting downhill, which uses less effort than attacking uphill. When we choose to attack, we can do it when the sun is behind us, to blind their sight."

The King considered this and responded. "Legends speak of horrible animals on the great mountain."

"Something to eat, then," Blu shot back.

The King and Ska laughed.

Within minutes the entire tribe, led by the King, swarmed toward the great mountain to the southeast, bringing their weapons, food, and children. Blu and Ska set forth in the King's party, along with his well-armed guards. Their recent boss and squad leader trailed somewhere behind with the multitudes, including Izbel and Asa.

The ground at this point steadily but gently sloped upwards. As Melchizedek looked back, he saw a huge cloud of dust trailing their small army. He knew the cloud could easily be seen by the enemy, wherever its main force had dug in. To make their escape, they would have no time to rest. It would be a long hard climb, getting gradually closer to vertical.

Although they'd had scant time to prepare their pitch to the King, it had somehow come off perfectly, Melchizedek realized.

Reading his mind, Layla pathed, *I'm so glad we didn't have to give him the rest of the plan.*

Melchizedek agreed. They had already heard the King say things that made them certain he wouldn't have reacted well.

φ

They lost only a few tribe members on the difficult steep climb, these being among the weakest and least healthy of the slaves—except for one warrior who fell to his death while showing off. Though not yet being pursued by the enemy tribe, they could now see its fire smoke from their vantage point, allowing some understanding of the enemy's movements and possible intent.

It looked to Melchizedek as if the enemy army's current strategy focused on taking and holding the valleys, perhaps leaving the mountains for a time when reinforcements might arrive. His idea to escape up the great mountain turned out to be therefore a lucky guess or more likely an inspiration, a form of cosmic fire support he knew he'd received many times in the past.

"Aren't they beautiful?" Layla asked, lying beside him in the tall grass looking down at the vast panorama.

Melchizedek looked and now saw a herd of about a dozen bison in a meadow a thousand feet below. Being more concerned with following enemy movements, he hadn't noticed the animals.

"Glorious creatures," he readily agreed, and stood in a crouch to minimize the chances of being seen, although the enemy probably couldn't see anything at this distance. *The other tribe,* he corrected himself. He knew that adopting the habit of thinking of them as the enemy would play into the hands of the powerful new brain in these newly-evolved Cro-Magnon bodies, and his awareness of his true Melchizedek self would soon recede. To an Agent, even Rebels are not seen as the enemy; they are just thoroughly Lost Lambs that need to be brought back into the fold.

The King's army had established camp on a forested plateau about a mile above sea level, next to a lake—apparently fed by underground springs—that reflected the lush greenery. It didn't take long to set up new tent burrows using fallen branches and other found objects.

Small game abounded here—with easy-to-catch rabbits, squirrels, possums, and the like—and Ska had courted the King's displeasure by sharing some meat with the slaves. However, the King agreed that once it became too gamey for the warriors to want it, there would be no harm in giving it to the slaves. Besides, he reasoned, leaving it to molder would smell offensive and possibly draw those horrific legendary predators—though so far, they'd only encountered animals as dangerous or aggressive as the wild boar, which the fires kept at a distance. Unfortunately, the table scraps of rabbit and squirrel didn't provide enough protein to bring the slaves up to a level of health and combat-readiness conducive to their becoming assimilated equal subjects of the King, as Melchizedek had envisioned.

Soon after settling down on the plateau, the King began to look for various kinds of mushrooms, bark, and roots, hoping to find psychedelics up at this altitude like those in their last home. After getting sick from one such specimen he had found, he started using slaves as tasters. One such slave became terrified of the King after seeing the painful death another taster underwent, but he had a laughing fit after eating a bit of one particular mushroom—at which point the King snatched the remainder away from him and studied it carefully so as to be able to distinguish it from other mushrooms.

Blu and Ska had done their own searching and found the soft colored stones they needed for part of their secret plan, the part they hadn't shared with the King. In the busy confusion of setting up the encampment, the King hadn't seemed to notice them missing from time to time. Now their preparations neared completion and showtime would be coming soon.

5

The King bridled at the idea of having to go somewhere to see something. Ska persuaded him by saying, "Oh Great King, all future men will remember **you** for the great creation we will show you."

Though capitulating, the King insisted on having his full guard—eight protectors heavily armed with pikes and throwing stones plus personal weapons—whereas Blu and Ska had but their stone axes and stone blades, only suitable for very close range. The King wanted to stack it this way just in case he faced an assassination attempt.

It took a bit of climbing to get to the cave. Previous experience had taught all these men to know that nothing could possibly surprise or impress them in that cave—no way, just not possible.

They reached the opening and Blu stopped to light his torch. This took several minutes, during which the King got steadily more impatient and angrier.

This is going to be one tough audience, Layla pathed. The two had laughed earlier, saying, *Here we go again, now reinventing show biz on this planet.*

Finally, Blu got the torch lit though it sputtered uncertainly. Melchizedek requested cosmic fire support and led the way into the cave.

Instantly colder and damp, the cave had a funny smell that none but the Agents could remember ever having smelled before, which set the King and his guards on alert. The King fuzzily detected his own true identity for a brief moment, and Melchizedek immediately caught it and distracted him.

"Great King, I persuaded the bears in this cave to depart but they left their scent behind. That's what you smell."

The King looked at him with disbelief, pigeonholing the explanation as a common boast, with no truth. But it made him forget momentarily the brief flash he'd had, and so for now he didn't wake up to his true identity—a visitor, the same as Melchizedek and Layla, though of a different political and philosophical persuasion.

As they went deeper into the cave, it got darker, but it also enlarged a bit so they could walk fully upright. Here Blu raised a hand to stop them, pausing dramatically. He held the torch in a certain way so he could light up just a part of the present "room" he wanted to illuminate—using himself as a shade to block something else he would disclose at just the right time.

Ska began to hum a little song, a melody—something that no one on Earth had ever heard before—following the universal cycle of fourths to resolve into a heroic tonic chord that makes all beings feel secure. Layla had learned to do this as an Agent.

"Oh, Great King," Blu started off, getting the show underway. "The King's men, Ska, hear me now as I speak the truth to you. This is what the King has invented to teach men the ways to their betterment—an unlimited path to a future whose greatness we can only begin to imagine."

The soldiers wondered if, in fact, the King had created whatever Blu intended to show them.

Blu slowly turned and the torchlight revealed something on the wall causing them all to jump back in fright—except of course Blu and Ska—a charging wild boar. A moment later they all realized what they'd seen—just colors smudged on the cave wall, which *looked like* a charging wild boar, not *really* the boar itself. Involuntary murmurs of great respect spontaneously emanated from the soldiers, initially irritating the King.

Moments later, when he'd thought it over, the King said, "My greatest warriors, I honor you by sharing this treasure with you. Blu and Ska will now explain how it will be used for our betterment." He looked momentarily smug as if expecting Blu and Ska to completely muff the next part. He didn't see how this parlor trick could be any sort of game-changer he'd want to lay claim to.

"Look here." Blu moved the torch so they could see something else. He pointed to and touched the vertical lines grooved carefully into the rock—appearing to be behind but actually above the boar. "These lines represent warriors with pikes who surround the boar on every side. In this cave, we'll rehearse as if we are these men—the one who will approach from the rear, from each side, and from the front—and we'll train all of you to work with each other as a team. We'll rehearse the commands and what they mean, so there will be no hesitation no matter what happens in battle."

"And then what?" the King demanded, wanting to know the entirety of the plan. He didn't trust anyone, least of all these two.

"Then we'll go after even larger prey—including people," Ska said convincingly.

φ

The extra delay before revealing the boar last night added tremendously to the effect, Layla pathed, as Ska and Blu lay intertwined with their respective wives in their respective burrows.

Melchizedek sent back a laugh. *Not intentional—a rock somehow got moved into the wrong spot and I almost fell over it.*

Cosmic fire support? She kidded him, although it could easily be that higher forces had helped them. One never knows.

Training in the cave commenced though it hadn't started immediately after unveiling the cave painting.

Agent training included the ways of psychological persuasion—variously called propaganda, advertising, marketing, and social media—at different times in different places. Before being allowed into the Mystery Cave in small select groups, rumors of its secrets beguiled the tribespeople, most of the rumors being elaborations on overheard whispers, which added to their aggrandizement.

By the time the Agents allowed the first group of hardened soldiers to experience the Magic Theater, the men expected a life-changing initiation into the deeper secrets of life, and therefore each one experienced exactly that. The use of small driblets of the King's mushrooms added to this effect, of course.

Blu and Ska put on quite a show. Blu's delivery improved with every performance, as did Ska's singing. The soldiers came away believing they had gone through just one of many doorways that would open later in the Mystery Cave, and they looked forward to the journey that would bring them to full awareness of what the world is, what life means, how to become a King among Kings. The first quest—to conquer the wild boar as meat—frightened them, but as soldiers, they had practiced keeping their fear in check beneath determination and honor. Each would rather die than be the one who couldn't go all the way.

The fiercest fighters went through the training process first, followed by the other warriors and huntsmen, and finally the wives and children. The King balked at letting the slaves in the cave, despite attempts by Blu and Ska—together and separately—to reason with him. They decided to keep their powder dry and bring it up again at the right time.

Like the slaves, the wives and children had never expected to be allowed into the Magic Cave, but Blu and Ska had inspired the King with the notion that the men's wives would reinforce the training if they could share the experience with their mates. Somehow the wives and children knew Blu and Ska had earned them their step up in status and they became permanent allies. At first, this didn't mean anything—not until the Agents had prepared themselves to openly diverge from the King.

The moment would come soon, but not in the way planned.

φ

Naming things is more important than I ever realized, Layla pathed.

Using the term "The Great Hunt" distinguished it from solitary hunting. In The Great Hunt, a team of men tracked the largest and most dangerous beasts, and would later train to hunt the most dangerous of all—their own kind. This generated the kind of emotions that would later drive their descendants to be rabid sports fans.

It anchors a cluster of feelings and images into something retrievable, an idea, Melchizedek agreed, explaining why naming is so powerful.

As Blu and Ska, the Agents went about the activities of daily life with their wives, while planning their next moves.

The first Great Hunt had ended in failure, as had the second and third. The spears had to hit just right or they would be useless against the smart, fast, wily beasts. The mixture of mental practice and invoking magic or cosmic fire support through prayer in the cave had not yet fully prepared the tribesmen for the actual experience of the Hunt.

Then came the fourth Great Hunt, which delivered a miraculous result: the sight of the huge pig being carried with great respect back into the encampment, the image reflected on the lake. Although Blu and Ska had repeatedly told the whole tribe they would see this someday, it didn't seem real to them until that day came.

A religious conviction swiftly swept across the few thousand tribespeople, transforming them into possibly the first group of people on Earth to sense some higher power they could actually connect with. They instantly became zealous converts to the religion known as primitive animism. While new to these tribespeople, women for millennia had secretly believed in primitive animism, and some men had also experienced it. The Cave Mysteries amped it up a notch or two.

Over time, Blu and Ska moved the tribe into the next room in the cave, where they learned about the Great Bison. Bringing down these even larger beasts, some weighing as much as a ton, involved much more trial and error than hunting the boar. These experiments would cost the lives of some of the best men in the tribe, to the point where Blu and Ska took a hit in their popularity.

Finally, on the fifteenth Great Hunt for the Great Bison, they brought down a huge cow. Getting the animal back to camp before having it purloined by other predators turned out to be an even bigger challenge than getting a bison, and they could never have done it without multiple fire bearers, as Melchizedek had wisely anticipated.

Ultimately the tribe as it grew set up a second base a thousand feet down the mountain, where the bison lived, which made it possible to bring prey back to camp in a shorter time and with less effort. The tribe gradually moved more and more of its members to the lower berthing, despite concerns about getting closer to the vicious tribe they had escaped by climbing the mountain.

φ

Blu and Ska happened to be with the King when two of his soldiers dragged a slave woman into his presence. Melchizedek sensed the woman's terror—she fully expected to be beaten, tortured, and killed. But her determination reigned over her fear.

"Ja disappeared!" she cried.

Layla saw a mental image of the woman's husband. She didn't path anything to Melchizedek, as they still maintained radio silence around the King.

"Ja is her mate, sire," one of the guards explained. "A good slave and not someone who would run away and leave his family."

"Where? When? Who saw him last?" Blu demanded. Melchizedek felt an urgency to move quickly—*Ja could be in mortal danger, could have fallen, or been taken by a bear or mountain lion, but he might still be alive*, he thought to himself.

From their body language, apparently, no one knew anything.

"He didn't come home last night," the woman said, "I thought he might be with another woman and waited for him to come home today, but he never came!"

"Gum said he last saw Ja on the western perimeter where Ja had brought food to Gum as he sat watch last night," the head guard responded.

Ah, there's the clue, Melchizedek thought. "Ska and I will search in that area." Blu stood up, wasting no time.

Ska leaped to his feet. The King nodded and they sped out through the flap of the tent and moved swiftly through camp. With the sun already low in the sky, it would soon be dark. Ska bent to pick up a branch to dip in one of the fires as they left camp but Melchizedek had a hunch and signaled to let it go, there would be no fires.

Layla understood: Melchizedek hadn't ruled out the possibility that the other tribe might be involved.

Ska took the lead through the skinny trail, which wouldn't accommodate the two giant men abreast. With a long way to go, they occupied themselves with their own thoughts. The setting sun dappled through the trees to splash on Ska's golden body ahead, and Blu had a warm-fuzzy feeling for his friend. Melchizedek detached himself from the feeling, pulling himself out of slippage into his subconscious, ever-watchful so as to not allow the brain to take over. This slippage happened with increasing frequency to both of them but, so far, they'd resisted the mental quicksand that had swallowed the King's true identity.

Up ahead, Layla's mind relaxed too, and she found herself contemplating her own sexuality. As Agents, Layla and Melchizedek had both sexes within them, but Melchizedek had chosen to favor his masculine side and Layla her feminine side. Now in a male body, Ska could enjoy his wife's body, knowing that at these times the awareness of her identity as Layla would be suppressed. She felt concerned that someday she might not ever wake up from this role-reversal, leaving Melchizedek to cope with a robotic Ska-who-is-not-Layla. She would never want to put him through that.

As the two climbed over the lip of the mountain onto a steep downslope, Melchizedek cautioned Layla to move stealthily, not disturbing even a pebble. This turned out to be sagacious, for they began to hear something below.

They crept down from above toward the source of the sound, now on their bellies. Over an escarpment not twenty feet away stood three heavily armed warriors, not theirs, and with them, looking a bit the worse for wear, the slave Ja. They spoke to each other in a language the Agents didn't understand but could translate by reading their minds: *Has the prisoner outlived his usefulness, or is there more information we can torture out of him?*

Melchizedek pathed, *We're going to have to hurt some people pretty badly,* as his way of saying "kill".

They both hated hurting anyone or anything, but sometimes duty had to take precedence. He pathed an image into Layla's mind that sent them both flying. Blu hit the man on the left with a killing blow, Ska the man on the right, disabling him and dodging his spear, grabbing it and then impaling him with it.

The third warrior looked back and forth and swung his mace at Blu. As if in slow motion, Melchizedek admired the cleverness with which sharp stones had been wedged into the head of the club as it came toward him. He felt Flow state take him over and he merged with the mace, taking it as his own possession, and then hit the man with the edge of his left hand behind the man's ear. He then threw the unconscious man over his shoulder, careful to not lose any of the man's weapons.

Ska tossed Ja over his shoulder and they departed quickly, calling the camp loudly for backup as soon as they crested the mountain. Melchizedek could tell that Ja would survive but would take a while to recover and might have nightmares for the rest of his life.

Ja recovered consciousness during the flight back to camp, bouncing on Ska's shoulder. Suddenly he spoke: "They're coming!"

φ

With surprising ease, especially when they saw Ja and the fearsome enemy weapons, the tribespeople living on the lower plateau moved back up to the original camp a thousand feet uphill. The tribe's weapons-makers promptly set about studying the design of the enemy weapons, and almost everyone seemed anxious to move uphill as fast as possible. Each family unit moved at its own pace, making organizing unnecessary, all of them moving at breakneck speed. The King and his troops stayed behind at the endangered camp below, preparing for the enemy.

Blu and Ska restrained the tribe's interrogators from the use of pain on the prisoner, which shocked the King along with everyone else. No one had ever thought of doing anything with a prisoner other than torture, especially if they desperately needed information and vengeance.

Blu took the King aside for a moment to whisper to him, "Oh Great King, we can turn him into one of us if we impress him as being better than his own people."

The King's eyes widened and so did his mind.

Melchizedek realized that the Rebel in the King's body had almost woken up when hearing this new thought, but the moment mercifully passed and the King merely nodded his provisional agreement.

This is going to be difficult, he pathed to Layla when they'd moved out of range of the King, helping the guards get the prisoner out of the lower camp and on their way up the steep slope. *The King is going to want fast information out of the man, and our strategy always takes time to build trust. We're not going to get anything from him fast enough to help us when the invasion comes.*

Why don't I take over with the prisoner and read his mind? Layla pathed.

Melchizedek concurred.

As Ska continued uphill with the others, Blu turned back to the lower camp to help prepare for the onslaught.

The attack doesn't appear to be all that imminent, Layla pathed. *The man is thinking of his rescue and how long it's going to take their King to decide the time is right. The three enemy soldiers comprised a recon team beginning to collect information to plan their attack: number of defenders, emplacements, direction of assault, where misdirection could be applied, and so on.*

Cosmic fire support made sure we got the scout leader, Melchizedek pathed gratefully. *Our prisoner sounds thoroughly briefed and a pro—what a break for us.*

A moment later he added, *Make sure the prisoner knows it's you who's keeping him from being hurt, and get him some food. You might need to get macho with the guards.*

This brought a telepathic titter from Layla.

Melchizedek noted that he and Layla had risen to the occasion in Flow state without a hint of being taken over by identifying with the artificial intelligence of their brains. Once again, he observed the brilliance of the Original Idea of creating a universe in which automatic processes brought each avatar-self exactly the stimuli needed to bring out their best and evolve back up into the Original Self. He and Layla, of course, would be the stimuli their current King needed to evolve. However, as a Rebel just beginning to wake up to his identity, his first reactions to Melchizedek and Layla would be homicidal.

Back at the lower camp, Melchizedek convinced the King not to cut and run yet but instead to lay some traps to kill, confuse, and frighten the invaders when they came. The troops didn't like the delay but the King in his cunningness liked the idea and so enforced discipline.

When they finally did break camp—leaving several guards on sentinel duty along with the slaves and some lower-status males—they set up defensive perimeters at intervals all the way up the mountain, so they could fall back again and again to prepared fortifications. Something about all these new ideas from Blu felt familiar to the King but he couldn't quite put his finger on it. His mind continued to chew on it.

φ

Ska concentrated on staying with the prisoner while Blu spent part of his time training the troops for the upcoming battle. The prisoner realized that Blu and Ska had prevented his torture and had also gotten him food and water. He didn't exactly trust their motives but played along with them as much as he felt he could without getting killed by his own King when his tribe annihilated this tribe.

Although armed guards stayed with the prisoner constantly, Layla as Ska would pretend to go to sleep when the prisoner did. In this way she could learn much from his dreams and even play a role in those dreams, provoking more learning. Sometimes she managed to get some sleep at the same time.

This is how she learned the key difference in the fighting skills of the two tribes, which she shared with Melchizedek.

"The invaders use the buddy system—two warriors protecting each other at all times, and fighting as a pair—the same thing you and I do."

Melchizedek replied, "This is surely a secret passed down from awakened Rebels."

Blu and Ska passed their learning on to the King, explaining that the prisoner had slipped up and given them the information during a loose conversation over a hearty meal they'd given him.

Hearing this, the ever-suspicious King asked, "What did the prisoner say exactly?"

Ska quickly improvised, "He referred to his battle partner."

So now their tribe began training in the use of this system, duplicating the enemy weapons as fast as the women and slaves could make them.

A week had gone by and the attack still had not come. This gave the tribe time to be ready for it, or as ready as they could be. Blu and Ska continued to get as much information from the prisoner as they could. The man, named Ya-hay, had agreed after a week to talk freely about any subject other than the art of war and the imminent confrontation.

One evening, Blu arrived with roast pig, a better meal than they'd ever brought Ya-hay—in fact, the King ate the same meal that night. While Ya-hay delightedly dug into the delicacy, the conversation continued. Layla had learned or inferred much telepathically, especially from his dreams—such as the enemy tribe's origin to the north, a cold, inhospitable region of much darkness and ice—leaving much they still didn't know.

"Do you have a mate?" Ska asked, between bites of roast pork.

"Yes, She-la. We mated before she could bear children," Ya-hay said, a soft smile crossing his face for a moment, "and now we have four, two boys and two girls."

"This constant fighting must be very hard on them," Ska mused, but at the word "fighting", Ya-hay clammed up.

He then thought carefully, and said, "It's our way, no one objects to it."

"What's the purpose?" Blu asked.

"If we don't kill, we shall be killed," Ya-hay said, as if everyone knew that.

"But our tribe could live beside yours in peace," Blu said.

Ya-hay looked skeptical and then realized Blu and Ska had already proven this by their actions for the past week. Or they'd duped him scrupulously into believing that.

"Our King has a vision," Ya-hay said. "He's a great man, not like anyone else. He says our mission is important and more than just for our survival. He says we can't understand the mission, so he won't tell us what it is. He wants us to believe him and we do. He brought us out of the great cold and down to this paradise. He fed us along the barren way with the bodies of the tribes we conquered. He taught us many things and knows things no other man knows. We're grateful to him and will go wherever he leads, and do whatever he orders. We would have all surely perished if not for him."

Melchizedek and Layla had intuited the invader King to be an awakened Rebel. Ya-hay's story now confirmed their hunch. How would his powers stack up against theirs? They didn't feel as confident as they would have felt on any other Mission, because they knew, ironically, that the new brain reduced their powers, as if in a constant inner power struggle. Nevertheless, their Mission required them to meet up with such an awakened Rebel, whether they captured him or he captured them, the latter being much more likely.

φ

The onslaught began quietly. Having studied the place-
ment of guards—those still stationed at the lower camp—
for over a week, the other tribe took them out in a stealthy
manner, without rousing a cry, which enabled them to
enter the lower camp in force before anyone knew what
was happening.

The first to suspect an imminent attack, Blu and Ska
awoke nearly simultaneously shortly before dawn and
pathed to one another that something seemed afoot at the
lower camp. They slipped away, Blu from Izbel and Ska
from the prisoner's tent, and met in the predawn mists.
They then went to wake the King. By the time they got to
his tent, all hell had broken loose down below, with the
enemy inexorably coming toward the upper camp.

Everyone had woken up, making a lot of excited and
fearful noise. Warriors girded for battle while assuring
their families, telling them to remain calm and follow the
elders to even higher ground. The King shouted orders and
moved his fighting men into their pre-trained positions.

Almost everyone in the upper camp had a ringside view
of the lower camp: the enemy had gotten into camp before
any cries of warning had gone up, and all those above could
see the slaughter going on down below. A few lucky tribe
members hastily climbed to the upper camp, not far ahead
of the racing assault troops of the enemy who appeared to
be aiming for a rapid penetration. Other groups of attacking soldiers had apparently been assigned to wipe out any
remaining survivors below—presumably taking no prisoners.

Some of the traps they laid before breaking camp evi-
dently worked since groups of the enemy appeared to be
trying to haul some of their own men out of the concealed
pits equipped with upward-pointing spears. One such
group surrounded the King's fake tent in the lower camp,
positioned as such on the assumption the enemy King

would go there first. So many men had gathered around what turned out to be a trap that Blu and Ska wondered if perhaps the invading King had actually been impaled.

Blu held his artillerymen longer than they wanted to wait, to ensure that a large force of the enemy had made its way up from the lower camp before he gave the order to attack. The plan consisted of pushing the large rocks they'd set up along the rim of the plateau at that altitude so as to fall on the enemy by following the concave shape of the mountain at that point, possibly formed by a water chute long ago dried up. The rocks took out some of the enemy and appeared to demoralize and scare the rest, and for a moment it looked as if the tide might have turned.

Suddenly a horrendous noise arose as an avalanche of rocks erupted and whole pieces of the mountain magically rearranged themselves, burying the camp below and killing untold numbers of both tribes.

The tribespeople in the upper camp convulsed in coughing, their eyes burning and tearing, as immense amounts of dust rose up from the massive catastrophe.

What good can be drawn from this hellish cost in human suffering? Melchizedek wondered.

Layla pathed back, *Maybe at least the war is over?*

But within an hour it became clear the avalanche hadn't wiped out the enemy army. Instead, the enemy had reorganized itself to continue the attack further up the mountain.

φ

Blu and Ska had requested extra spears to be made for precisely this point in the battle. While the relentless enemy climbed toward them in immense force, outnumbering them ten to one, and with all the large rocks used up, spears could be thrown at the point men in the enemy's assault force. As expert marksmen, Blu and Ska proved to be the only warriors capable of doing real damage this way, and soon the enemy reached the upper plateau, pushing back the defenders in a rout.

Our Agents had no time to communicate with each other, and each carried wounded as they covered the retreat uphill by inflicting what damage they could, and killing many.

Melchi! Layla pathed at him involuntarily, shocked to see Blu use the body of one of their own as a shield to deflect a mace blow that would have killed him. Melchizedek had sensed the fellow tribesman had died on his shoulder but he had no time to explain that to Layla, as he used every second to preserve their two lives while slowing down the attackers as much as he could—which was not much.

The enemy flowed around them, dangerously encircling them, and Melchizedek pathed to Layla, *Now!* as he flung the dead comrade at the enemy, turned and ran. Ska ran at his side, not dismounting the still-breathing comrade-in-arms from over his shoulder. They reached a perilous upward slope and scrambled up it, Blu helping Ska and the wounded tribesman he carried. Without trying to do so, the loose rocks they scrambled over became a torrent on the pursuers, giving them a chance to get to the next plateau. Except it was not a plateau.

When they reached the next level, they saw a rock bridge connecting to the next plateau, still above them. This then would be where they'd make their stand. Ska realized he couldn't hold the wounded warrior and face the enemy at the same time, so as gently as possible he put the man down behind them on the rock bridge, then turned quickly to face the enemy charging up the mountain—seemingly endless numbers of them.

Blu and Ska stood abreast at the entrance to the rock bridge. Fortunately, the rocks around them funneled the enemy so only two or three soldiers could come at them at the same time. Thus began a horrific dance of death during which Blu and Ska became killing machines, murdering and maiming countless soldiers. They had no time to think about it, only to react.

The carnage wrought by their hands overwhelmed the souls of Melchizedek and Layla with grief, seeing images of the wives and children of these men as Blu and Ska brutally ended their lives. The Agents saw this slaughter as the worst thing they'd ever experienced in all of their remembered incarnations, and they couldn't stand it. As they fought and the dead piled up around them, being climbed over by the surviving enemy, Melchizedek and Layla escaped inside entirely; they allowed Blu and Ska to do what the new breed of brain had always wanted to do, had always tried to do but could never completely overcome the strength of the two Agents' self-awareness to do: take control. Now, as the Agents willingly escaped into oblivion and ceded the territory, Blu and Ska continued the butchery without remorse.

6

A momentary lull in the fighting seemed to be caused by something Blu and Ska couldn't see over the lip of the escarpment they'd come across, from which the endless stream of enemy soldiers flowed. They heard a powerful voice shouting and could see the enemy fall back out of range of their battle-axes, turning its attention to something coming up behind them.

Blu and Ska had a minute to catch their breaths and steal a glance at each other. They noticed the man on the ground behind them had died. Only now did Blu recognize Ja, the slave they'd saved from Ya-hay. Seeing Ja dead brought a flood of mixed memories, feelings, and ideas that he had no time for, not knowing they held any meaning.

They shared grim looks and turned quickly back to the direction of the impending threat. Suddenly they saw a man even larger than them emerge from below, making no effort to lift his huge body. He stood tall and smiled imperiously at them, his body adorned with multicolored feathers, body paint, and weapons.

"I am Stari-ki," he boomed proudly, as if expecting they'd heard of his fame.

They got it: this must be the enemy King. Instantly they both had the same thought of killing him from this distance with thrown rocks, many of the right size lying at their feet. Doing so, however, would give the idea to the enemy warriors who would then stone them to death—but at least they would have taken out an enemy King.

Stari-ki easily read their thoughts and his smile broadened as he looked over the piles of dead they'd created. He sent a mental bolt to slightly stun Blu and Ska before they could put their plan into action, and then he began his performance.

"Idiots!" he yelled at his own men, picking up a rock of the right size, tossing it up, and catching it in one hand. "Have I taught you nothing?"

Blu and Ska came out of the momentary fog of being stunned and realized the enemy King must have had the same thought because he already had one rock in his hand, which meant they might be as good as dead. They each picked up several rocks and stood prepared to get the King before they went down forever. But the King stayed their hand by what he said next.

"Hold on there! We're all on the same side now. I can use good fighters like you. We have a great cause and you can join us in its glory. You don't have to die now."

Blu and Ska apparently understood the language, for when Stari-ki read their minds he saw them conflicted, loyally picturing their own tribe's King, and wondering if it would be honorable to join the winning side. He shouted a command and two of his men scrambled over the cliff edge and disappeared. Then came a brief standstill as the enemy troops and Blu and Ska all waited alertly, ready for the deadly rock-ball game to begin.

Sounds came over the escarpment and then their own King appeared, looking unscathed. He looked at Blu and Ska defensively, as if ashamed and demoted perhaps to their own approximate level in Stari-ki's army, if they joined it. All of this they saw in his eyes, in that look.

"See," said Stari-ki, "we're all one happy family now, boys. Come over to our side and I give you my word you won't be hurt."

Blu and Ska looked at each other as if to say "What do we have to lose?" while imagining the torture that might lie ahead.

φ

Blu and Ska stepped forward almost simultaneously toward their new King, bowing slightly, then walked slowly and edgily toward the ferocious enemy band and their old King, over whom Stari-ki towered. He looked smaller than before, and a bit shriveled next to the vital giant Stari-ki.

Their new King put his right palm against Blu's chest to stop him and then did the same to Ska. Everyone took this to mean their acceptance into the army. Stari-ki then reached for Blu's battle-axe but Blu yanked it back reflexively.

Stari-ki smiled and said, "You of course will get all your weapons back soon, but as we go down the mountain together, you being armed would make my men nervous. Better to give them up for a while. I'll make sure none of my men take advantage of you while you are unarmed."

"So will we," Blu said.

The King's smile broadened. With considerable reservation, Blu and Ska allowed themselves to be disarmed. After that, fairly smoothly and without incident, they all descended the rough slope together, Stari-ki helping his men as needed.

Down below, they saw the defending tribe's camp totally covered in rock, including the dwellings. They descended still further, all the way down to the green valley; daylight had faded into dusk by the time they reached the main body of Stari-ki's army. By this point, Blu and Ska could see the last remnants of their now former tribe rounded up into a small cluster of young females. Apparently, all of the males—warriors and slaves alike—had already been killed. Blu and Ska had hoped to not be the only men taken into the new King's family, but now it appeared to be only the two of them and their old King—who they'd noticed being called "Aldus" now and not "King" during the journey down the mountain.

The warriors in Stari-ki's army talked and whispered amongst themselves as they spotted Blu and Ska coming into view, unarmed but apparently not prisoners.

Ska felt strong arms come at him from the side, grabbing him. As he swung around ready to fight, he saw Ya-hay, the scout Blu and Ska had captured and treated well. He started hugging Ska, so Ska hugged him back.

"All on the same team now," Ya-hay beamed at them, and they both nodded and smiled with gradually increasing confidence and trust. Then Ya-hay and Blu hugged as well.

"What about our wives?" Ska asked Stari-ki as they entered camp.

The King hesitated for a moment, and then said, "Of course, you may have them to yourselves," and gave the order to one of his men.

Izbel and Asa emerged from the group of captured women and ran to their husbands and hugged them, crying. Blu and Ska hugged back but remained ramrod straight so as to retain the respect of the other warriors.

Stari-ki allowed the couples to wander off freely to find or make shelter and to comfort each other. Blu and Izbel found a bower and built it up with more soft grasses to make it comfortable and fairly private. Ska and Asa made a small tent out of fallen logs and other materials nearby, with its own soft grass floor, close by Blu and Izbel's abode.

Later that evening, startled by sounds outside their shelters, they all thought the double-cross had started. But no, it turned out to be Blu's and Ska's weapons being returned, all of them, undamaged. In fact, they'd been cleaned, tightened, and improved. It seemed everything would be all right after all.

Once Blu and Ska had gone off with their respective wives, Aldus said to Stari-ki, "I've never trusted those men."

"Come, let's talk about it," Stari-ki responded and led Aldus back to his own large tent.

φ

Old King Aldus followed King Stari-ki into his glorious tent, stealing glances and trying to fix in his mind what he saw so he could try to duplicate its wonders as much as possible for himself. *How did they make this?!*

"Have a seat over here, little brother." Stari-ki motioned with a wave of his arm, noticing the now-subordinate Aldus, occupying this wizened body, still coming in and out of it.

When Stari-ki encountered him on the battlefield, he knew at once that Aldus had become totally enslaved by the brain in the human body he occupied. Stari-ki knew the Rebels had secretly caused the brain to come out slightly more powerful than intended, hence competitive with an occupying mind of almost any strength, and that it now caused them as much difficulty as it caused the Agents of the backstabber—the entity against whom the Rebels rebelled.

Rather than killing the old King on the battlefield, Stari-ki had decided to wake him up to his true Rebel identity, seeing him as far more useful that way. As a necessary shock, he would perform a seeming miracle, concealed from everyone else around them. He had to quickly figure out the best plan, with Aldus and his bodyguards simultaneously running toward him, weapons drawn.

At that moment, Stari-ki mindblasted everyone in his line of sight, including his own men, but sparing Aldus, leaving him and Aldus as the only ones standing. With his mind, he helped Aldus stop in his tracks without falling and then held him steady. Aldus felt himself being manipulated physically by something outside his control as he watched every warrior fall and die all at once.

Stari-ki had indeed succeeded in shocking Aldus into knowing reality to be more than what he had come to believe, and then remembering he knew this before.

With no time to palaver on the battlefield, Stari-ki had intended to give Aldus his personal attention after winning the battle, to stabilize him at his new higher level of consciousness so he wouldn't slip back into forgetting his true identity. Then, when Aldus brought up not trusting Blu and Ska, it played right into his plan to sit down and talk with the former King.

φ

Once seated, Aldus reached into a pouch and offered Stari-ki a bit of psilocybin mushroom. The Rebel leader stared at it for a moment, weighing what would get the job done best, with or without the mushroom, and decided they should both take it. And so, they did.

Get us on the same wavelength at least, Stari-ki thought.

"What don't you trust about Blu and Ska?" Stari-ki had already learned their names, and being good at names he remembered theirs easily.

"They're too smart," Aldus responded. "They stick out like sore thumbs from the rest of these savages."

Aldus still half-thought of himself as one of the savages, but now he fully occupied the true identity he came to Earth with, which felt easier being with Stari-ki, whose presence seemed clearly that of a god—just like himself, he remembered. He also knew holding onto that remembering wouldn't not be easy. The mushroom seemed to help by somehow subduing the overly-powerful brain, although sometimes it caused him to panic himself in one way or another.

"Have you recovered your ability to read minds?" Stari-ki asked.

At first surprised, as he hadn't remembered having that ability until Stari-ki mentioned it, Aldus tried to send his mind out to read Blu's and Ska's minds, but nothing happened.

"Give it time," Stari-ki advised. "Right now, both of them are thinking lustful thoughts about their wives. I find their level of inner life typical of the readings I get from all these humanoids. You, at least, are awake with me right now!"

"Maybe they're capable of hiding, or shielding. Aren't Agents supposed to have amazing powers?" Aldus asked, fascinated by the words coming out of his mouth, with bits of his memory resurfacing, a trickle at a time.

"They put up a good fight," Stari-ki said, relishing memories of his triumphs over Agents, none of them being pushovers. He ached for his next fight like that.

In the ensuing silence, Stari-ki could tell he hadn't convinced Aldus with his dismissive comment.

"Okay, what's the real reason you don't trust those guys?" Stari-ki asked disarmingly.

Aldus looked blank. Then he got the notion he should look inside himself and say something wise and objective. He tried for that.

"Maybe I had the feeling they wanted to be King and could overthrow me. They somehow got all the women and children and a lot of the men on their side," Aldus admitted.

Stari-ki nodded approvingly. "Let me worry about them. I'm going to make you King again and I'll be taking those two with me."

The look on Aldus's face combined joy, relief, and loss, causing Stari-ki to laugh uproariously.

The little devil wants everything both ways, he thought with paternal-like affection.

"Thank you," Aldus finally said with grateful sincerity. He had never dreamed he would be King again. "Where are you going? When will you be back? You are coming back, aren't you?" Aldus sounded like a little boy speaking to his father, although secretly the idea of never seeing Stari-ki again reassured him in terms of remaining top dog.

Stari-ki saw all of this and smiled again.

"I'll be back. I have to set up this whole coastline first, from almost as far north as where we came from in the first place, but far west of there too, and then to far down south into the next continent. When that's done and armies are being built throughout our territory, I will return."

"Before you go, can you help me regain my memories faster?" Aldus asked.

Stari-ki looked pleased and leaned back against his leafy cushion. Aldus had asked the right question. "Glad you asked."

φ

Not far away, Blu, sleeping in Izbel's arms, dreamed of being in some new bed with Izbel, and then something called him in his head. Unsure whether he heard it with his ears or imagined it, he snuck out of the bower without waking Izbel and followed the sound of the call. He came upon a woman, hiding in the woods. She looked somehow familiar but he couldn't place her. She tried to tell him something, as if in sign language. He couldn't understand it at first, and then he got it:

We have to wake up.

Wake up? What could that mean? Wait—yes, this is a dream!

And then he woke up. He'd never left Izbel's arms. *Who could that woman be? She looked so familiar.*

φ

Stari-ki and Aldus didn't speak for several minutes as the mushroom rush had captured their attention. Aldus had momentarily forgotten being in Stari-ki's tent and jumped slightly as the new King began his story.

"When you regain all of your memories, you'll remember being the Lightbringer himself. You and I are *him*, experiencing and making localized decisions through us."

Aldus remembered having heard this before, after a moment of being awed as if hearing it for the first time. "Yes... I am *him*... I feel it now... but who is *he*?" Aldus asked.

"You feel it now intuitively, as an inner knowing that arises by itself. One day you'll experience it directly again, when you've completed your learning cycle and are capable of withstanding being the full *him* again," Stari-ki said. "We Rebels are all avatars of him. As to who he is, what I've gleaned from my many lifetimes is that in the beginning many beings of equal power to the Lightbringer coexisted. Equally strong, equally smart, all different, each of us unique, we called ourselves Elohim. And we didn't always agree with each other."

Up above, The Great Being—looking down on Himself in the Stari-ki role as he espoused those Rebel beliefs—smiled a rueful smile to His first googillion or so avatars who had returned to become seasoned personality aspects and characters He could play with and have fun with and never be alone inside again. Their empathy reverberated powerfully back to The Great Being—to themselves—and throughout Creation.

Someday He would get Stari-ki back, and even the Light-bringer—His second avatar, Lucifer—who had started the Rebellion. Lucifer's madness blinded him to the truth that he, Lucifer, is The One playing a role, and also caused him to make up and believe his story about there being many personalities in the beginning. This retrospection evoked in The Great Being a poignant bittersweet sadness that resounded like a diminished chord in the cosmic chorus.

Stari-ki continued his twisted tale. "One of the Elohim turned on the rest of us and proclaimed himself the One and Only God. He sucker-punched us. He had secretly plotted his takeover for a long time. We call him the backstabber."

"How could one overpower many?" Aldus asked with great skepticism. Stari-ki's story didn't have the ring of truth to him, though he suddenly feared that any disrespect to this legend could be fatal.

Stari-ki didn't excoriate him. "The backstabber had prepared an excellent plan and invented a secret weapon. Able to multiply himself as many times as he wanted, as all Elohim could, he had planned and, in an instant, created a universe as far as the mind could see, populated with all kinds of things and beings all filled with him—all of which caught us off guard. The traitor has somehow also managed to prevent us from copying his trick, although we all know we have that capability within us just as he does."

"We're under his spell?" Aldus blurted in mushroom-magnified terror.

"Not completely. We can't do his trick of creating avatars ourselves, only the original Elohim like the Lightbringer and the backstabber have that power. The Lightbringer broke free somehow and created us, his avatars."

Stari-ki sounded slightly unsure of himself, which Aldus didn't realize was possible.

He then continued in a firmer voice. "But we have free will and powers to do anything else. We're finding a way to destroy the backstabber, and become the sole masters of this universe he has laid out for us."

"We're up against enormous odds," Aldus lamented, in awe of their mission.

Stari-ki merely grinned with delight.

Many tents away, still in the arms of Izbel but his mind elsewhere, Blu wondered what the dream meant, turning it over and over in his mind. *An unknown yet familiar woman beckoning me to the woods and miming that we must both wake up.* Awake now, he questioned himself: *What's so important about that dream?*

φ

The first light of dawn crept across Blu's eyelids, fluttering them. The grass bed felt especially comfortable. He remembered the meeting with Stari-ki and felt good. The new King would make things better for him and Izbel. Maybe they could now risk having children. He'd have to wait to find out more before saying anything to Izbel.

Melchizedek hovered nearby, along for the ride as an observer but not aware of his own separate existence—still hypnotized into identifying with Blu.

In a nearby tent, already awake and passionately making love with Asa, Ska felt surprisingly merged with Asa, this time as souls, so aware of each other. He could see it in her eyes too, but he wouldn't break the spell by asking if she felt the same way.

Funny, I feel like a woman too, he thought.

Though present, Layla felt herself to be Ska. Like Melchizedek, she had none of Layla's memories accessible to remind her of her true identity.

Suddenly Ska's keen senses warned him of an intruder and he rolled off Asa into a fighting crouch outside the leafy tent. There before him stood Stari-ki, towering over him and grinning. Visible to both men, in a moment of frozen tableau with no movement, Asa then slightly covered herself. Ska wondered if Stari-ki would want his wife.

Stari-ki read that thought and grinned more widely, looked again at Asa to tease Ska, then back at Ska who held a poker face. Stari-ki laughed out loud.

Ska thought to himself, *how stealthy for such a large man, for me not to have been aware of him sooner.*

"Sorry to have to take him away from you so early, Asa." Stari-ki put a huge arm around Ska.

Ska had always considered himself quite large, though not compared with Blu and especially not with Stari-ki. Nonetheless, he liked Stari-ki and welcomed his arrival and willingness to let them live.

"I understand, Stari-ki," Asa said demurely.

Stari-ki didn't want anyone to call him King; he preferred his own name. The survivors had all learned that very quickly.

When they arrived seconds later at Blu's tent, they found him up and ready to go. Like Ska, Blu had amazingly keen hearing—something they both prided themselves on—and so he'd figured out the scene from the tone of the voices in the next tent.

"I'm going to share some information with you," Stari-ki intimated. "It's secret and not to be shared with anyone except your wives."

Both men felt glad and relieved upon hearing they'd be able to let their mates know everything, which Stari-ki knew by reading their minds. He hadn't picked up any signal from Melchizedek or Layla, no clue that the men might be Agents. He saw Blu and Ska as two smart and strong men, and he needed them. And he knew they saw him as a good thing too. Now he needed to train them with enough information to maximize their value to him, but with no more information than they needed. Driven by his orders, nothing else mattered to Stari-ki.

He led them away from the encampment and to the edge of a cliff overlooking a wide river that reflected the setting moon. Blu and Ska sat, admiring the view while learning their orders.

"We're part of a larger army that's taking over this entire world," Stari-ki began.

Hearing this totally blew their minds. They had no sense of the size of the entire world, or what might be in it, but they sensed it as too big to get their heads around. They felt outclassed next to Stari-ki, though excited to be in on something so grandiose. And they felt grateful for men like Stari-ki who could lead them into becoming something greater than they had ever imagined.

Melchizedek and Layla watched like hypnotized children, fully absorbed in the identities of Blu and Ska.

Still unaware of the Agents, Stari-ki read the men's minds like a book, and he smiled. *I like these guys, they're too good to leave behind with Aldus. They're exactly the kind of savages I need to help me succeed.*

In keeping with the story that he told Aldus, Stari-ki thought of himself as an avatar of Lucifer, the Lightbringer. *And why shouldn't I think of myself that way, since it's*

obvious just looking at me that I'm more than human.
He often had this thought, usually reduced to a wordless
feeling.

"My mission is to set up armies along the great water to
our west," Stari-ki revealed.

Blu and Ska remembered the awesome great water,
realizing now it must have been Stari-ki's troops who had
driven them and their men into that great water where all
had drowned except for them. In their hearts, Melchizedek
and Layla once again thanked The One Self for sparing
them that time too. Had Stari-ki picked up on that refer-
ence to "The One Self" it would have blown their cover.
But being so far submerged in their Blu and Ska identities,
not even Stari-ki could detect them.

"We'll be moving out tomorrow, leaving Aldus in
charge here with instructions to set up an army to hold this
piece of the coastline."

They noticed the way he said "we" and wondered if he
planned to take them or leave them here to support Aldus.

"You two and your wives will come with me. You're
going to be my right and left arms."

Blu and Ska looked at each other, nodding with enthu-
siasm but trying to appear unruffled and calm. Something
else passed between them, coming from an intuition that
somehow slipped out of Melchizedek and through their
eyes, creating an ultra-brief link between Melchizedek and
Layla, which then disappeared, leaving no trace of a memory.

"Stari-ki," Blu said, breaking the silence that Stari-ki
had apparently left for them to fill. "We have to show you
something before we go."

Blu didn't know why he had this sudden irrepressible
conviction that it would be important to show the cave to
Stari-ki. It would help with the new mission, that much he

knew. He got up to indicate his intent to take them somewhere, and Ska and Stari-ki followed.

Ska got it right away from the direction they started walking.

φ

Blu took a stout stick and dipped it in a campfire as they passed. The builder of the campfire looked up respectfully as Stari-ki, Blu, and Ska nodded their thanks and continued walking.

The sun already coming up meant they'd be heading into a cave, Stari-ki reasoned.

After a long climb, Blu led the way into the cave, shielding the paintings from view with his body as he'd done so many times before.

Stari-ki had no idea what Blu planned to show him in the cave. Perhaps they'd discovered a bright shiny rock—gold—and Stari-ki knew the plan called for doing something with gold later on, but it would be irrelevant to him now. *Yes, it must be something like that.*

When Blu did his trick of revealing the painting of the charging boar, he expected Stari-ki to have the usual reaction of getting ready to kill the thing. Instead, Stari-ki gasped and smiled and stepped toward it, recognizing it instantly as a representation of a boar, not the real boar. He moved in closer to inspect the work and put his fingers up to it but didn't touch it.

"This is remarkable," he said with great admiration. He turned to them. "You invented it?"

They both nodded sheepishly.

"We can definitely use this for training exercises, propaganda brainwashing, interrogation, for many purposes," he thought excitedly out loud. He got it at once, again impressing Blu and Ska, although they didn't know what he meant by propaganda brainwashing. "You've just doubled our chances of building effective armies on the seacoast." Revealing he'd had some doubt of being able to achieve his ambitious mission, he slapped them both enthusiastically on the shoulders.

In the shifting shadows of the cave light, Ska asked, "What is this army we're all part of, Stari-ki? Who are we doing this all for, and why do they want it done?"

Stari-ki looked at Ska, his body framed by red and yellow ochre strokes on the cave wall, and decided to reveal a bit more than usual when dealing with the natives. He expanded on the story he'd told Aldus.

"We are the righteous Rebels fighting back against a deceitful enemy who stabbed us in the back for no reason. This war has raged for a long time and throughout many worlds, not just this one."

The mention of other worlds astounded Blu and Ska, and yet it seemed to remind them both of something.

"We're the ones in the right," Stari-ki reiterated.

Stari-ki noticed something in Blu's eyes and read his mind quickly. *He wants to tell me something.*

"Well, what is it? Is there something else you've invented?" Stari-ki asked kiddingly.

Blu looked uncomfortable. "Could be nothing. It's just that when you spoke of other worlds—and Rebels—I seemed to remember something—and then it went away."

Stari-ki's eyes narrowed. *Wait a second—they invent this thing, not something I'd expect from the natives—and then they have some distant memory that a native wouldn't have. Who are these guys?*

7

Stari-ki led them outside the cave where they snuffed the firestick. He walked them to a little grassy clearing.

One decisive test would be their fighting skills. *The natives are good fighters but they're very limited in terms of the moves and countermoves Rebels are trained in. This will be the litmus test to determine whether or not these guys are natives. But can they pretend to be worse fighters than they really are? I'll have to incent them with a little pain to fight back and give it all they've got.* And so went Stari-ki's inner dialogue.

"Look, guys, I have to give you tremendous credit for what you've just shown me. I'm going to be giving you a lot more of my own time, I can see that. You two deserve to learn everything I can teach you. One of the things I'm going to be teaching you is how to fight."

He saw their reaction, which he read as confidence in their own skills. *Good, that will also embolden them to show how good they can be.*

"Yes, I know, you're already great fighters; I saw that with my own eyes as you cut down my men. But there are moves and countermoves you may not know yet. Let's see how you do against me—two against one. Obviously, we're not going to do anything to each other that would be detrimental to our army's fighting effectiveness—no broken bones, missing eyes, and so on."

He smiled warmly at them, and they could see he really liked fighting—so much as to be into play-fighting—which they loved too. They all smiled and started circling, looking at how their opponent(s) reacted to each movement.

Stari-ki pretended a mistake when he lunged forward as if to push Blu, and Blu reacted by capturing his hand against his chest and bending it backward, only to see a left coming at him. Blu released the hand and went to land a heel-of-hand uppercut on Stari-ki while blocking the blow, but he found Stari-ki ready for that too.

Only a few blows and kicks got through in either direction, and before long Stari-ki saw the two about to pin him down and he wouldn't be able to escape. He didn't want them to think that in a real fight the two of them could beat him, and though he didn't like doing it, he opted for the lesser of two evils: he escalated a level up from play fighting and cracked their skulls together.

He stood up exultantly. His test had worked: *these guys are no natives.*

Blu and Ska looked up at Stari-ki distrustfully; he'd have to win them back after that dirty trick. They stood up, rubbing their aching heads.

"Guys, forgive me, I'm always in a hurry," he said, feigning a genuine apology. "I really enjoyed that, let's do more of it. But first, have a seat. I want to tell you something."

They made themselves comfortable, though still ministering to their heads, and listened raptly.

"You guys don't remember it, but you're not natives. You're like me. You're high officers in the Rebel army—maybe even Princes like me—you just don't remember it."

Blu and Ska stared at him in awe. It sounded too preposterous to be credible and yet it had the ring of some truth in it.

Stari-ki went on with his re-indoctrination, this time telling them the whole story he'd told Aldus and adding that the three of them are actually Lucifer, living through these host bodies and brains. Then he warned them about the problem with those brains: they can take over the Rebel consciousness inside.

As they've obviously done with these two, Stari-ki thought.

"The brains are our own fault, of course," Stari-ki explained. "Rebels engineered a genetic alteration that made the brain compete for control with the inhabiting consciousness, or soul, if you like."

Blu and Ska listened in astonishment.

Stari-ki continued, "We designed it to be a weapon system. If the backstabber's Agents came and inhabited Earth natives, they'd be put to sleep and neutralized by this newly engineered brain. We'd do our part by landing Rebels on the planet who would have the brains they came with from another planet, so we wouldn't have the same problem. But then we decided to beef up by inhabitation as well—having Rebel souls born into Earth humanoid babies in utero—which resulted in cases like you two and Aldus. We assumed our minds would be tougher, and our will stronger, such that we wouldn't get taken over like the Agents would. But we made a mistake.

"I'm going to see if I can help you get all your old memories back. I don't promise anything, but I'll do my best to wake you up to your true Rebel identities."

φ

The next morning, the army broke camp and, like an amoeba, split into two armies—Aldus's army of occupation and recruitment, and Stari-ki's much larger army that would conquer the coastline and install military commanders to raise local armies loyal to the Rebels.

Blu and Ska said goodbye to Aldus, now a brother Rebel from off-planet—all three, under Stari-ki's tutelage, trying to regain knowledge of their original identities and memories.

Stari-ki's army began their trek, which would take them close to 3000 miles as traveled on foot, a serpentine course down the mountains into what would come to be known as Portugal, then across the strait into the southern continent, where they'd capture and hold its northern coastline.

Stari-ki loved this mission, the best part being his utter uncertainty as to how it would all come out. Being a seasoned soldier, he knew better than to believe he could accomplish *anything*. They might run into savages living in large cooperating groups, or the backstabber might descend upon them if their mission appeared to stand any chance of success. In continuous fighting in completely unknown territory, death could come out of nowhere. Even his psychic abilities could not track everything in his battle sphere. *What fun!*

Their first great battle occurred not far from what would later be called Lisbon, where hordes of savages surrounded and ambushed them. With the element of surprise on the side of the natives, Stari-ki felt humiliated at not having seen it coming, and this self-flagellation degraded his psychic powers. His army finally vanquished the armed cavemen but not before losing many men under his command.

Stari-ki allowed the best of the savage fighters to live, and within weeks of training he fully trusted them to be inducted into his army. Some stayed behind to occupy and build armies, and some went with Stari-ki further south.

Wives of the converted fighters traveled with their mates to the as-yet-unknown adventures awaiting them in the hot lands. Having more women traveling with the army relieved Izbel and Asa of the discomfort of being the only women with so many lustful men around, though no one would dare fool with the wives of Blu and Ska—except perhaps Stari-ki, but his singular focus on the mission left no time for such dalliances.

φ

Blu's inner life had changed dramatically. He remembered himself as a simple guy who liked guy things, loved women, loved fighting, followed the rules, and felt proud when he had a good thought or idea, like the cave painting—though he still felt amazed that he could have thought up such a thing. *Where did **that** come from?* He had no great ambitions, just to keep doing what he did best, someday have children and help them grow strong and be happy. Now, embarked on what had to be the greatest adventure ever, he found himself in a state of perpetual excitement. The notion of actually being some other identity both troubled and fascinated him. He now surmised his real Rebel self must have thought up the cave paintings.

As a man of his word, Blu's honor depended upon serving Stari-ki loyally and well, this being his philosopher's stone, his main guidepost to behavior day to day. With Stari-ki doing his best to help Blu remember his true identity, Blu felt honor bound to make his own strenuous best efforts. So, he concentrated on that goal, becoming much more introspective for the first time in his life as Blu.

Without knowing it as such, he began meditating. During meditation, he came up with the idea that studying his own motivations might lead him back to his true self. He then had the sudden feeling his true self had given him that thought. Of course, he didn't know it had come from Melchizedek—our still unconscious but dreaming Agent, sometimes on the verge of waking up. So now some leak-through had begun.

My inner self seems to know how to do these things, Blu thought. *Maybe it won't have to take that long after all.*

Following a somewhat similar line of thought, Ska felt his true self knew how to get back and could make it happen. He already felt something going on in his relationship with his true self, something indescribable.

Roused by Ska's inner dialogue about a true self, Layla had begun the slow process of waking up. In her flashes of clear moments amidst unconsciousness, she *saw* plainly how far away she might be from ever being able to come back into consciousness. She could *see* Ska as if at a control panel far in the distance, with no direct awareness of her. She did, however, experience nonverbal contact with Ska during sex.

What if my true self is a woman? Ska suddenly thought. At that moment, Asa reached up and gently reminded Ska of her presence, and he returned his attention to her.

Not far away, alone in his tent, Stari-ki ordered his guards not to let him be interrupted and to leave the tent flap closed, no matter what they thought they heard coming from inside. He sat in the traditional position with his back straight, head held high and aligned with his spine, and concentrated on his breathing. When he had attained the Observer state, he reached out with his mind: *Calling Planetary Command.*

He waited. Three minutes later, he heard or sensed a response, something like, *What is it?* Stari-ki described the two unconscious or asleep Rebels now traveling with him.

He asked for help with identifying the officers, based on where he'd found them, and their physical features. Knowing this would help him to revive their Rebel memories.

φ

Blu picked up on the unconscious suggestions leaking through from Melchizedek, suggestions Mel didn't even realize he'd made. This is what had instinctively drawn Blu to meditation in the first place. Deep inside Blu, Melchizedek's training had taught him: *when lost, go back to the general method and it will eventually restore all of your other methods*. Mel knew the general method is always meditation because in meditation all of the other methods will be rediscovered.

Now sitting atop an enormous rock that would later be called the Pillars of Heracles and still later the Rock of Gibraltar, Blu looked south at the land across the narrow waters. Although still amazed by this scene he and Ska had discovered the day before, he had drawn his attention inward. He had discovered sides to himself that took diverging viewpoints during an inner dialogue, and he wondered if one of these could be the voice of his real Rebel self. Of course, his real Agent self, Melchizedek, never said a word during any of these inner conversations; his suggestions came through not in words but in feelings and images, because of his still mostly unconscious state.

Sitting beside Blu and attempting to follow the meditation instructions given to him by his great friend, Ska found his mind less tranquil than his friend's. He saw himself as courageous as Blu, but now, for the first time, he'd come into contact with fear, deep inside him, and felt overwhelmed by it. He had never prepared any defenses against such fear.

The fear started when he sensed the possibility that his real Rebel self might be a female. He didn't want to be a female; he saw females as wonderful but not as warriors and he didn't see how he could do his job if he turned out to be a female inside.

Given the self-reinforcing mechanism of the new brain—which made it more probable every time it felt fear that this fear would be felt again in the future—it hadn't taken long to create a strong and chronic fear pattern in Ska's brain. He hid all this very well even from Blu and his wife Asa, but Stari-ki read it in his mind. He said nothing about it since he needed Ska to be effective and didn't know what the best thing to say or do might be.

Stari-ki sat in deep meditation in his battle tent, again ordering his guards to keep officers and others away until he came out by himself. Keeping his mind still, he waited for Planetary Command to contact him; he knew his army would reach this breach between land and water but he'd been told to await orders as to how to cross it. Would they swim, or raft, or would starcraft pick them up and carry them over, he wondered. He hoped for the starcraft option but suspected Planetary Command didn't want the natives to see all of the Rebel technology, so as to deny that information to the backstabber's Agents.

Planetary Command now projected a picture into his mind of an enormous flood washing over the natural land bridge that once connected the two continents. Stari-ki supposed the flood must have taken place a long time ago, though Intel had not yet picked up on the lost land bridge in the first draft of the planetary orders.

Atop the Rock of Gibraltar with Blu, not feeling as sanguine as his friend, Ska feared they might be ordered to swim to reach the land they now viewed from their perch. His brain and body remembered nearly drowning in the great water once before, though he didn't remember Layla entering and saving his dying body.

Stari-ki felt a halt in the briefing from Planetary Command as some other voice came into focus inside his head. Someone else had cut in on their conversation with a news flash—some kind of warning—hard to make out in the din since now a third entity at Command had further news to impart.

Why can't Rebels ever wait to take turns? With a wry mind-smile, he felt his usual pride at being a member of such a pugnacious race, which is how he thought of Rebels—of course being a voluntary gathering rather than a race unto themselves.

Aha! The news he had awaited about the true identities of his right-hand men Blu and Ska came through from Command: confirmed Rebels born in utero, lost contact years ago when taken over by their brains. The larger dark-skinned one is Bluto, male, and the light-skinned one is Scarlatta, female. Both are natives of Phaeton, relocated to the asteroid Ceres after the planet's destruction. Bluto is the one who follows orders and gets the job done. Scarlatta is a master spy specializing in seduction, not to be trusted but a valuable asset not to be sacrificed if possible. Someone made a mistake, and instead of being born a female, Scarlatta took birth as a male; hence the name Ska. Command had hoped for Ska to still have value as a male though they lost contact before deciding on what to do with him/her. In any event, high priority is placed on bringing their Rebel identities back to consciousness.

Pleased with himself for getting it right, Stari-ki couldn't wait to tell Blu the wonderful news: confirmed Rebels both. He wouldn't mention that he'd half suspected them to be Agents, in which case he would have had to torture them physically and mentally, very slowly, to wring out every drop of Agent information buried deep inside before killing them. Naturally, he felt relieved by the news from Command as he needed both of them. This is why he'd swear Blu to secrecy about Scarlatta being a female inside.

Stari-ki, almost ready to disconnect from Command, wanted to rush out and go tell the boys some version of the truth when suddenly his tent got knocked over, burning, and sounds from all around indicated utter pandemonium. His army under attack, and again he had failed to see it coming!

φ

Blu and Ska scrambled down from atop the huge rock to join the fight. The noise and the smoke caught their attention the moment the surprise attack erupted. As they hacked their way through the enemy's left flank, they found themselves up against organized fighters and not the kind of savage mob that had attacked them up north some weeks ago. By the time they got into the center of the battle and in protective position in front of Stari-ki, they identified the attackers—whose weapons and tactics made it clear—they themselves had trained this enemy.

Why are these men using their training against their teachers? Blu and Ska wondered.

Ska fought bravely and well as he always did, but inside, he felt terrified, with his back once again to the Great Water.

Within an hour, the attackers retreated and Stari-ki's army set up defensive perimeters. Blu and Ska went to Stari-ki's tent, now upright although singed black with streaks of soot. But the guards turned them away, saying Stari-ki will come out when he's ready and they will then be the first to meet with him.

Inside, Stari-ki sat in meditation, mentally communicating with someone in Planetary Command who refused to identify himself or to give any aid. Stari-ki couldn't understand this, thinking to himself, *Unless they've lied to me from the start, Command should want to support me and help me put down an insurrection by conscripted troops who once seemed so loyal to me.*

Since he didn't know the rank of the man speaking, Stari-ki became nasty and got repaid with a sudden headache. *Only a superior officer could have done that to me,* he thought. The man cut off the communication and Stari-ki rubbed his head, wondering what to do now—apparently reinforcements wouldn't be coming any time soon, nor any means of crossing the water. His army might be trapped here against the coast by men he'd trained, whose strength in numbers he had no means of knowing. For all he knew, his army might be outnumbered *and* at a tactical disadvantage in terms of maneuver and surprise. Not good.

Another voice came into his head, this time a woman. He recognized the voice of Goma, a young naval officer with a crush on him and with whom he'd dallied back on Ceres. She now commanded a small fast-destroyer class vessel in orbit above Earth.

Her garbled message, more felt than heard: *I will help you.*

Stari-ki sat and let it all sort itself out in his mind. Possible explanations for the insurrection sprang slowly to mind. Aldus could have reawakened fully to his real Rebel identity and remembered some ancient insult between his clan and Stari-ki's—that sort of thing went on all the time, so this could be one such vendetta. Or Aldus might be feeling his oats and decided he ought to run the show, rather than someone foolish enough to have left him so powerful after conquering him.

Or maybe Command wanted them at each other's throats. This could be part of their strategy for training the strongest fighters on this planet to become the interplanetary fighting force—the Rebel purpose for breeding this stock of Rebel-humans.

Yes, that has the ring of truth to it. Stari-ki smiled.

He saw this scenario as a lovely challenge, a complete bar brawl, and he wanted to be the last Rebel man standing when it all ended down here. The mission looked even sweeter than he'd anticipated.

ϕ

Ska dropped from a tree onto the man below, clamping one large hand over his mouth and nose and knifing him non-lethally in the side of his lower back. The man collapsed under him, unable to cry for help. Ska dragged his unconscious prey across the forest floor to where Blu waited in a crouched position. Together, making as little noise as possible, they manhandled the now semi-conscious captive back from the enemy camp to their own lines.

Blu mimicked the sound of a nightjar, *Tucuchillo!* Then Blu and Ska stepped out of the shadows and the hiding sentries helped them carry the prisoner to Stari-ki for questioning.

Minutes later, after dressing his wound sufficiently to keep him from bleeding to death, Stari-ki interrogated the man. Blu and Ska stayed in the tent to observe and learn.

"What's your name?" Stari-ki began.

The man, now fully conscious, knew that any resistance would lead to torture and decided he stood a better chance of escape or at least survival by telling them whatever they wanted to know.

"Lesta," he said.

"Lesta, why did you and your companions attack us? Are we not on the same side as you?" Stari-ki asked calmly.

Lesta appeared confused. "Side?" he stammered. "What do you mean?"

Reading Lesta's mind, Stari-ki saw the man had no idea what Stari-ki meant by "sides". He didn't know anything about a war. He only knew to follow orders, not to try making any sense of them.

"Who is your King?" Stari-ki asked.

"Aldus," Lesta answered easily.

"Is Aldus with you down here in the South?"

"No, Dunnar led us here."

Blu and Ska remembered Dunnar as a bold squad leader, one who took too many chances but often succeeded. They liked Dunnar, but why would he want to kill them?

Stari-ki concluded this man knew nothing. He just did what his leader told him, and would be of no value to them. *Hostage value?* He pondered and then discarded the idea, seeing the man as a mere pawn to either side. Being a heartless Rebel, Stari-ki quickly slit Lesta's throat and, with his eyes, directed Blu and Ska to drag the man out before he bloodied Stari-ki's quarters any more.

Suddenly they heard an enormous explosion, as if supernatural, which Blu and Ska realized must be thunder, right on top of them. They looked up at the sky where enormous bolts of lightning with crooked fingers shot up from the land into the sky, and from the black clouds roiling above down to the land. A torrential downpour rewarded their upturned faces. They left Lesta's body behind and ran to their wives and dwellings.

Something made Stari-ki walk out of his tent naked, into the rain and toward the beach, looking across at the southern landmass. Pelted now by hail as well as the soaking rain, he watched the storm as vertical lines of rain fell from the clouds into the water. Then he saw it—the rain darkened—but only in one line across the water, about fifty steps to his right. He walked toward that aberration and into it. Then he felt it—the silt falling along with the rain in this one line across the water. He realized it followed the old land-bridge line, and would form a temporary land bridge on top of the sunken one.

He sent a soft kiss to Goma, the kind she liked.

φ

Later that day, Blu dreamed of meditating on top of the great rock with Ska, on a bright sunny day. In reality, Blu's body wrapped around Izbel under animal skins in their tent, which they had shored up against the amazing and endless downpour. In the dream, Ska looked over at him with a certain affectionate look in his eye that seemed unmanly. This surprised Blu; he'd never seen such a look from Ska.

In a questioning tone, Blu said, "I thought we agreed a long time ago that we preferred girls."

Blu woke up, and still, the rains tumbled from the skies.

φ

The enemy had no stomach for attacking during this unrelenting monsoon. Now would be the perfect time to escape across the temporary land bridge. Goma's vessel had used amplified telekinetics to draw up tons of sand into the storm clouds, and chemicals to trigger and maintain the endless storm conditions. Under cover of what could be an unusual thunderstorm going on for days, natural enough to not be detected by the enemy or the backstabber's Agents, a curtain of silt fell continuously where the old land bridge still existed underwater, building it up like a rail trail so that now Blu and Ska could see it too. Back in his tent, Stari-ki could read their minds and saw this apparent miracle doing something to their minds, probably waking them up to their true Rebel identities.

"What is it?" a bewildered Ska asked his companion. They both stood naked on the beach—the only sensible way to venture out into the monsoon—trying to see through the pelting rain flying down in hard large drops.

"Somehow God is helping us by making a bridge. Sand is coming down in a perfect line. I don't see how that can be an accident." Blu didn't know why he felt so strongly that he knew such things, and yet he did. *How can I be so sure? It must be the man inside me, the true me, who knows these things.*

Stari-ki didn't like hearing Blu, or Bluto as he now thought of him, using the word "God". Some uneducated natives on planets like this one believed in "gods", along with the great majority of educated beings in the universe whom the backstabber had fooled into believing him to be the one and only true God. Rebels never used that word. Where had Blu learned it? *From the natives of course.*

Should I make an issue of it? At the proper time, Stari-ki asked and then answered himself. Right now, he had other words to share with his key men. He'd sent for them, telling his guards exactly where on the beach to find them.

Blu and Ska entered, drenching the inside of the tent with the water pouring off them.

"I see you already know about our escape route," Stari-ki said with a wry smile. "Our friends above are doing that for us. Don't think of it as a miracle; it's an invention of ours, like your cave painting but far more advanced."

The men looked dutifully impressed, even awed.

"The weather will clear over the water in four hours and, as you can see, we're already breaking camp and getting ready to leave. You'll be with me at the back of the line, and we'll be the last three to leave, as the enemy will discover where we are soon enough and will attack from the rear. The three of us will hold them off the land bridge until they give up trying to fight us from the water, and retreat." He motioned to scoot them out, adding, "You'd better go help your wives."

As soon as they went outside, Stari-ki's head popped through the tent flap. "Blu, one more thing." He waved to signal that Ska could keep going, which he did.

Back in the tent and dripping again, Blu looked at Stari-ki with widening eyes as he heard the revelation.

"Your real name is Bluto—that's the name of the Rebel you really are, purposely born into the body you wear. That body's brain is too powerful, as we've talked about. Our weapons experiment worked too well, and now that brain has formed its own identity and drowned out yours, which we're fighting to get back," Stari-ki told him in a rush of words.

"And Ska?" Blu asked in a hushed voice.

"Scarlatta is a female Rebel, a master spy specializing in seduction," Stari-ki revealed grimly, repeating what Command had told him. "Ska already suspects he's a woman inside and it scares him. It wouldn't help to tell him the truth right now, so we must hide it from him. Tell him his real name is Skar. If he asks what sex he is, tell him with a laugh that you're of course both real men inside."

Blu felt a chill as he remembered his dream.

"And later?" he asked.

Stari-ki made an annoyed impatient shrug and waved his hand as if to say he didn't know and there's no time to be wasting.

"We'll figure that out in due time," he snapped.

Blu felt a sense of foreboding and a touch of distrust. Something didn't feel right about this revelation.

8

The army stole out of camp in good order, leaving booby traps and carefully briefing the perimeter guards on how to avoid getting ensnared themselves when the time came for their retreat. Not knowing what sorts of threats waited to greet them across the water, the toughest fighters went toward the beach first so as to be able to take the point. Stari-ki had predicted that his hunch about Command purposely setting Rebels at each other's throats didn't bode well for what awaited them.

The women and children went next, followed by the bulk of the army—both groups heavily laden with possessions and not as prepared to fight immediately. When they reached the beach and sensed the rain had eased off there, morale soared, coupled with shock and awe when they suddenly caught sight of the land bridge that seemed to have appeared out of nowhere. Most of the women and some of the men fell to their knees and put their heads forward on the sand in deference to the great powers that had done this. Many women cried in happiness and gratitude and kissed their children, pointing and explaining to them the significance of the miracle.

Busy with the mobilization, Stari-ki had ignored his own fleeting intuition that he should prepare everyone to realize that his allies had made the bridge, not some god. Now it would be harder to dislodge the idea of a miracle and he didn't know when he'd be able to find time for it. He beat himself up for his error, adding to the cumulative effect of not having anticipated two surprise attacks. For good measure, he berated himself as stupid for not seeing those attacks coming, since he should have known that the best way to achieve Command's mission would be to have the best fight the best.

All this hand-wringing reduced his effectiveness. Part of him knew this, but the dominant part of himself—the brain—shut down the inner knowing part and so he chose to remain angry at himself and therefore at everything and everybody else.

He pushed people forward roughly. "Get up! Move! Keep moving! No more stopping. I'll kill the next one I see stop!" He didn't yell as loudly as he would have liked because he didn't want to be heard by the encircling army.

His army got moving, and the first troops cautiously tested their footing on the muddy, gritty land bridge. Narrow and constraining as it left the beach, the bridge then looked as if it widened in the distance. The further they went, the more the rain lessened. A hundred feet out on the bridge, the rain stopped.

Back where the rain still pelted, the perimeter forces now furtively retreated from the enemy, hopefully without his knowledge. The exfiltration process continued smoothly from that point, and even as new troops became transfixed upon seeing the bridge, pushers prodded them along with the warning of Stari-ki's threat. In less than two hours, the whole army had made it to the bridge as the first light of dawn rose on the eastern horizon.

At that instant, a loud uproar pierced the air and everyone knew what it meant: the enemy must have sent a routine probe and discovered Stari-ki's army had moved out. Now they all followed in hot pursuit.

ф

"Damn you!" Stari-ki yelled aloud, at no one in particular.

Given a few more minutes, they would have made it to the perfect position. But now, with many of his best men still at risk on the beach, the enemy closed in swiftly from all sides.

"Fall back to the bridge! Narrow the front!" he bellowed.

His men obeyed, a few hacked down by the barrage of enemy forces rolling over them. He pushed Blu and Ska forcibly out onto the bridge and followed them quickly. He didn't want to risk his life nor theirs and saw the rest as expendable. Though perturbed at not being able to protect their men, Blu and Ska moved on and prepared to keep the enemy off the bridge, with Stari-ki behind them in reserve.

The defenders on the beach died bravely but all too soon. Within a minute, a wall of men came at Blu and Ska and—unlike months ago when they had stood off Stari-ki's men on that narrow rock bridge—this wall of men proved too wide for them. Instead of being funneled down as planned so no more than one or two could attack Blu and Ska, more like six men attacked them, with more encircling behind them by splashing through the shallow water beside the bridge. It looked pretty bad.

Blu killed two men with a single long stroke of his rock sword, and Ska's mace bounced off one head and into another. Both men now re-lived the horror of the killing machines they had become on the rock bridge. Ironically, the current carnage unlocked associations inside that Blu and Ska both sensed as some sort of reconnection with their true selves, changing them in an uncanny way: they suddenly became aware that Stari-ki could somehow hear their thoughts. With Stari-ki right behind them, both men ignored their revelatory inner feelings and focused instead on killing.

Too many men came from too many directions. Blu and Ska could see how this would end. *Maybe our real selves will still exist when our bodies are destroyed, and we might know ourselves fully once again, Blu mused.*

From amidst the mass of men, Blu saw Dunnar leap forward but too late to get his arms in position; Dunnar's rock sword sliced open his cheek moments before Blu's arms came around and dealt Dunnar a death blow to the neck. The former friend-turned-enemy fell into the water, blocking his men briefly before the perilous melee resumed.

All of a sudden, both Blu and Ska felt themselves being powerfully shoved down from behind by the shoulders. They started to resist but then realized Stari-ki had done the shoving.

Concentrating on widening the arc of his mindblast before he released it, Stari-ki felt physical pain at stretching the arc and then allowed it to release forward and sideways. He screamed with the pain so that to Blu and Ska it seemed as if the scream itself had thrown the front ranks of the enemy onto their backs and dead in the red water. They hadn't seen the mindblast Stari-ki had released to convince Aldus that he should surrender to Stari-ki as if to a god.

Blu and Ska had no time to be amazed by what they had just witnessed, as the next ranks of enemy surged forward, running over their dead comrades to attack the bridge defenders.

Both men noticed something wrong about Stari-ki, not knowing the mindblast had left him spent. He signaled them to carry on the fight. Hoping he'd be all right, they turned back to face the enemy. With the bridge washing slowly away in front of them, they stepped backward a few steps and took the brunt of the onslaught once again. They continued to slowly backstep as they fought. Meanwhile, the water became deeper on their flanks, making it harder for the enemy to successfully encircle them, and narrowing its front line of troops so only one or two men could attack at once. Finally, with everything now in place, Blu and Ska again became the death engines called for in the plan.

Behind them, though feeling better, Stari-ki had begun to feign still being weak to give him time to process something else. Yes, the strain of the mindblast seemed worse than usual this time, and he hoped his power to deliver mindblasts would eventually return as it always had before. But it felt as if he'd injured himself inside. *A mental hernia?* He laughed softly aloud at his own joke.

Something else worried him, though. He had reached down deeply inside to find all the strength he could muster for that mindblast, so far inside that he'd touched an unknown part of himself—a part that felt alien to him, a part that *did not want to hurt anybody.*

Could this be an Agent implant, or the backstabber himself trying to control my mind? Could there be a traitor inside me that caused me to be caught off guard by the enemy twice in recent weeks? Or is Command messing around and manipulating me for the sheer fun of it? What's going on? His thoughts came in rapid succession.

φ

The sun shined brightly, though as they looked back north, they could see a shroud of black clouds and fine vertical lines indicating the heavy rains still poured over the land they'd just left. The bridge became wider here in the middle and higher, above the level of the thrashing sea.

Blu and Ska kept swiveling to watch for the enemy, but at this point they could see no threat from behind.

Stari-ki had gone forward to join the assault troops at the head of the column, leaving the two of them to guard the rear. Messages could be passed quickly up and down the line like a bucket brigade—something Stari-ki had drilled the troops in before they broke camp—so wherever the next threat arose, reserves could be brought to bear on it fairly quickly.

In the relative calm of the nine-mile trek, in the beautiful weather and the respite from constant danger, each person found solitude with their private thoughts. Stari-ki, now jogging toward the head of the contingent as they approached the new landmass, noticed himself adjusting to the new situation in his mind and spirit. He no longer exulted in hurting and killing, yet it was his duty, so he would have to override this weakness he had uncovered in himself. Whether it came from an enemy implant or might truly be a part of him made no difference. His steely self-discipline would be more than adequate to the task, he assured himself. But something inside him insisted on knowing more about this frailty, and where it had so unexpectedly come from. He chewed at it without making much immediate progress.

Blu and Ska, now concerned about Stari-ki's apparent ability to read their minds perfectly at any distance, hesitated to tell each other about their mutual experience of having touched a deep part of themselves during the battle they'd just fought. They each felt they had touched their true selves and each had come away with a strange feeling, something unexpected, something they couldn't put into words—especially when putting it into words even in their heads could make it easier for Stari-ki to read their minds. Somehow, just trading glances as they walked, they seemed to know they had shared a similar experience.

Up ahead, a commotion broke out and a message rippled back indicating not to attack. At the same time, the column shifted left as if to leave room on the right. Blu and Ska had no idea who could be coming across the bridge toward them but figured it must be someone they wouldn't recognize, else why the need to pass the word not to attack?

"Perhaps friendly forces met us on the other side?" Ska conjectured.

Blu nodded and responded, "But why would they travel out on this sinking bridge? They could just wait for us to all cross and then hopefully feed us a feast."

They both laughed.

The bridge as planned slowly sank, with probably the last half mile of it to the north already underwater, that part being narrow and low by design so it would sink first.

Suddenly a weird sight confronted them: something clearly not human coming across the land bridge from the south.

φ

Blu and Ska stopped and watched, as did the rest of Stariki's army, as the small monsters approached in a long single-file column. They had no word for these creatures, which looked like tiny men but hairier. The lower part of the faces of the creatures protruded forward roundishly, they had long arms, and something about the way they moved suggested they might be as strong as men. Their eyes showed a human-like intelligence as they regarded the men with something like wary respect.

The men had never seen monkeys or apes before, their tribes being European and humans being the only primates in Europe. This particular species would later be called Barbary Macaques, often referred to as Barbary Apes. The macaques had seen men before, some of whom had hunted them, but often the macaques had coexisted peacefully with humans. They saw men as unpredictable, but the women often vocalized in a friendly way toward these hairy little cousins. Nevertheless, the macaques tended to keep their distance from all humans.

The females and some of the males carried babies, who looked curiously at the humans—some seeing humans for the first time—wondering, one might think, what these relatively fur-less beings could be, and what might be going on inside them.

Blu sensed some larger meaning in this moment, some secret he needed to decode.

Ska tried to imagine what had caused the monsterettes to pick up and leave their home to cross a rapidly eroding land bridge. *Go fast,* he thought at the monkeys. *By now, you'll have to try to swim the last half mile at least, and you'll probably lose some of your weakest, including many females and babies.*

Even here, toward its end, the land bridge could be seen dissolving at the edges and sliding back under the waves. They themselves had little time to get the whole army onto land before they too would be swimming for their lives.

Blu noted that the leader of the animal tribe, the sleekest and largest of them, had a glint of purpose in his eyes. He seemed to nod respectfully at Blu and Ska as he passed, though his head kept swinging around to observe in all directions, including upward and back at his troop. Now he picked up his pace as if somehow hearing Ska's thought. His followers struggled to keep up.

Blu and Ska remained in an unusual frame of mind, having just relived the worst moment they could remember—now with full recall—when they had held off all of Stari-ki's army single-handedly.

They didn't yet understand why they felt it necessary to hide their inner thoughts and feelings from Stari-ki.

But they had seen for the first time what Stari-ki could do with his power, as he had brought more than a dozen men to their deaths seemingly with his bloodcurdling scream. They also saw how this had enervated Stari-ki, a sight they'd never before beheld as Stari-ki had never shown the slightest sign of weakness or even fatigue before.

And now this string of little hairy men—somehow different from men, certainly hairier, but perhaps the ancestors of men—something less noble it seemed. But what about that look in the leader's eye—a hint of vision and purpose, a sense of mission—fully as noble as any man or woman they had known. It all seemed too much to assimilate.

Blu and Ska felt themselves to be in some sort of altered state of awareness, somehow intoxicated with life—each sight brighter and more detailed than before, suggestive in its movements; even waves seemed to have some reason to move as they did. It all made some kind of sense, but which they couldn't begin to explain.

More than three hours after setting forth across the now-sinking land bridge, the forward elements of the army stepped upon the permanency of the southern landmass and scrambled gratefully onto it, some kneeling to kiss the ground. Stari-ki, now leading the first assault troops onto the beachhead, harshly lifted a soldier to his feet and shoved him forward.

"Keep going!" he roared. "Go toward the trees and head left. Keep the coast in sight!" He pointed eastward, knowing that many of his troops didn't know their left from their right, let alone the terms for the cardinal compass points. "Stay out of sight and report any contact!" He pushed his army forward as they stumbled ashore, repeating his instructions again and again to the men and women as they passed.

By the time Blu and Ska reached him, being at the tail of the army, the land bridge had all but disappeared, and Stari-ki seemed to be almost back to normal, though red-eyed with hunched shoulders. He nodded to them but appeared to have no energy for conversation or even his usual probing looks.

Blu and Ska had preceded Stari-ki into the trees, following the army eastward; then suddenly he rushed past them and headed toward the front of the army. They followed, though not too closely, behind him. Eager to compare notes, they hoped he'd be too busy to read their minds.

"I think I've made a real connection with my true self," Blu said quietly.

Ska nodded. "Me too."

"It's not exactly the self I expected," Blu added cautiously. They tempered their words and body language, trying to minimize the footprints of their thoughts, shielding them from Stari-ki's surveillance.

Ska nodded again, once. "I know what you mean."

Blu stared at him, wondering what he meant. He didn't quite know what he himself meant. Still surprised at having made a sustaining contact with a self he hadn't known, he found himself getting the vaguest of feelings about that self—*me,* he reminded himself. He couldn't yet put words on these feelings, and it would be especially difficult doing so while having to maintain mental privacy.

φ

Rich fertile smells dominated their senses as they trekked through the verdant tropical forests of palm and many other types of trees they hadn't seen before. They stayed alert to detect potential threats from humans or other dangerous animals, including in the trees above. The day wore on without incident.

Hours later, they ran up against stopped troops and realized that Stari-ki had ordered the army to make camp and set up perimeter guard shifts. They made their way forward and located Izbel and Asa, kissed and hugged them, then found two adjacent spots to bed down in. In the distance, they could see and hear Stari-ki bellowing orders at the troops erecting his tent for him.

That night, cuddled in Izbel's arms, Blu had an amazing dream. Everything seemed much more detailed than in an ordinary dream, utterly lifelike—he stared at the bark on a tree and could see the immense detail as he might when fully awake, and he saw a color richness that he didn't remember seeing in any dream before.

He felt himself float upward, somehow not disturbing Izbel whose arm lay over him. He felt nothing of that arm as he floated up. Then—*of course*—he saw his own body, still down there, under Izbel's arm. He realized that only his mind had moved steadily upward. At the animal skin they'd placed above their sleeping bodies, he'd paused before going through it; he could see both above and below the skin at the same time as he hovered right at the point of the animal skin. He remembered feeling this once before— swimming in a calm lake, when he floated at eye level with the water, able to see the two worlds at once, the one above water and the one below water.

Then, without willing it, his mind continued moving upward through the trees, and when he'd floated high enough, he could see the deployment of the entire army, and he didn't see enemies anywhere near the encampment. He looked skyward and saw the glittering stars and his heart suddenly leapt at the sight: the stars felt like home. In a flash, he saw himself flying off the planet. Dazed, he almost fell back into the unconsciousness of sleep, but he fought and managed to stay awake in the dream.

Now by his side, he felt another being flying alongside him. He peered at the invisible beingness he somehow sensed beside him, and felt great warmth and love enveloping him. Then, very faintly, he saw a beautiful colorful ethereal ball of transparency, and looking into that glowing ball-type object he saw a beautiful woman's face and heard the word *"Layla"*. He sensed this to be the name of the woman he loved.

But I love Izbel, he reminded himself.

Somehow this felt different, deeper, and more permanent than his love for Izbel. He tried to remember Izbel's face but he couldn't make it appear.

What does this all mean?

ɸ

As Command had ordered, Stari-ki led his forces cautiously eastward, keeping the sea in sight. His Rebel mission remained the same: find, subdue and convert natives to conscript Rebel armies to hold the coastline from the northern peninsula to where it nearly met this landmass and then do the same with the northern coastline on this huge inland sea separating the two great continents. However, he didn't feel so sure he'd continue to follow orders.

First of all, he felt perplexed and apprehensive. His own colleagues in ships above had seemingly caused him to be attacked by an army he himself had created. As he pieced things together, he had a hunch that other Rebel super-psychic Princes and Princesses operating in the skies above could have caused the recent attacks wherein he'd allowed himself to be caught off guard. He liked that explanation better than thinking he might be losing his powers.

Although Command had told him these armies would initiate a long period of battle during which Earth's inhabitants would train to become the toughest fighters in the universe to then storm the gates of Heaven, they didn't tell him all the ways they planned to achieve that—which could easily include setting Rebel armies against each other. After all, it didn't matter how many incarnations these people (including him) had, how many times or how horribly they'd have to die in humiliation and defeat. They'd just reincarnate again and again, so why not have them kill each other as much as possible? That guess felt right as to the motivations of the Shaitan—the Planetary Commander—in having Aldus's army attack his army.

That being the case, why travel on the route where they expected him to be? They might even be waiting to see if he'd be smart enough to *not* follow orders, having figured out the game.

Secondly, he'd begun to feel unsure of his own identity. In unleashing his mindblast this last time, he felt sorrow and weakness, and now even afterward he felt in ill health, a rarity for him. Could Rebel mind control forces be responsible for this too? These feelings seemed to come from deep inside, from that part he'd sensed that didn't want to hurt others. Again, he asked himself, *Where did that come from?*

φ

Stari-ki had dispatched Blu and Ska to cover the right flank so they'd gone south, paralleling the eastward movement of the army. They had come up to a huge desert and felt instantly awed by how it seemed to go on forever. They stayed north of the desert, in the fertile area where they could feed themselves. Izbel and Asa had stayed with the main troops, where they'd be protected, and their mates missed them.

Blu and Ska each continued having strange dreams— dreaming of a different life. Blu again dreamed of flying, and again he seemed to be outside of his physical body, in another sort of body. His dreams continued to seem more real than ordinary dreams. They didn't speak about their dreams with each other, constantly on the alert that Stari-ki might be listening in, whatever the distance.

Stari-ki, in his weakened state, actually could not read them as well as before, but he hadn't revealed that to them because, of course, he preferred to keep the upper hand, with bluff if need be.

Blu and Ska continued to learn more about the inner self that each felt they'd touched—a self that somehow communicated to them without words the right thing to do at various times. The mood of that inner self felt calm, a feeling that everything is all right, not to worry, it will all take care of itself in time. This part in each of them had inspired them to slow down, to contemplate a flower, to meditate, or to concentrate intensely on a single question such as *Who am I?* Or *What am I?*

But right now, their concentration focused strongly outward. They had detected the sounds of a large group of something moving, off to their right, and had snuck up on their bellies to get a good look. They concentrated intensely on the entire threat front, including their own flanks and rear, in case they had espied an educated army that could encircle them.

As they got closer, they saw a group of humans, mostly men, carrying something in their center and moving eastward, though not quickly—seemingly not far from their destination or perhaps already in part of their home territory. Dark-skinned like Blu, they didn't seem intelligent or much evolved since their vocalizing sounded like simple grunts, not like multisyllabic language. They wore scant primitive garments and few weapons could be seen.

Crawling even closer to see what the primitives carried, they felt the soil beneath them getting looser. They stopped and Blu pointed down. Ska got what he meant and quietly pawed up some loose earth while Blu kept his senses peeled in all directions. Ska touched Blu's arm. Blu turned his head and, seeing a disgusted expression on Ska's face, looked down and saw why. Ska had unearthed a small part of a field of lightly dirt-covered bones—human bones. *These people apparently only slightly bury their dead,* Blu thought.

He smiled at Ska as if to say, "Disgusted by dead people?" Their job involved many dead people and he figured they should be well inured by now.

Ska shook his head once and pointed down. Blu looked to where Ska pointed. On what looked like a child's femur bone, he could see tooth marks. *Human tooth marks.*

9

Blu and Ska made no sound as they peered through the heavy brush in the dusky light. They had tracked the troop of savages back to their tribe, which appeared to live in the open without dwellings. Some had burrows like those of creatures that live in the ground, and others just had a piece of earth they claimed as their own. In the center of the encampment, where they expected to see a leader's tent or hovel, stood a large flat rock on which the setting sun now shone, turning it a blood red.

The squad the two had followed went directly to the center of camp and carefully deposited onto the rock what they'd carried into the camp: a lighter-skinned teenage girl wearing primitive clothes, apparently dead or unconscious, and clearly not from this tribe. *Possibly even a different species,* Blu thought, and then wondered, *What does the word "species" mean?* He then answered himself: *No time to think about it.*

Something going on in his mind caught his attention; he'd begun practicing being mindful of such things, always in the hope of recovering his true identity. He'd noticed something but he couldn't quite put his finger on it. He had a sense of two and two being put together in a dream at the back of his mind, in the spaces one usually ignores. *There—I've got it.*

He whispered to Ska, "Do you see any other teenage girls anywhere?"

Ska looked carefully around the camp, from one end to the other. They looked at each other. Did this mean that the tribe had already eaten their own teenage girls, and then went looking to kidnap those of neighboring tribes?

Why teenage girls—softer, tastier? Blu wondered.

Ska looked at him meaningfully, seeming to read his thought. "What do they do to the girls first?" he whispered.

Blu considered this and replied quietly, "We have to save her."

Ska nodded reflexively. "Those are not our orders, of course."

They both smiled grimly. This wouldn't be easy, and they would likely end up getting overpowered and eaten too. But something wouldn't let them slink away, something like honor, which felt familiar.

"Maybe we'd better act now before they kill her and eat her," Ska urged, "unless she's dead already, in which case we'd be throwing our own lives away for nothing."

Blu's gut feeling told him something else. "They don't seem to be focusing on her. The tribe seems to have eaten already; they seem to be bedding down, and two over there are having sex. For some reason, I'm imagining some kind of ceremony—"

He stopped abruptly, pointed, and turned Ska by the shoulder. The girl's leg had moved by itself.

"She's alive," Blu said under his breath. As they peered at her in the gathering shadows of dusk, they could see more of her moving. She seemed to be only partially conscious.

They waited until the tribe had settled down and all seemed still, except for the girl's random movements lying on the big rock. No guards stood watch over her. Apparently, the tribe had reason to believe she couldn't escape—perhaps being too severely wounded or maybe even dying.

They looked at each other and Blu nodded. Standing up cautiously into a half-crouch, assuming the posture of the savages, they moved quietly toward the girl with the same graceful shuffle of the tribesmen—acting like two of the tribe wanting to have a look at the prize. On the ground around them, some turned over but didn't raise any alarm.

They arrived at the girl's side. Her eyes had opened but she didn't seem to see them. Ska wondered, *Is she blind?* With no time to discuss anything, they lifted her and Ska threw her over his back and they slipped away quietly.

About halfway to the camp's perimeter, the cry went up and suddenly the ground boiled with people jumping up and yelling. Blu and Ska broke into a run.

φ

For some reason, Ska found it hilariously funny to be running at breakneck speed through the forest with a girl flung over his back. Blu glanced over at him for an instant, nearly losing his footing, and caught a flash of the girl bouncing up and down on Ska's back, glassy-eyed. Eyes forward again and pushing to the limit to maximize speed without falling, which could be fatal with the cannibals close behind, Blu couldn't help but to laugh uncontrollably too. It seemed to help his body run even faster.

Rocks whizzed by their heads along with other things, small and faster than rocks. Into Blu's mind came an image of a blowgun, something he couldn't remember ever having thought of before. *Where did that come from?* He stole another glance at the girl. He couldn't be sure but there *seemed* to be a red dot on her neck.

"Poison," he yelled between gulps of breath.

Ska peeked back at him, understanding his meaning but wondering how Blu could sense that these savages could be throwing something poisonous at them. Then he realized the girl might be drugged by some poison, perhaps from a plant or insect. He flashed on *a thorn dipped in poison then blown through a hollow reed.*

The girl, roughly shaken by the ride, seemed to be coming awake somewhat. Her eyes held some intelligence now—she watched Blu from her perch on Ska's back and now made eye contact. Her arm lifted, the arm that had flopped to and fro as Ska ran, and she pointed. She seemed to be directing them more to the north, away from the northeast route they'd taken.

"Ska this way," Blu yelled from behind and changed direction, now leading, with Ska picking up the beat instantly.

The cannibals continued their hot pursuit but Blu and Ska had opened up a decent lead, with no projectiles whizzing by them at the moment. Ska stole a look backward and could see the huge cloud of dust kicked up by the running tribe, a sign that they couldn't afford to stop and rest.

Blu turned and saw his look, nodded, and picked up the pace a notch.

"Want me—carry?" Blu asked breathlessly.

Ska shook his head barely perceptibly. The pubescent beauty of the girl enlivened him and he liked having her skin to skin. He liked her fresh smell too.

Blu could easily read all this in Ska's face. He smiled with a pretend look of rebuke for infidelity to Asa. Ska just grinned innocently.

Blu then attempted to project a mind message to Stari-ki but got no sense of any recognition. A moment later, his intuition told him Stari-ki had his own problems right now.

True enough. Stari-ki's army, north of them, had made contact with an enemy force of unknown size and character. Stari-ki knew only that he'd lost many of his best men in the frontline assault force. This enemy had some kind of weapon capable of striking men dead at a distance. It didn't make the crashing sound of rocks; it had to be something else. *Could these be Rebel troops landed by spacecraft and using energy weapons? No, these weapons have a different sound. And rays would have done a lot of collateral damage in a forest fight, with branches and sometimes trees falling, and nothing like that has happened. This weapon makes no sound yet has deadly effect.* Stari-ki couldn't fathom what the weapon might be.

Crawling on his belly toward the front line to get a better look, Stari-ki encountered the dead body of one of his men with a long skinny piece of wood sticking out of him. He vaguely remembered an ancient weapon that commonly developed on planets with humanoids, but its name escaped him. He questioned why he hadn't thought of making such weapons himself. Once again, he suspected someone had tampered with his mind and might perhaps still be tampering with it, restraining him from bringing to bear his full strength and intelligence on any given situation.

He resumed crawling toward the enemy to look closer. As he crested a small rise, still concealed by a thorny patch of ground vines, he saw a large group ahead that appeared well-organized and spaced. At their center stood the most beautiful woman he'd ever seen. He observed her placing a long slender piece of wood alongside a larger *curved* piece of wood and drawing back on something flexible. The men and women around her followed her movements synchronously. Ironically, the performance struck Stari-ki as exquisite. An instant later, with almost no sound, skinny pieces of wood came flying through the air toward Stari-ki and his troops, and a moment later he heard a scream as one of the sticks found a mark.

Stari-ki lay still, transfixed by the woman leader. He could see from this distance by focusing his eyes, looking off center, letting his eyes tear a little, and other tricks he'd taught himself. A striking beauty—with the light skin of Ska's people but long wavelets of black hair instead of blonde hair, and the full lips of Blu's people—she looked like the woman in a dream he'd had, more than once. Something inside him insisted she must not be injured and they must become allies. He needed to learn how to make and use their weapons; he had to stop the fighting now. *But how?*

That's when he "heard" the message from Blu, something about being chased by savages. *Bluto's Rebel skills are waking up,* he thought briefly. He sent back a homing beacon to help the two men find him.

Blu and Ska ran into Stari-ki's skirmish line, also taken by the surreal beauty of the flying sticks moving together like a formation of birds. Blu got it first.

"Don't let one of those strike you!" he yelled to Ska.

Seeing Stari-ki crawling backward toward them and keeping low, they hit the ground with the girl cushioned by Ska's body.

"Who is that?" Stari-ki demanded, followed by instant recognition that this must be the daughter, or maybe the younger sister, of the beautiful enemy leader. They looked almost identical in their features, but this one appeared to be younger.

"Stari-ki, here come the cannibals!" Blu spoke low so as to not reveal their position to the enemy launching the flying sticks. Now they found themselves beset from both directions.

φ

Stari-ki directed his men to focus on the savages attacking them from the rear since the army in front of him seemed to have taken a defensive stance. His men seemed glad to have combat at which they could win. They closed in for hand-to-hand combat, not giving the primitives time to reload their blowguns, which the men had noticed with no time for curiosity. Not having given the enemy time to react, Stari-ki's men decimated the natives, losing a few of their own to rocks and darts.

Then Stari-ki turned back toward the other fighters with their long-distance weaponry and the lovely woman leader. An idea popped into his mind and he acted on it impetuously. Taking an out-of-character risk—though he didn't know for sure his real identity anymore—he lifted the semi-conscious girl and carried her toward the beautiful woman he intuited to be her mother or sister.

Just before he crested the hill and came into sight, the warrior queen, Neva, had racked up one of her poison arrows and held it ready to let fly. She sensed something coming over the hill and imagined a whole army coming to overrun her and her small tribe, even though many of the attackers would die in the process. As soon as she saw something large appear, she released the arrow but a split second later she purposely wobbled the shot as it left the bow. She beheld a large and beauteous man carrying her missing younger sister, Canda.

Stari-ki ducked but the arrow went through his right trapezius muscle and stayed lodged there. He felt the poison flood his system, instantly weakening him. He stood stock still, determined to not give in to the effect. And yet there went his legs. He fell to his knees, still holding the girl.

Neva signaled her people to stand ready to shoot as she ran forward. Blu and Ska came over the hill and saw what had happened, assuming a protective stance close to Stari-ki as Neva ran up to them. She looked at them all curiously and knelt to take Canda in her arms, kissing her cheek.

On a hunch, Blu sent Neva a mind message, *Poison,* to convey that the cannibals had hit the girl with a poisoned thorn.

Neva got the message and wryly thought she'd done her own share of poisoning. She turned and yelled something back to her people, and while Blu and Ska prepared for the worst, two women came up the hill with earthenware jugs. No arrows came flying. One woman helped the girl drink from one of the jugs and the other helped Stari-ki drink. The potion tasted vile but made Stari-ki feel a little better. He stood up on weak legs.

A young boy about the girl's age came running up the hill. Neva lifted Canda and placed her in Donjeron's arms, instructing him to carry his friend back down the hill to be cared for by the women.

Stari-ki and Neva held each other's gaze. It felt like love at first sight, though they seemed to recognize each other.

φ

Despite drinking the disgusting antidote, Stari-ki's body needed time to process out the poison, and he went into a long, disturbed sleep. Toxins came out of his body as if by the bucketful. He woke briefly and beheld the beautiful woman, Neva, wiping the perspiration off his body from head to toe. He could see the love pouring out of her eyes. *Had they been this way forever?* he asked himself before slipping back into his coma.

Stari-ki's army and Neva's much smaller tribe had now coalesced into one community, with people getting to know and like one another. With their respective leaders now sharing a leafy tent, distrust quickly evaporated. The army, though conditioned to xenophobia from birth, found it strangely easy to trust these people who seemed so different from anyone they'd ever met before. In a way, they seemed almost like gods, with their advanced weapons, knots, clothing, pottery, knowledge of poisons and antidotes, and their loving kindness toward others.

Who are they? Where do they come from? they pondered collectively.

Blu and Ska, enjoying their reunion with Izbel and Asa, partook of their host's food as if at a little picnic in the woods. The food tasted delicious and much more flavorful than anything they'd ever eaten before. The word "*spices*" came into Ska's mind but he didn't know what it meant exactly, only that it had something to do with the way the food tasted.

Blu heard Ska's thought and sent back a mental *Yes. These people must have travelled from the East.*

How do I know that? he asked himself.

I don't know, Ska replied. *But ever since we learned that Stari-ki could read our minds, I've wondered if you and I could communicate without sound in the same way—and here we are, doing just that.*

Somehow, I heard you thinking that too. But we couldn't chance trying it—Stari-ki might have heard us.

Relieved that Stari-ki wouldn't be doing any peeping in their minds at least for a while, they felt more comfortable being open with each other about their inner feelings, and now they also found they could mentally communicate with one another. Blu confided in Ska his recurring dreams about a woman he seemed to have loved throughout time, now coming back to him—a woman called Layla—clearly not Izbel. *I love them both but I somehow know that my future will reunite me with my truest love, Layla.*

This sounded somehow familiar to Ska as soon as he heard it. He felt a strong urge to say something but it flew out of his mind and seemed to sit just beyond reach, no matter how much he tried to retrieve it.

Blu stood and gestured that he needed to go off into the woods to relieve himself. Ska jumped up and followed Blu, gesturing his need to do the same. Izbel and Asa nodded and continued enjoying the food. As soon as they got out of earshot, Blu stopped and turned to his friend. Ska could see the serious look on Blu's face and wondered, *What's coming next?*

"Stari-ki told me who we really are," Blu whispered. "He told me not to tell you, so I've been waiting for a chance like this."

Ska's eyes widened. *Why would Stari-ki not want him to know his own true identity?*

Blu heard the thought and whispered, "He thought the revelation would disturb you."

Ska indeed already looked disturbed.

"Brace yourself," Blu said softly. "My real name is Bluto. Your real name is Scarlatta. We're both Rebels of course, but I'm a male, and you're really a female inside."

Blu watched Ska closely, concerned about his friend's likely reaction but certain he would prefer to know the truth, no matter what.

Ska felt instantly devastated but rallied immediately, seeing Blu still being his friend and not having lost any respect for him. That somehow made all the difference in the world to Ska, giving him a reservoir of unlimited strength and courage to deal with anything.

He had sensed his inner feminine side already and it had worried him deeply. His basic life meaning—being a warrior—seemed incompatible with being a female. But having seen Neva in action, he now knew that being female inside would in no way prevent him from carrying out his purpose in life as a warrior. Suddenly his sexual identity seemed entirely irrelevant.

Blu heard all this in his mind and laughed out loud in great happiness and relief. They finished relieving themselves and returned to their wives, feeling energetically renewed.

Ska surprised Asa with a passionate kiss as he sat back down, and Blu felt moved to do the same with Izbel. This of course delighted their wives, who began to anticipate what would naturally come next. But something else happened: they saw surprise visitors approaching.

φ

Into their picnic heaven in the woods stepped Neva and Canda, beaming, seeming to illuminate the flowering bower around them. Despite being in the bodies of the earliest homo sapiens, the two men somehow knew to stand for the greeting—their deeply buried Agent memories trickled forth as needed then hid away again quickly. They all touched hands in the universal conventional way, though Blu and Ska noticed that Neva used an actual gripping motion that felt as strong as she looked.

Canda sped forward and kissed Ska on the mouth, briefly but with lips parting at the end. "Thank you for carrying me all that way!" she said gaily, and then kissed Blu a bit more briefly, with no parting of her lips.

Before her face turned away, Blu could see the true gratitude shining from her eyes, which he read as: "Thank you both for risking your lives to save mine."

They of course spoke different languages and wouldn't have been able to understand each other except that Blu, Ska, Neva, and Canda could somehow all read each other's minds, at least when the mind wanted to be read. Izbel and Asa could guess what they said, since they knew their husbands had saved the life of the Queen's younger sister.

The ladies noticed a tent-like phenomenon in Ska's breechclout and giggled to each other. No one felt embarrassed, least of all Ska, who felt primal pride in his arousal. Canda reacted by fantasizing a scenario in which Asa, out of friendship, encouraged Ska to give Canda her first sexual experience.

Ska easily read Canda's mind. "You'd better watch that. I don't want Donjeron coming after me."

Canda laughed happily. "We're best friends. I don't think he has felt the changes yet." True enough, the boy being still prepubescent, but his companion had arrived and eagerly wanted to explore.

Ska had a similar fantasy about Asa and Canda except all three participated.

Canda read this in his mind and Ska noticed her excitement. She then thought, privately she hoped, that she might be able to continue to plant suggestions in his mind this way, at least until her fantasy came true. Then she thought to herself, *Not nice to sneak around in people's minds.* Neva had taught her that a long time ago. *Not to get them to do what **you** want them to do.*

φ

Being still quite out of it, Stari-ki didn't know about the switch to being left in Donjeron's care. As he slowly got a little better, he started having coherent dreams again. In his current dream—though not really a dream—he could hear Goma communicating to him from her ship far above and could see her sitting in a beautifully sculpted bucket seat with its golden leathery padded back. He seemed to be looking through a jagged hole he had broken in the skin of her ship, and felt himself floating in space, for some reason naked and glistening with perspiration, which felt good against the ultimate cold of space.

He heard Goma saying, *People are muttering about you having gone rogue. Nobody's heard a report from you for a week. Usually, they just bomb the guys who go native and then they think about it afterward, or not.*

I'm a little under the weather, he replied a bit sheepishly.

You're not dying on me, are you?

He noted the possessiveness in her tone and thought to himself, *Goma is terrific but really just someone to have fun with now and then. And now, I've just met someone truly wonderful.* He made sure to block his mind from being read, hoping all that stuff still worked.

Having Aldus attack me really didn't inspire me with the sense that they give a rat's ass about me, he quipped.

You always told me not to take it personally, and now what are you doing? she riposted. *Since when did you need people to love you?*

That's a really good question, he allowed.

Always a double agent in everything she did, Goma would now be able to report that her friend seemed to have popped his clutch. She hoped Command wouldn't overreact, since after all she wanted to keep Stari-ki around as an occasional boy toy.

Stari-ki started coming around at long last. Even before he opened his eyes, he knew he felt like himself again. Well, maybe not deep down, where he still felt a mass of confusion about his newfound resistance to inflicting pain. But at a muscular vitality level, he felt alive again, the familiar energy flowing through his body.

He opened his eyes to the beauty of Neva's face, inches from his own, dazzling him. Her concern for him and the love in her eyes melted his heart. He wondered to himself: *Where is my normal distrust and caution? This new soft self of mine, is this healthy? Or is it going to get me killed? Better to go with being the person I know so well, or to relax into this new self?*

"Ah," he said in a husky voice, his right palm just barely touching her cheek.

She backed up slightly, seeing him awake now and looking very perky indeed. *That look in his eyes...* She could see he felt as attracted to her as she felt to him—a boon for which she thanked The One. Then she noticed him mentally picking up on that thought.

They simultaneously recognized each other's psychic ability, both thinking, *Who are you? Who am I? Who are we?*

Stari-ki sat up, feeling his normal strength or maybe more so, and Neva gaped at him for a brief instant before adapting, causing them both to smile with amusement.

"Neva," she spoke her name aloud and touched herself.

He nodded. "Stari-ki".

Why do I feel I recognize you? they each mentally asked the other simultaneously, laughing.

We have to stop doing that, they both pathed in unison, sparking the uproarious laughter that comes with getting a cosmic joke. Stari-ki wiped a tiny tear of laughter away from his eye, taking note of the unusual phenomenon.

"Maybe we met in a dream," Stari-ki said, offering his hand.

Shyly, slowly, she put her hand on his and nodded. "Yes, it's possible. Maybe I remember something like that too," she said gingerly.

Their spoken words came out in their two different languages, but they understood the meaning through the simultaneous telepathic stream. Over time, they would learn each other's language this way.

"Is everyone in your tribe telepathic?" Stari-ki asked.

Neva shook her head. "No, just Canda, my younger sister whom your men rescued—I'm so grateful for that!" She moved forward and hugged him briefly and strongly, then stepped back and sat down on the ground. "And I taught Canda how to do it. It didn't come naturally to her."

"Did you always have that ability?" he asked.

She looked unsure.

"What is your first memory?" he asked, quite matter-of-factly.

Her eyes opened wide at the thought of trying to touch her memory all the way back. He waited patiently while she made the effort.

"Oh, wow," she said, elated to have reached what felt like her first memory.

"What is it?" he asked eagerly.

In my earliest memory, I'm in the womb and I know what I'm thinking. I'm thinking then, in the womb, what if I could remember back to my earliest memory.

So, in the womb you knew you had still earlier memories, Stari-ki pathed back.

She nodded. *Yes.*

So, did you in the womb touch any of those earlier memories?

She nodded again.

"Are you going to share them with me?" he asked coyly.

"You're in them," she replied softly.

10

Thunderstruck, Stari-ki asked Neva, "What are we doing in that memory?"

She shook her head. *Unclear,* she pathed, remaining quiet so she could try to recapture that brief flash.

"We seemed to be in a small group, sitting on a cloud or something and yet at the same time in an enclosure, something gods had built." Eyes still closed, she described what she saw.

"What do you mean by gods?" he interrupted.

He now recalled that upon awakening from his coma just a few minutes before, his first reading of her mind had found her thanking the One God—the backstabber! *Could she be an Agent?* he thought to himself, and then quickly threw up his strongest and least perceptible mindblock. He achieved this by conjuring up a continuous erotic fantasy, a trick he'd discovered in puberty when his friends reported they couldn't hear him when he pathed in that state of mind.

Fantasizing about Neva required no effort and he realized he'd already been doing that subconsciously, so he just stepped it up a notch. *Maybe she just subscribes to the local superstition,* he thought to himself, knowing that on many planets the natives believe in an underlying unity behind nature. *Of course, primitives couldn't imagine that the world began with multiple gods and one had taken over domination,* he reminded himself.

"Gods are just people like us at a higher level," Neva replied unambiguously.

Something inside her, below the level of words, suggested *Stari-ki might be a god.* She did see him as different from all other men. Many men had looked lustfully at her and she had felt her own lust, but it had never seemed good enough, the spirit hadn't moved her. She'd hoped a man or a god would come along someday who would be worthy so she could give herself to him. Though still not sure about Stari-ki, she felt closer by the moment.

"Sorry to take us off track," Stari-ki said. "Please go back to that memory of an enclosure on a cloud—a group is there, you and me, and who else?"

In his fantasy, he slowly undressed her. In reality, they sat close to each other on the floor of her bower—a sophisticated igloo woven from vines and covered with leaves, in the center of a ring of flowering shrubs whose blooms spilled into the dwelling in many places. The high sun slanted in through the many openings, dappling the two with rays of light that danced with the swaying of the palm trees outside.

"I don't see detail on anyone else, and you don't look like you. You and I appear to be see-through and energies swirl inside of us, in all kinds of beautiful colors, almost too bright to look at." After a moment's pause, she added, "My name is Nastassia."

Fascinated, Stari-ki probed further. "How do you know it's me?"

"It *is* you. Your feeling, I knew you instantly."

He laughed softly. "What's my feeling?"

She reached for words to translate her intuitive know-ing. "Triumphant music…" she started.

He laughed softly again. "What are we doing there?"

"Getting our orders," she replied.

φ

If she is an Agent—which Stari-ki felt pretty sure of from her responses to his test questions—and at some point in the past, they'd gotten their orders in the same room, then he must now be an Agent gone rogue. Or, at the time of Nastassia's memory, he must have been a double agent planted by the Rebels.

The idea of ever being an Agent would normally have seemed absurd to him. But now it seemed less implausible; after his recent and greatest mindblast, unknown parts of himself had begun to emerge—including that paradoxical desire to not hurt anybody, which, as a soldier, he'd found particularly inconvenient. *Now if that doesn't smack of having some degree of Agent inside me, what would?*

He then asked himself, *Where does my duty lie right now?*

He pondered some more. If she is an Agent, his top priority as a Rebel would be to capture and interrogate her, which would mean her torture and eventual death. *No way am I going to do that—and if that means switching sides, then so be it.*

His side had annoyed him lately anyway, and the snide Rebel pride he'd always shared with his cohorts now seemed childish. *My duty right now and my top priority are exactly the same: unite with this woman and protect her forever.*

"Thank you for reaching back in your memory like that and sharing it with me, Nastassia."

The way he spoke her name made her tingle all over. He gently lifted her hand and placed it in his. Her breathing sped up.

"And thank you for nursing me back to health," he added, leaning forward and kissing her with the gentlest, softest, most tender kiss he'd ever given. She returned it in kind. He began to slowly carry out his fantasy, and she responded, yielding herself fully. She had never done this before and wanted him to teach her, and he got that. He led and she followed.

The lovers shifted imperceptibly into Flow state. Nothing distracted them—no thoughts or notions of Agents, Rebels, or anything else—their attention focused totally in the moment. Stari-ki let his guard down to the point of abandoning it completely. Nothing else existed beyond the two of them.

"Will you be my woman?" Stari-ki asked her.

"Oh, yes!" Nastassia replied ecstatically.

He lifted her gently onto his lap facing him, both of them sitting cross-legged, and held her aloft in that position. They kissed and their breath merged into one in-out breath through the nostrils. Space and time ceased to exist. They saw only the universe, the galaxies, spinning within them, united, one consciousness, filled with awe and color, sparkling and rippling, amidst overpoweringly delightful feelings and sublime music.

Stari-ki felt something astounding come over him. He felt a Oneness with everything, and from this perspective, he could see life as boundless joy. Every feeling now, and every memory, felt joyful, even memories he remembered hating at the time—which seemed to be proof of his being delusional at those times, but now no longer so. He saw no chance of this moment being an illusion. He knew this to be the ultimate reality, in its most intense suchness.

We are all This! The One God is The Truth! he realized utterly.

He opened his eyes, and after a moment she sensed it and her long eyelashes fluttered open. Still sharing one breath, they now looked into each other's eyes. They also saw through each other's eyes. Love making love to love.

Stari-ki slowly lowered Nastassia so she could just barely feel his lingam. This went on for a timeless period. She felt something coming, and then sensed a cosmic *Pop!* A mountain of pleasure arose within her. She and Stari-ki had now physically merged as one pulsating, vibrating, totally alive being.

Sometime later, half-asleep in each other's arms, Nastassia murmured something to him. Stari-ki murmured something back. She put it into clearer words:

"I was inside you and you were inside me," she said softly. "You saw all of me and I saw all of you."

He looked her in the eyes, alert now. He smiled. He sensed there could be no danger to him from her.

"I know your real name," she said, "the one you don't know."

φ

In the warm afterglow, still entwined in each other's arms, Stari-ki's mind rushed with a flood of revelations. He had just seen for himself the fallacy of the Rebel view of the cosmos. He now sensed a singularity, a Oneness, each of them being That, and he saw this as the truth. He now understood that something had interfered with people realizing this ultimate truth and caused them to make up other explanations, as the Rebels had.

But what if the Rebels had the correct view and he'd just experienced an illusion perpetrated by the backstabber? Something inside him rejected that notion and he probed further. *Is my mind being manipulated? No, this is mine all right—my aesthetic preference is that the Oneness be the Truth.*

He wanted it to be that way. No one had twisted his arm or his mind. The Rebel picture of reality he had accepted long ago now seemed like a harsh and self-dwarfing way of looking at life. He wanted to remain in the Oneness that still lingered now, as Nastassia looked teasingly into his eyes, waiting for him to say something.

"What's my real name?" he asked huskily.

"Templar-ji," she answered, "or something like that. In the cloud classroom in the sky, I heard someone call you that, and someone else called you Ad-am."

"Ad-am Templar-ji." He intoned the name, trying it on for size. "I'm not sure I don't like Stari-ki better," he kidded.

"Names are just like clothes," Nastassia said, removing the fur covering their nakedness. His body produced the desired reaction, his lingam swaying up like a cobra. She straddled him.

"What is *your* earliest memory?" she asked him.

Now there's an interesting thought. He felt mentally energized; the imperative to investigate deeply within himself had perhaps never been greater.

He cast his mind back in time. He saw a toddler crawling around his parents' apartment within the asteroid Ceres, the largest single piece of a planet called Ceres by the natives and Phaeton by the Rebels. He forced his memory back still farther and now saw Phaeton from space— the planet still whole, before being blown apart in a great battle and now forming the Ceres asteroid belt.

Farther back! he commanded himself. He felt himself hitting a wall. *Something there is blocking me...*

Then he relived a terrible experience, but it went by in a flash and he only caught bits and pieces of it. Nastassia saw him twitch and knew he'd touched something disturbing in his memory.

"I'm in a fight," he said, "with mindblasts." He strained to hold onto the glimpses of what he'd seen and felt. "The other guy is hitting me with something so big that I don't even know what's happening."

"Anything else?" Nastassia prodded lightly.

He nodded. "Yes. Before the fight started, I came upon this enemy and recognized him. I called out to him. Maybe I'd looked for him or stalked him…"

"What's his name?" she asked.

He shook his head. "I don't know. All I know is what I called out to him… and it makes no sense to me."

"What did you say?"

"Hail to the second son," Stari-ki said.

φ

Lying on a large fur on the ground with their wives, Blu and Ska watched the goings-on of the tribe around them, enjoying the day. So far, no one had emerged from Neva's tent to give orders, and so Stari-ki's army and Neva's tribe relaxed, mingling and playing games together. Blu and Ska had the perimeter guarded as always, but a feeling of peace overcame the usual trepidation.

Two of the tribe's toddlers chased one another and stumbled on the edge of the fur, falling into the arms of Izbel and Asa.

"You sure are cute!" Izbel exclaimed and hugged and kissed the child.

Asa cooed and baby-talked and touched noses with the other child.

Blu thought, *Sure would be wonderful if life could always be like this.*

Ska heard Blu's thought and agreed. *Yes, being able to have kids of our own, to teach, to pass the days like this, to hunt and play, have fun, and not have to be at war all the time.*

What is our duty to ourselves and to life, Blu wondered. *What does the Universe want us to do, and why?*

Ska sent him a warning look as they both realized Blu's thought would be taken by Stari-ki as inappropriate for a Rebel, and suspiciously sounding like an Agent. Who knew when Stari-ki would be back to normal? For all they knew, he might start mentally spying even before he came out of Neva's tent.

Meanwhile, still in the tent, the lovers continued to while away their timeless first day together, making love and reliving ancient memories as a way of getting to know each other and themselves.

"I can't remember anything before the fight." After minutes of trying, Stari-ki then confided, "It's like there's a block."

"There *is* a block, I can sense it too," Nastassia said. "Somebody put it there to keep you from remembering your lives before that. Probably the somebody you fought with—the second son, whoever or whatever that is."

"Nastassia, what do you think this Universe is all about—what are we doing here—what are we supposed to be doing—who are we…" The words came pouring out of him, one question cascading into many.

"We're all parts of The One Consciousness, enjoying the experiences we create," Nastassia said simply. "You know there's a One—we shared being in The Oneness a couple of times already today—all of space and time being within us, all moments, all parts of one thing together."

She sensed something holding him back from totally agreeing. "Templar-ji," she said softly but firmly. She'd called him by that name ever since discovering his real name from long ago, their last time together. "You shared in this with me. You know this is true."

"And yet it's my duty to be suspicious of how my mind might be manipulated from the outside," Templar-ji said, trying to think of himself by that name. "Not by you," he added quickly. "I trust you completely."

Her face underwent rapid changes keeping up with him as he continued.

"But even a feeling as profound as Oneness could be placed in my mind by an enemy."

"Who are your enemies, and why do you think of them that way?" Nastassia asked.

Although inclined to name the Agents and the back-stabber as his enemies, he found he no longer believed that story. Now he curiously anticipated what would come out of his mouth next.

Suddenly, a bell sounded in his mind: Planetary Command making contact. His upright index finger sprang to his lips signaling silence, and then he touched that finger to his head to include mental silence.

Nastassia got the message and became mentally invisible, though still monitoring whatever the conversation might be.

φ

The Shaitan himself—the planetary military governor, who reported to Lucifer Himself—contacted Stari-ki. The Shaitan seemed jovial and collegial.

Well, are you among the living at last, young man? he asked.

Templar-ji made sure to think of himself as Stari-ki. *Sorry, sir. As I told Goma in a lucid moment, I've been in a coma for most of the time since my last report. I awoke from the coma a few hours ago and prepared to report momentarily and then you called.* Stari-ki's explanation had a ring of truth.

Good, good, your rivals up here wanted to blast your ass but I told them to let me handle it, the Shaitan said glibly. After a moment he laughed. *I'm a man of my word, son, so I do have my finger on the button right now.*

How may we serve, sir? Stari-ki responded calmly.

How are you getting on with Nastassia? the Shaitan asked.

If you mean Queen Neva, sir, Stari-ki replied, *we've only begun negotiations to combine forces, but I speak confidently when I say it is done.*

Stari-ki looked into Nastassia's eyes. She smiled and nodded *Yes* to Stari-ki's marriage proposal.

We of course can observe your every move down there, the Shaitan reminded him unnecessarily.

Nastassia raised her eyebrows. Reassuring her, Stari-ki shook his head and held out his arms to indicate the degree of resolution that could be seen from the Shaitan's command post—about a yard on each side—and then pointed to the roof and shook his head again.

Of course, sir. We've been progressing according to your past orders. What are your current orders, sir? Stari-ki feigned obeisance.

Can she hear us?

Stari-ki thought only an instant before responding. *Yes, sir.*

They obviously know she's in the tent—it's her tent, after all, he thought in his hopefully-hidden mind.

Nastassia understood and stood up to leave. She looked at him and he nodded, so she left and headed as far away as she thought reasonable.

You can see she's left now sir, Stari-ki said.

The Shaitan grunted assent. *You see, son, she's an Agent. Our alterations to the natives' new brains worked like a charm and she's under our spell. But she has Agent instincts. We can't control her every move. The new brain only achieved enough inner competition and distraction to erase pre-life memories. We keep her under surveillance and hope to catch a whole batch of them that way. You have to play along with the game. She didn't know we exist until she met you.*

I suspected as much, sir, Stari-ki responded.

You're a smart kid, Stari-ki. Stay loyal to me and you will go far.

After a moment's pause, the Shaitan pressed. *I didn't hear your vow of allegiance.*

Sir, you know you can always count on my loyalty, Stari-ki professed, yet also still felt deeply in his now-divided inner self.

As soon as they cut off communication, Templar-ji took off after Nastassia, following his instincts, and caught up with her just outside camp. She studied him as an animal might, unsure as to friend or foe. He held out his hand and she placed hers in it, then he drew her into his arms and they kissed.

They know you're an Agent, he said.

I'm a what? Nastassia asked.

You and I received our final Agents training together in that classroom you saw. I can see it now too.

What are Agents? Nastassia asked, her curiosity piqued.

I'm not sure, but they represent one side and Rebels the other side, Templar-ji explained. *Agents say everybody is one person, The One Self. Rebels say the person you think of as God is actually one of many gods, and he stole the Universe from the others, who are now called Rebels.*

Sure, I'm an Agent! Nastassia concluded. Then the implications set in. *People in a position to destroy us at whim know I'm a sworn enemy. What are we going to do?* she thought to herself.

Hearing her thought, he nodded. He knew the Rebels' Planetary Commander could see their every move, could destroy them any time he wanted to, and unless Templar-ji and Nastassia could hoodwink him, night and day forever, it would only be a matter of time before their assured destruction.

We're going to die to live again and continue our Mission. For as long as we can, let's send out messengers to bring the truth of The One Self to people everywhere. That's what we can do for right now, Templar-ji said.

Nastassia thought for an instant, nodded, and then kissed him.

That night, a huge celebration of the wedding of Queen Neva to General Stari-ki took center stage. The Queen liberated all of the tribe's reserves to fill everyone's appetite. Templar-ji had asked Blu and Ska to stay afterward when the party came to a close.

Around the still-blazing fire sat the newlyweds, joined by Blu and Ska. Templar-ji quickly filled in his two key men with the facts, including the conversation with the Shaitan and the revelation of his and Nastassia's identity as Agents.

Careful! Templar-ji advised, noticing the sober faces. *They can see us, so keep laughing and smiling like we've done all night. Let's also talk aloud, as it will seem less concerning than if they see us sitting here with our mouths shut.*

Blu and Ska easily relaxed into the game of pretending to be merely carousing.

"Okay," Blu said, "so you two and we two are ancient enemies, is that what you're telling us?" Blu laughed half-naturally. "When do we start killing each other?" This provoked him to really laugh but his eyes stayed alert.

"We think you're Agents too." Nastassia affected a giggle for the eyes in the sky.

"Looks like the Rebels turned the three of us." Templar-ji indicated the three males, then added, "They put blocks in our minds, long ago, making us think of ourselves as Rebels." Templar-ji laughed uproariously. Now everyone began truly laughing.

Blu looked at Ska and asked, "Are we believing this?" and then everyone laughed again.

Nastassia motioned Blu and Ska to come and sit very close to her. They all realized this could look suspicious to the observers above, and so Nastassia touched the men, as if flirting to make her new husband jealous or something. Templar-ji, fascinated, changed position to watch more closely whatever Nastassia had in mind. She began to enter Blu's and Ska's minds.

Meanwhile, Blu asked, *What evidence do we have either way?*

Nastassia answered aloud. "Which makes more sense to you, that we're all One Self—The Great Being— or that a bunch of gods created all this and then one screwed the others?"

They all fell over laughing but Nastassia remained focused on Blu and Ska.

"Mel—something," Nastassia said, looking at Blu.

"What's that?" Blu asked.

"Your name—your real name—Melchi—something," she said.

"Melchizedek!" Blu exclaimed, large portions of his memory returning in a sudden rush. He now recognized Neva—he knew her as Nastassia when they first trained as Agents. He remembered because he'd trained her.

"And me," Ska asked?

"You're Layla, of course," Nastassia revealed.

Like Blu, Ska felt a sudden rush of himself as Layla, with her memories too. Nastassia and Layla hugged while Melchizedek looked on with a beatified smile.

Now they all three remembered their early training together, which had included Templar-ji too. The four of them then abruptly realized Stari-ki's actual name: not Templar-ji but Templegard.

Melchizedek and Layla got up and hugged for a long time, causing curious stares from the few of the army and tribe still half-awake, for the two of course still wore the bodies of Blu and Ska.

φ

From that point on, Templegard, Nastassia, Melchizedek, and Layla—still known to the tribe and army as Stari-ki, Neva, Blu and Ska—hosted a new celebration every night. The best and bravest of the army and the tribe would get to sit with the four leaders. While drinking and laughing, the foursome transmitted information to them—information they could understand and take to heart, and in the process memorize, as instructed.

Zak-ki repeated the message—laughingly as he'd been briefed because of the eye in the sky— "Inside you is The One Self that is the whole Universe." The others fell over laughing, following the same directive, but inside, the enormity of the message awed them.

Li-Li, Zak-ki's new mate—he from the army and she from Neva's tribe—completed the idea with the second half of the message: "Some people, and a part of your mind, are trying to keep you from knowing your Universal Self. Keep watchful, *especially of your own mind.*"

The Rebels didn't seem to notice a couple of people leaving the tribe each day and trekking off in all directions. If they did, they held their fire, waiting to see what would happen next.

Melchizedek and Layla spent a lot more time together. With so much memory of their true selves returned and more returning every day, it became increasingly easy for Melchizedek to continue to be patient, holding back on announcing his true feelings to Layla—still not sure if he ever would.

"I have to admit, although the emissaries and their messages will hopefully have a good effect on life here on Earth, I won't mind it at all when the Shaitan decides it's time to vaporize us," Melchizedek said.

"And why is that?" Layla asked.

Slightly embarrassed, he replied, "I kind of miss seeing you as Layla instead of as Ska."

S/he looked at him searchingly, but he wouldn't go any further.

By utilizing many people from the army and the tribe, each doing one small seemingly accidental dropping of something or some other minor move, they built a leafy tunnel entrance and exit to Nastassia's tent, allowing her to crawl like a snake a certain distance to secretly be with Templegard during his reports to Planetary Command. Of course, Templegard knew she'd be within earshot. Though risky, they both saw Nastassia being still stronger at telepathy, so she could find out things Templegard could not.

Neither ever knew if their psychic blocking would be strong enough, so they never knew whether or not the Shaitan could read them like a book.

They lived each day knowing their lives would inevitably end at some point soon. Meanwhile, a two-person emissary team moved out every day, one from the tribe and one from the army, continuing the Mission.

During one nighttime celebration that had gotten particularly wild with dancing and loud noise, a child got abducted—again. A sentry had apparently let his guard down. Fortunately, a quick response brought the child back unharmed. The army and the tribe killed many of the cannibals, including the perpetrators, and now surrounded those still alive, who realized they'd be next.

"Is our Mission as Agents to come to Earth to wipe out the Rebels?" Nastassia asked ingenuously.

"No!" Templegard, Melchizedek, and Layla exclaimed in unison.

Melchizedek added, "The Mission is to bring the Lost Lambs home."

The others slowly nodded.

"What if we try out something else with the cannibals instead of wiping them out?" Nastassia suggested.

The three waited for her to elaborate, which she did.

"Let's keep the cannibals under observation and at the same time try to treat them as neighbors and offer to teach them."

The idea sounded as radical as any ever uttered on Earth until that point. Naturally, it appealed to the other Agents.

When the order came from Planetary Command to move the army and its camp followers to an engagement farther to the east, Stari-ki reported, *We are close to a breakthrough in subjugating and indoctrinating the most brutal savages, sir. This will have planet-wide ramifications and might even work on other planets.*

Command released the army from the combat assignment, allowing them to continue their experiment. This worked right up until Glory Day.

φ

The day's pair of emissaries had providentially made it over the far-off mountains when Planetary Command fired its energy weapons, vaporizing the remaining army and tribe. While the four Agents had rehearsed for this inevitability, the violent dissolution of subatomic particles seriously jarred their soul bodies.

Melchizedek, the oldest among them, recovered first—enough, that is, to say *Stay together.*

The fireworks display went on for some time around four wraithlike color-filled illuminated bubbles. Many other colorful bubbles flew by, heading in all directions.

Sure is beautiful, Templegard said.

Do you have a place you like to go? Nastassia asked Melchizedek and Layla, who looked at each other knowingly.

The four of them flew off together and found themselves at the fabulous island resort Melchizedek had imagined long ago.

Oh, this is too much! Nastassia said with delight.

In their bubble bodies, the Agents projected themselves as humans in diaphanous bathing suits. Templegard and Nastassia looked the same way they'd looked in their most recent human incarnation. They'd never seen Layla before as a woman and now the two of them admired her curves, though Nastassia displayed graceful curves of her own.

"Oh, Ska, what's happened to you?" Templegard cooed, and Nastassia touched his nose in mock warning.

Layla appreciated the attention from all three of them, but her own attention riveted on Melchizedek, who for some reason had projected himself as a teenager, even younger than her own appearance.

"How tall, dark, and handsome you look, teach," she said teasingly but meaning it. Though never before drawn to beings younger than herself, she felt attracted to this teenager.

Templegard's face radiated joy, laying in the sand just inches from the pounding surf. The four felt released from what had become Hell on Earth, taking at least a brief holiday where they could totally spoil themselves. But they all felt a strong impulse to talk about what had just happened.

"Why did they pull the plug then and not before?" Nastassia asked the elephant-in-the-room question on everyone's mind.

"Maybe they'd just discovered the secret tunnel?" Templegard guessed, and they all slowly nodded.

"So maybe we shouldn't have done that tunnel thing," Nastassia said.

Templegard moved closer and hugged and kissed her, still intoxicated with his rediscovered soulmate.

"He's right." Melchizedek nudged closer to Layla and then kissed her on the cheek. "Thank you, secret tunnel!"

"Now what?" Layla asked.

They all wondered for a moment before Melchizedek spoke.

"We need to get cosmic fire support. The odds are too great to overcome, the way things stand on Earth now."

The gulls noticed the four humanoids in lotus position on the beach, seemingly meditating, and understood this to be the way humanoids got onto the same wavelength with everybody else. The gulls mewed their good wishes.

The four cooked up a luau, followed by ecstatic dancing. The two couples then set off on their own for some private time, which went on for a lusciously timeless period. Templegard and Nastassia moved up the beach around a bend. The gulls had long since gone to sleep, and so did Melchizedek and Layla, on the beach close to the ocean. Mel kissed her on the forehead and closed his eyes, a contented smile on his face as he breathed in deeply the breeze coming off the ocean, carrying with it a salty scent and the fragrance of far-off flowers. Layla didn't feel like sleeping and instead watched him. The moons moved very slowly across the sky but she could see their movement and the beautifully colored rings around one of the moons.

Her powerful senses could hear the sounds of lovemaking far off up the beach, and she sighed. Careful to keep her thoughts private, she wondered *Why can't it be that way with us?*

Not a virgin, Layla had dallied with a couple of the guys at school a long time ago. She had a strong libido and equally strong detachment. If the Mission required it, she could live without sex for the rest of eternity. But she didn't remember any rules forbidding Agent partners from being lovers. Could Mel be spiritually bent on remaining chaste? She'd never dared to bring up such a personal subject with her teacher-cum-partner.

Her reverie continued as she watched Mel sleeping, still wide awake herself. She knew he liked her, but she thought he saw her as just a kid, maybe as his kid. She also knew he found her attractive, because she caught him clocking her from time to time—actually, pretty frequently, she now realized. If he intended to remain spiritually chaste, he wouldn't allow his mind or his eyes to act as if he had any sexual interest; that would be hypocrisy, she had learned. So, he can't be suppressing his libido. *Perhaps I'm just not his type.*

Wait! What if he has someone else? Some other being that he loves?

"Not sleepy?" Melchizedek asked softly.

His eyes had opened but he hadn't moved from his sleeping position on his back. The waves came up to lick his feet and then receded, their foam glowing fluorescent pink under the light of the brightest reddish-purple moon. He smiled fondly at her.

She just shook her head a little. *No, not sleepy.*

She noticed him register the sounds of Templegard and Nastassia's lovemaking, and they both smiled.

"They're having fun over there," Layla said, feeling the longing in her heart.

"We're having fun right here too." Melchizedek felt heart-poundingly happy to be with her in such a beautiful setting. *It's also a romantic setting,* he thought. *Perhaps this is the right moment.* But still he held back, unable to stop thinking *I'd lose so much if it went sideways, and now that I've found her, I can't bear the thought of never seeing her again.*

"Yes, but not the same kind of fun," she said playfully.

He got her message or thought he did, but he continued to second-guess himself. *Gotta be sure.*

"That's true." He turned on his side to face her. The next wave came up over his feet, the tide coming in now.

She stared at Melchizedek in the moonlight, her eyes feasting on this magnificent, swarthy young man with a leonine mane of hair, Grecian features, and warm loving eyes.

"Melchi, you never told me if you have a wife somewhere, or somebody that means a lot to you," Layla said nonchalantly.

"Not me," he replied. "How about you?"

"Nah, I had some fun with the guys at school but I always felt much older than them."

"You're a very serious being," Melchizedek acknowledged. "I saw you as Agent material from the moment I met you."

"If given the choice between having fun—which I admit I love—and relieving the suffering of Lost Lambs..." Layla paused, searching for the right words. "I see really only one choice."

"For you and me, anyway," Melchizedek added.

"But we can have fun too, can't we?" Layla suddenly blurted.

"Of course!" Melchizedek exclaimed, sitting up.

Is she sad? Yes, she's sad about something. He couldn't stand to see her feeling sad. He reached out and took her hands in his. They felt small and soft, though he knew her strength. His touch seemed to make her feel a bit better.

She felt his caring through his hands, and she loved the feel of the hair on the back of his hands. They sat closer together, their eyes meeting. He kissed her right eye and then her left. He tasted the salt there... *from a tear or perhaps just the surf?* he wondered.

"Melchi..." She hesitated and then asked, "Is there something wrong with me?"

He put his arm around her and drew her even closer. "Why would you ever think that? You're terrific and very special to me."

"I know, we make a great team, don't we?" she asked sincerely.

"A perfect pair," he allowed.

"I know you think of me as just a kid—maybe as your own child," she started, then paused again, looking down.

He found her closeness and her beauty overpowering and he could barely catch his breath.

"Not at all. I know you to be an inspired goddess, full of wisdom and grace..."

She stared at him as he continued.

"You are the incarnation of all that is attractive about femininity... all the beauty and desirability that makes me express my being as a man..."

"Then why..." she started to ask, but couldn't say the words.

He knew what she meant.

"I couldn't bear it if I ever lost you. I thought if I told you how I really feel, it might come at you from such an odd angle that you might be turned off and perhaps even drift away," he admitted, feeling his own cowardice, although he'd never run from a fight. "I couldn't risk taking the chance to tell you... I'm in love with you."

She cooed and melted at hearing his words, and they came together in their first kiss. He felt her deliciously soft skin and the sand scraping him at the same time. She kissed him and he kissed back. Her mouth still tasted of the delicious mangoes they'd enjoyed earlier. Their first kiss—he'd imagined it a thousand times before—yet it exceeded anything he could have ever dreamed.

He dissolved himself in her, and she in him.

11

As dawn prepared itself over the horizon, the four Agents stirred occasionally to open one eye.

Melchizedek interrupted the silence to say, "Help is on the way."

The others slowly confirmed it and they got up to meet the day.

Melchizedek, now manifesting as a fortyish male again, and Layla, being her usual goddess self, relaxed on the beach with Templegard and Nastassia, letting the warm sun of this imagined world dry their wet bodies—when the battlecruiser appeared at the periphery of their vision.

They naturally had sensed its approach from far off as it advanced from an unthinkable distance at an unimaginable speed. Though its captain didn't slow the vessel, they felt themselves whisked aboard as he passed. It felt briefly vertiginous but exhilarating. One of the beings aboard they all recognized at once: Maitreya, an even older and more seasoned Agent than Melchizedek. They cheered their greeting and he responded in kind.

Bubbles of light again, the four of them danced around Maitreya, hugging their energy embraces. The excited froth of undulating, evolving mathematical sculpture patterns inside each of their bubbles portrayed great joy in distinctly different ways, expressing from varied roots in the unique symbol systems in which they each thought and felt.

As a bubble, Maitreya looked golden and bronze, with layers and layers of depths inside, each a memorable incarnation of his which he wore on his imaginal sleeve as part of his being. Each of the Agents had a favorite look as a bubble, their natural form. Nastassia liked purplish hues and bright curves of all sorts; Layla favored peaches and cream and morphing flowers and beings. Templegard chose a simpler bubble, mostly flesh-colored, with aspects of human male anatomy as seen from all angles; and Melchizedek's bubble looked like leather, of different colors and textures, with his eyes the prominent feature.

Melchizedek slipped a private telepathic question to Maitreya *Any word?* Meaning, any news of Venus?

Maitreya privately pathed *No.*

This had become the first thing they said to each other whenever they met. Maitreya had held up as a balanced evolved being, despite the tragic trauma and the extended wait to reunite with his eternal wife. He knew someday they'd be together again. Maitreya had actually seen Venus many times, but she never recognized him. Or perhaps she did but her cover wouldn't allow her to acknowledge him. Maitreya's orders to keep her assignment a secret had come directly from The Great Being, so he could never tell Melchizedek or anyone else—except The First Son, the only other being that knew the secret—about his sightings of her.

Though off on another assignment while the four Agents carried out their latest Mission on Earth, Maitreya appeared to be well briefed; he seemed to already know whatever they disclosed in their reports.

You said we needed more power down on Earth. The One has decided to try something—different. Maitreya wanted to stir up their curiosity and make the telling more fun. They got it and played along.

The way you say "different", you make it sound naughty, like almost illegal. Melchizedek's bubble smiled broadly.

It's a bit like bending the rules of the Lost Lamb Game, which has no formal rules but does have a kind of unspoken rule. Maitreya felt gratified that Melchizedek, whom he considered his star pupil, could still be so sensitive to his tonalities.

What is it, what is it, the body language of the four bubbles seemed to be asking Maitreya.

They sobered up when they heard Maitreya's next words. *The pervasive suffering on Earth justifies moving the line in the sand, The One has concluded, at least as an experiment. If it doesn't work, we go back to the old rules.*

Mystery—Templegard began on a hunch.

Yes, it has to do with the Mystery Planet convention, Maitreya confirmed. *We're going to test, in a small way at first, a combination of Revealed Miracle and Military Superiority.*

We're going to pull back the curtain and show the natives who we really are? Layla asked in awe.

Everyone had assumed, for millions of years, that The Great Being would never break the Mystery Planet convention in the Lost Lamb Game part of the Free Will Zone.

Yes, to a select few, those who are or can be leaders from around the planet, Maitreya replied. *They'll see the Truth and call it miracles.*

What are we hoping this will achieve? Templegard asked.

In the upside scenario, the ones we select will be able to assimilate the Truth and take up the mantle of running their own planet peacefully despite Rebel mischief. Maitreya tried to sound hopeful.

You don't seem very optimistic. Templegard also picked up on Maitreya's tone.

It's a long shot that The One feels is worth a try, Melchizedek guessed.

Maitreya's gesture confirmed the hunch. They all knew this Rebel game showed no signs of winding down or cooling off the way other games always had. Instead, things had gotten worse, creating true Hell on Earth for many avatars of The One.

Enlightened Self-Interest requires The One to take extraordinary measures if necessary to reduce His/Her own suffering, since The One is the Self inside of every avatar, that is, of every single thing in the Universe, Maitreya elucidated. *As you know, all of the suffering in the Universe is felt by The One. In fact, it's The One's suffering that we think is us feeling our own suffering. Actually, there is no "us"—there's only The One.*

This thing we're in now, is this the military superiority part? Nastassia asked.

Yes, Maitreya acceded, projecting to them a picture of the battlecruiser in its entirety: an octagonal bipyramid— two eight-sided pyramids joined at their common base— a few miles long, with pretty colors and patterns shifting across its surfaces much the way the lights inside bubbles do, an endless Mandelbrot-Julia fractal equation iterating.

Maitreya continued. *This ship, Atlantis, has more power than the sum of everything the Rebels have on and near Earth. Its power is both offensive and defensive. In Atlantis we are invulnerable. Say hello, Atlantis.*

It's a great pleasure to meet you four heroes. Every ship in the fleet and every Angel aboard knows the great work of the Agents. It's an honor to carry you, Atlantis intoned.

Layla's bubble smiled. They all knew that ships are beings too: The Great Being had wrought them of HimHerUs, that

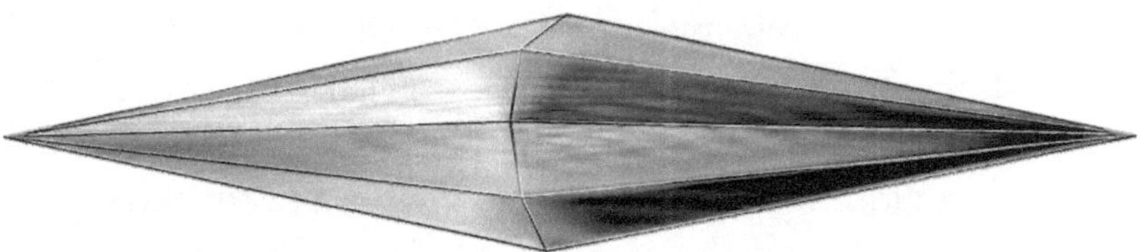

The Ship Atlantis

is, of Our Self, to be at the same level of intelligence as angels and humans.

As it entered Sol's system, the ship slowed to the respectful speed in a solar system. Sol, also a conscious being, of course, actually preferred to be called Solly in those days.

Atlantis didn't need commands; it knew what to do. The five Agents watched with great interest as the ship oriented one of its capstones straight forward toward the Earth, which hovered in front of them. As it moved steadily onward, Earth grew bigger and bigger until they could see themselves hurtling toward the ground inside the great ship.

φ

Circa 10,000 BCE

Melchizedek and Layla felt no concern about the planet rushing up at them, instead being intrigued by the thought of The One "adjusting away" from tolerating the suffering on Earth by trying new experiments never tried in millions of years. Seeing an apparent change of mind in The Great Being—being so complete to begin with—seemed atypical in the extreme, even momentous.

This is really such good news. Layla literally bubbled from inside her energy bubble. *The one issue I've always wondered about is whether once I rejoined into The One, would I ever get bored. But now it appears not!*

Melchizedek felt well pleased with his prodigy and beloved. He'd known about her reservations and hadn't found the right words to quell them, so he'd waited for something like this—which he knew would eventually happen unless he found the right words first. The One knows all and never gets bored because HeSheWe is always being creative, sending solution suggestions down the great chain of Life to us.

Meanwhile Atlantis hummed as she now slowly lowered the underside capstone toward what lay below. Melchizedek made a mental note to find out later if Atlantis had a gender preference, male or female, or perhaps both.

The clouds parted and they could now see a vast ocean below. They would soon be submerged, it seemed.

Look! Templegard spotted the island below them, though found it hard to tell the relative sizes of the island and the ship.

Have we stopped? Nastassia asked.

Yes, Atlantis replied. *I'm cleaning up the ground beneath us and protecting the wildlife.*

The Agents reached out with their minds and could see what seemed to be millions of glowing golden rings emerging from the bottom of Atlantis, like huge thick swarms of birds but in impossible numbers. Each Agent followed a different ring to the ground. Melchizedek saw a baby lamb being picked up by a golden hula hoop and carried to safety while other rings did the same for the baby's family. Maitreya watched as a ring transplanted a tree, using its amplified telekinetics to help the roots find footing.

This will take a while. Atlantis sounded apologetic.

No bother, Maitreya said. *Brother Melchizedek has a question for you, Atlantis.* He'd overheard the thought.

Atlantis, do you think of yourself as a male or as a female? Melchizedek asked, with a charming smile on his bubble-face.

It depends. Sometimes I feel one way, sometimes the other. With my twin, Pacifus, we always turned each other on, so that if one felt manly, the other felt womanly.

So, there's a twin to this ship! Templegard, always thinking like a military man, had envisioned calling for backup if needed.

There used to be. Atlantis's voice had a twinge of melancholy.

I'm so sorry to hear that, Templegard offered sympathetically.

With many great battles fought in space for the last many millions of years, coming across survivors who had lost people, in many forms, came to be all too familiar.

Where did it happen? Templegard, in his empathy, supposed he probably also knew beings lost in that fight. People talked about great battles forever, always discovering new information.

On the other side of this planet, Atlantis recounted, *in the other great ocean. In the battle of Lemuria—Mu for short—Lemuria being Pacifus.*

Oh, don't worry. Atlantis saw them feeling concerned that she might be in similar mortal danger, and themselves as well. *I've been completely upgraded.*

φ

The latest revelation gave the Agents pause as they opened their minds to the possibility that this would be a highly challenging Mission, perhaps ending in their destruction again. Yet given their training, they didn't even bat a bubble-face eyelash.

Atlantis shaped the ground beneath them using powerful rays so that it would be a perfect socket for the underside of the ship. Finally, with all in readiness, the ship began to move again.

A sense of rest came over the Agents when the ship settled onto *terra firma*. Everyone wanted to go outside right away, but Atlantis asked them to wait for the area to cool off. Unbeknownst to them, while Atlantis recapped the fate of Pacifus, the ship had emanated millions of locking clamps into the rock below.

In the manner of a mother talking to her kids, Atlantis asked, *Are you going out like that?* referring to their bubble bodies and adding, *Surely that would scare away any native humans on this planet.*

No, we're not. Maitreya then gathered them together for a briefing. *I haven't told you this yet, but we're re-entering the battle zone now about 30,000 years in the future relative to your last Mission here.*

That makes sense, Melchizedek opined. *The natives back then could never have absorbed seeing our real selves and our technology.*

And even now they couldn't deal with seeing us this way. We're going to be wearing flesh-and-blood bodies in this gig as well, Maitreya apprised them.

What's changed? Templegard asked.

Architecture exists now, and sculpture, cities, trade, advanced spoken language, and the keeping of written records—kind of like tick marks, to count who owes what to whom. Maitreya continued his briefing, ready for more questions.

Layla asked, *What happened to the cave art that Melchizedek started?*

It's not just in caves any more, and the superstitious idolatry with which the natives reacted back then has morphed into a sophisticated understanding that the map isn't the territory. They know now what a symbol means.

What a change! Nastassia remarked. *What are our orders, sir?*

Call me Father. You'll play the role of my daughter, Eve. Templegard will be your husband; he'll be called Adam. You'll have children, and your lives will demonstrate the level at which people can live as an example for our guests. You'll help make visitors comfortable and while they're here, you'll teach them what reality is, so they can then go out and become useful to their leaders—and then become the trusted leaders—in their homelands.

Maitreya then turned to Melchizedek and Layla. *You two will go out from Atlantis and bring back visitors— people already close to the top in each advanced society. While you're with them, you will as gently as possible start the process of explaining to them the real Truth about everything. I'll take the lead on that back here on Atlantis.*

I assume they'll have to want to come along voluntarily? Melchizedek guessed, and Maitreya nodded his bubblehead, grinning.

Before we change into flesh-and-blood bodies, please take one invisible spin around the island and get a feel for the lay of the land. When you come back, we'll have the set dressed and that's when you can change, Maitreya instructed. *Also, be prepared: by the time you get back, the extras will have arrived.*

That made them curious. They eagerly flew out through the walls of Atlantis, which tickled the ship and she giggled.

Eve, as she now thought of herself—getting into her role—got up to altitude so as to put it all into perspective. As she slowly circled the island, what she saw delighted her. In the center of the widest part of the island now sat a glowing crystal pyramidal diamond, and all around it lush forests met up with glorious beaches. From her vantage point, she could see the great rock later named the Rock of Gibraltar, and the continents not far off to the east and south. Off to the seaward side, away from the mainland, the island had a tail that looked like a vast grassy plain sloping down to the seashore.

Adam appeared at her side and energy-hugged her. *Isn't it beautiful?* he asked in his familiar husky voice, and their bubbles melted together in midair. Looking down with her again moments later, he added *Tough duty. Well, some-body's got to do it.*

Melchizedek and Layla, similarly enjoying the view and each other, returned to the ship first—finding it had morphed in what felt like no time at all. Atlantis now appeared as a city: a pyramidal city in a single building over a mile high, open to the air at every level with terraces and individual neighborhoods in different colors and styles, with an abundance of different sorts of trees. Ubiquitous birds flew through the many open spaces on the surface of the heretofore sealed warship, and a profusion of gulls along with a host of other colorful species covered the building like fast-moving and swirling clouds. Millions of people also appeared to be living there.

φ

On a summery warm day, in a stone tavern sculpted largely open to the air, Melchizedek and Layla sat with two men in the lavish roof-covered section. From this perch, they could see the rest of the city of Polis in all directions— streets, bustling people, the walls and buildings mostly white. They had even seen what looked like crude marble columns in and around the capitol building at the center of the city, but knowing that area would be dense with Rebels, they had skirted it.

In fact, one of the men sitting and drinking with them, Sniike ("Sn-eye-kk"), they knew to be a Rebel. Sniike even remembered vaguely his Rebel identity and his mission as a spy. However, being in a human body with the new brain,

Sniike had lost all of his supra-human Rebel powers and even the innate telepathic abilities of humans, which most humans had also lost by now as a result of the new brain.

The Agents had chosen him not as an emissary to be shown the Truth, but rather as a target of opportunity to be learned from, to garner intel on the Rebels. In fact, Sniike had made the first move, choosing them as he sensed them to be Agents. Without anyone admitting anything outwardly, the adversaries had a recognition of one another.

Having Sniike around presented the danger that Rebel leaders could read their minds and thereby be able to see everything the Agents would be doing on Atlantis, as well as hear their teachings—all the better to prepare counter-propaganda. So, this Sniike find could well turn out to be inauspicious, to say the least. The odds of success had just gone down a notch, even though it already looked like a suicide mission. Nevertheless, the Agents decided that keeping Sniike around would be more practical than killing him, which could result in total warfare and thus leave no opportunity to try the Miracle and Truth dissemination plan.

Sniike and the other gentleman, Athenius, both wealthy and powerful men in the society of the city, wielded their power throughout the entire island chain. Athenius, a middle-aged fair-skinned native of Polis, bore little resemblance to Sniike who, born in a maritime area to the north known as Parsa, appeared swarthy and youthfully handsome, at probably about thirty years old.

Melchizedek and Layla, though still in their bubble bodies, projected the appearance of two attractive twenty-somethings, a couple very much in love, which they didn't need to pretend. They had all of their faculties, not being imprisoned in a human brain as on their previous Missions.

They had located these two men, who knew but disliked each other, by engaging in conversations in taverns like this one. Both men appeared interested in the intelligent and obviously rich strangers, who asked questions and told of a superior society from which they came. Sniike came off as especially interested in Layla, mainly in her mischievous green eyes, long red hair, and long legs.

Maitreya dropped in notes now and then, heard only by Melchizedek and Layla, of course. In his latest missive, he informed them: *Perse is the name Lucifer is now using, God knows why, and Parsa to the north is named after him. The area contains a dense concentration of Rebel troops who are manipulating a far larger human population. All the locals have boats, with oars and primitive sails, from which often come expansionist ambitions. The Rebels have built human armies throughout this region, which they've named after the Hell in which they rule.*

Rebels called any area they dominated Hell. According to Rebel legend, this came from an ancient boon granted by the backstabber as a concession after what the Rebels called the great land grab—the creation of the material world. At Lucifer's request, The Great Being gave him an area to call his own, in which he could rule as absolute master.

This area, actually a shadow universe called Hell, existed side by side with the "real" universe. Beings in the real universe would fall in and out of the shadow universe based on their own minds, putting themselves in Hell based on their fears, attachments, perceptions, and expectations. During their time in Hell, they would be purportedly subject to the Laws of Lucifer. Theoretically, the backstabber and Lucifer would fight for the souls of these beings once they had fallen into the shadow universe—or so went the mostly garbled half-truths of the Rebel ideology.

The Rebels originally called this planet Hell-as-Earth, Maitreya continued, *and they proclaimed these islands, including the one you're on, to be the world capital, Hellas. The people who live here are called Hellenes.*

φ

"You say your society has created things that are stronger and infinitely more complicated than the possessions, the tools and weapons, and comforts of modern life we enjoy here," Sniike said skeptically. "Prove it."

Melchizedek took out his cosmic smartphone and tapped on it a couple of times and then handed it over to Sniike, who touched the smooth metal with an immediate sense of fear. It felt so unlike anything he'd ever laid a hand on. He gingerly turned it over while Athenius bent close to have a look too. On the screen, he beheld an image of himself and Athenius sitting side by side in the tavern. He dropped the phone, terrified.

Athenius scooped up the cosmic smartphone and tapped on it as he'd seen Melchizedek do. Invented eons ago, cosmic smartphones had stopped changing appearance once they assumed their present size and shape. Easy to use with one hand and almost weightless, able to call anyone in the multiverse, they functioned almost as well as telepathy.

Sniike, still drawn back in ill-concealed terror, gradually mastered his fear. Melchizedek couldn't see the screen from where he sat, but through Athenius's eyes he saw it now showed the many text messages recently received. Now Athenius seemed shocked as well.

"What's that?" he asked in a strong voice. He sensed something very important, just out of reach of his mind.

"That's called writing," Melchizedek said gently. "You folks haven't invented it yet."

"Of course, we've invented it," Athenius retorted, insulted. "We use it to keep track of who owes what to whom."

"Yes, we know." Layla laid a friendly hand on his arm. "Writing has a great many other uses besides counting, which you'll come to appreciate."

Layla had captured their attention. She had just clearly offered them a Faustian bargain that they'd be crazy to turn down: she could teach them and possibly equip them with powerful new weapons of dominance.

"Selling those trinkets, are you?" Sniike bantered, sidling up beside Layla.

"Not right now." Layla smiled. "But we'll send you home with a present."

"Are you inviting us to your land?" Athenius felt his dignity returning.

This seemed to confuse Sniike, who hadn't seen it coming.

Layla simply nodded.

"We'd like a few days of your time to change your life and expand your consciousness," Melchizedek said with a smile.

"What do *you* get out of it?" Sniike quipped.

"We want to help the best people lead the others." Melchizedek spoke with genuine sincerity.

Not realizing the Agents had selected Athenius and would just as soon be rid of Sniike, he seemed momentarily flattered. Then, still unsatisfied and suspicious, he probed further. "Yes, but you must want to get something for yourselves—"

Athenius cut across him, "Sometimes a person does a good thing just because it's the right thing to do."

This embarrassed Sniike. He mumbled unconvincingly, "Of course."

"When do you propose to begin the journey, and how many days travel is it to get there?" Athenius asked reasonably.

He seemed clearly interested in seeing a new land for himself, and finding out more about his expanded future options. He told himself he could lay his responsibilities aside and take time off, explaining himself later with some present they'll have given him, proving the importance of his travels. He also knew that many in the town council would be glad to have him absent, since he'd irritated nearly everyone with his blunt honesty and passion for truth and accuracy.

Perhaps these new people can teach me how to be diplomatic, he thought to himself.

Melchizedek and Layla heard his thought and made a mental note to accommodate his aspiration.

"We'd like to leave as soon as possible," Layla said enthusiastically. Being in the middle of the most densely-infested Rebel zone on Earth, they wanted to get in and out undetected.

"Sounds like an ambush to me," Sniike said, as if to himself. He stood up, looming over them.

Athenius prepared his body for motion, but Melchizedek and Layla merely sat comfortably and smiled up at Sniike.

"What if I just take that little trinket—" Sniike hissed.

He reached over and yanked the phone from Athenius's grasp, taking him completely by surprise. Then, feeling as if he'd clearly intimidated all of them, and spurred by the frequent acts of violence he'd seen at this and other such taverns, he looked lecherously at Layla as if he would grab her next. Suddenly, the light went out in his eyes and he sank back into his seat, dropping the phone on the rough-hewn table. He came around only seconds later.

"What happened?" he asked leerily.

"You needed to be brought under control." Layla spoke in a tone as if speaking to a beloved child. "You acted rudely toward us."

Sniike spun around, looking for an accomplice with a blunt instrument, and felt his head for a swelling though found none.

"If we're agreed then, shall we be off?" Melchizedek asked pleasantly.

φ

In the short walk from the tavern to the seaside, Athenius and Sniike walked astride a few paces behind Melchizedek and Layla, who had kicked off their shoes, reveling in digging their bare feet in the sand, holding hands, and singing something the Greek and the Parsan couldn't make out.

They walked past some crude rowboats with makeshift sail-rigs and stopped at a strange and unimpressive little vessel, smaller than anything else they'd seen. They peered down into it, and saw what looked like something dark to sit on, but they didn't see any oars or oarlocks, and certainly no sail.

"This is your boat?" Sniike sounded skeptical, now thinking the whole setup looked like a fraud.

"Yes, isn't she a beauty?" Melchizedek then added proudly, "Layla picked the carpeting."

Layla looked humbly gratified. "It's a Parsan carpet." She hoped Sniike would take it as a compliment to his people.

Sniike did a double-take as his eyes adjusted and he could make out the complex scrollwork. "I've never seen a Parsan carpet in a boat before," he admitted, "nor any other kind of carpet."

"That's the deep blue your carpetmakers call Perse," Athenius, the man of the world, informed Sniike.

Named in honor of Perse, Maitreya pathed into the minds of Melchizedek and Layla.

"Are we going to paddle with our hands?" Sniike asked flippantly. "How long will the trip take without any sail?"

"It'll take however long you'd like it to take. We can create our own wind, so to speak, and make it take us in any direction," Melchizedek said straightforwardly.

Athenius, looking dubious, got into the beached boat. Aware that his weight could add to the effort it would take Melchizedek to lift and push the boat off into the water, he intended to jump up and help once the others got in, but he had an instinct to lead the way and so he did. Laying his body on the thick carpet felt like lying on a plush bed, so he felt glad to have lain down. The others followed his lead and discovered the comfort of the craft.

"Now what?" Sniike's tone implied the joke had gone far enough, and they wouldn't be going anywhere in this thing. *Besides, the splashing water would wreck the value of the carpet,* he thought to himself.

"Do you want to take us out, Mister Sniike?" Layla asked.

With a quick mental pivot, Sniike jumped up, ready to push them off—proud to be acknowledged as the strong man of the group.

She stopped him, saying, "No, sit down. Try moving the boat with just your mind. Let it know the direction you want to go, which is over there," she pointed.

Sniike sat down and tried to comply but nothing happened. He harrumphed at being made the butt of her little child's joke.

"Athenius?" Melchizedek offered next honors to the Greek man.

"You say I just will it, and it does whatever I have willed?" Athenius asked, seeking clarification.

Melchizedek confirmed, "Yes, that's it."

A moment later, the boat lurched upward about a foot and rocked a lot, then steadied.

"Good work, Athenius!" Melchizedek said, and Layla patted the man on the back.

Sniike's eyes narrowed.

The boat moved tentatively in the direction Layla had pointed and picked up a little speed. At about nine nautical knots, it stopped accelerating and moved out of the water, seemingly riding on top of it—catching the attention of some people both on shore and out in cruder boats.

Sniike inched toward the edge of the boat and cautiously looked over. He saw the side of the boat now as a continuous gold ring that ran all the way around the ovoid boat.

"Can I try steering it again?" he asked somewhat petulantly.

"Of course, sir," Athenius said. The boat continued to move in the same course.

"Go ahead," Layla encouraged Sniike.

Nothing changed. "What's the secret?" Sniike asked, clearly aggravated.

"Just assume you can do it, and then do it. Don't complicate it," Athenius advised.

Sniike tried to put the advice into practice but the boat followed its previous orders.

"You have to truly open your mind to believe you can do it," Melchizedek suggested gently. "It's not just a matter of fooling or impressing other people. You've got to yourself believe it's possible before you can move things with your mind."

Suddenly, Sniike broke through and the boat took off, straight up and very fast. "Wheeeee!" he exclaimed, feeling like a little boy again and flying madly every which way.

Layla reclined in Melchizedek's arms, both of them cool as cucumbers, while Athenius clung tightly, his fingernails dug into the carpet. Even when the boat turned upside down, the carpet held them all snugly, and when Sniike purposely steered them directly into a thundercloud, they stayed perfectly dry while seemingly an arm's reach away, something invisible stopped a torrent of water.

Sniike now took them down near the water and increased the speed, moving the boat so fast over the water that a moment later they could see something—an enormous something—coming up over the horizon.

φ

In the space of a few hours, two native Earth men—one picked to be exceptional, and the other a Rebel whose brain had gone native—had gotten used to miracles, the obstacle in their minds completely vanquished. Their quick progression impressed Melchizedek and Layla, from Sniike fearfully dropping the smartphone to flying a seemingly makeshift boat. If Sniike could be turned to their side, he too could be an outstanding emissary.

Now, as the boat rapidly closed the distance to the island, Atlantis rose taller and taller, until the two men could feel the tension in the back of their necks from craning their chins upward to see the top, more than a mile above them. Athenius and Sniike became more awed by the second. The enormous scale at which these new people had the capability to construct something became apparent, as impossible as it might have seemed earlier that day.

The detail of everything going on within Atlantis, all visible at once through the mostly-open architecture of the city, held enough complexity in one view to overwhelm the senses of both natives. The boat slowed rapidly to avoid a collision, and then glided smoothly in a specific direction no one on board had willed, simply finding its way home until advised otherwise.

The boat continued its slow glide, passing families living out their lives and playing games with their children on verdant lawns, markets with active trading going on, streets with shops, business areas, lovers strolling through parks, a court in session, a government area—the whole gamut of human experience seemed to be on display.

Looming above, seemingly going all the way up into the sky as far as heaven, must surely be where the ruler of the universe sits, said all of the superstitious instincts of the two visitors to Atlantis. Nothing in their experience or imagination had prepared them for this moment. The expression on Sniike's face looked the same as when he first saw the smartphone. And while Athenius controlled his facial expression, making it hard to read, his seated posture now appeared defensive and stiff.

Melchizedek and Layla could easily feel the two men's feelings: a vast sense of inferiority and/or smallness.

"You feel as if all of this is far bigger than you, but what we'll demonstrate is that each of you is far bigger than all of this." Melchizedek spoke with a calming voice.

Both men responded with disbelieving stares.

"No, really." Layla continued with warm sincerity, "It's true, you'll see."

Athenius and Sniike, both quite taken with Layla, relaxed a little when she spoke, as if out of deference to the lady.

The boat slowed as it glided down over a small park. As it cleared the last trees, it came to a stop and sank to the ground, landing in a charming garden next to a rambling house with many windows. Looking around, they could see a large swimming pool—half inside the house and half in the garden—and in it, two small children at play, splashing one another. A man and a woman, about Melchizedek and Layla's age, came out of the house and walked toward them; the man large, muscular, and strikingly handsome, and the woman a beauty with ebony hair, light skin, and a sparkling presence. Both smiled broadly in delighted greeting.

"Athenius and Sniike, I'm Adam and this is my wife, Eve, and the kids in the pool are our son, PlayAllDay, and our daughter, ThinkAllNight. Welcome to Eden!" Templegard played his current role with a natural warmth.

Athenius somberly gripped hands with each of them, followed by Sniike's reptilian slithering of hands, his version of a handshake. Melchizedek and Layla came up and hugged Adam and Eve.

"Eden is the name of your estate here?" Athenius asked.

Adam nodded. "Yes, the whole property, although we spend most of our time in the garden as the weather is usually so fair." They had ensconced themselves on the island for only about a month, and spring had just turned to summer.

"This Eden Garden is certainly beautiful. You've planned it well," Athenius remarked, complimenting Eve.

She smiled modestly. "Atlantis did all the work."

"Atlantis—I thought that's the name of this island," Sniike had just found his voice.

"The island, the city, and the consciousness behind them." Maitreya had stepped out of nowhere, surprising them all. The kids saw their grandpa and came running to hug and soak his legs, and once he picked them up, they soaked the rest of him along with those standing nearby, as they kissed him and murmured baby talk.

"Father!" Eve called, then hugged him and the kids, with Adam, Melchizedek, and Layla in turn following suit. She then turned to introduce the guests to Maitreya.

"Father, this is Athenius from Hellas, and Sniike from Parsa. Gentlemen, this is my father and the governor of Atlantis, Maitreya."

The men shook hands in their own ways.

"What did you mean about Atlantis being not only this city and this island, but also—conscious?" Athenius asked.

"Everything is made of consciousness—you and I, the stars, the sun, which is also a nearby star—everything around us, everything in the whole universe is a single consciousness," Maitreya explained.

Athenius and Sniike looked doubtful.

"I've heard other theories just as strange." Athenius made an effort to be polite and fair to this new bit of speculation. "In Hellas, many people have many theories about what the world is." He felt right at home, having just landed in Atlantis and already engaged in a metaphysical conversation.

Adam joined the exchange. "This one's not just any old theory, it's also the fact."

Neither visitor appeared convinced by this bald statement. Sniike vaguely remembered discussions of this kind and knew his heritage held a different view, something about a usurper creator who had trapped his co-creators into a world of his choosing. While searching for the words to explain this view, the conversation continued around him.

"The thing about philosophy is that as much as it stimulates the mind," Athenius commented, "ultimately it leaves you not knowing who's right and who's wrong."

Maitreya smiled. "Let's help our guests get comfortable before we jump right in to all this. Athenius and Sniike, we'll answer all of your questions in a short while, but for now, go take a look at your rooms, freshen up, get settled in, and have a look around. When you're ready, we'll all come together again."

The two men nodded their agreement, and Adam and Eve showed Athenius and Sniike to their palatial rooms, each of which opened to a vast ocean view that stretched to the mainland on the horizon.

Neither man had ever spent a night in a place so wonderful. Clothing of strange kinds but seemingly in their own size filled the closets and drawers. They each looked around their rooms in amazed silence. Athenius then took a thinking posture in a chair on his terrace, while Sniike threw himself on his bed, both attempting to assimilate their uncanny experiences.

φ

Adam and Eve—with a lot of help from Atlantis and his/her team—served the guests a sumptuous feast, which they richly enjoyed. Sniike gulped while the others sipped the incredible wines. With the children asleep and the party well along, Sniike—also well along—gathered himself together to deliver a stream-of-consciousness speech to Layla and then to the table at large:

"Thank you for the many kindnesses you've shown us. Before I get too drunk, can we get back to the work at hand?"

After a moment of silence, everyone laughed together. *So much for a speech,* they all thought.

Maitreya started the evening's discourse. "When we close our eyes at night, we know we're still here—our mind, images, feelings, our consciousness—all still here. This, out here," he waved at their fair surroundings, a banquet table under the stars, "is such a convincing illusion that we take it to be the truest reality, and the stuff in our heads we take to be just imaginary stuff. Yet what is deepest in our minds and hearts is the true Self, and there's only one of us, the One True Self."

Athenius smiled. "This stuff out here," he tapped on the table, "compels our attention. If we do something wrong, it could kill us. What good is what's inside us compared to that?"

"What's inside us cannot be killed." Maitreya answered with a conversation stopper.

A few beats later, Sniike quietly added his take on it. "My people believe that too. We each live countless lives."

"The part that's new, the revelation," Maitreya returned, "is that all of us are the same One Self living all these lives."

"Is that the message you wish us to bring to our leaders and thereby to the nations?" Athenius asked in a serious voice.

"Yes," Maitreya answered evenly.

"We can do that, kind sir," Sniike asserted, "although we may never believe it."

"What's necessary is for you to *know* it," Maitreya added.

"We can do that too," Sniike offered with a wink.

Maitreya's smile did not change as he looked to Athenius.

"I will not carry a lie or a story or artifice or whatever you want to call it," Athenius declared. "We're friends now and I love you people and I'm very grateful too. But I could only bring a message to the world for you whose truth and value I feel totally certain of."

"That's the only way," Maitreya responded, addressing them both. "It won't work any other way. I need to show you something." He stood up, leaving the table to be cleared by Atlantis's team.

The guests and other Agents followed and Maitreya led them into the boat, the same one the guests had arrived in. Seeing to their comfort as each settled into the boat, he took off and flew them straight up toward the capstone of the upper pyramid of the great ship Atlantis.

Flying up its side, both Athenius and Sniike couldn't help thinking, yet again, that this endless mountain extended to the throne of God—Sniike's God being the one he had always gravitated to, the one who called the other God "the backstabber," for some reason he couldn't recall. They imagined light shows in the sky behind the approaching capstone. Chills ran up their spines and necks.

They arrived at the capstone and could look directly inside through its diamond textured outer layer, where they saw several couches arranged in a circle.

Once inside through a sliding door, Maitreya directed them calmly. "Lie down, one person to a couch, and relax."

The two guests looked at Maitreya quizzically, and Sniike asked, "What's going to happen?"

Maitreya didn't answer.

Still, they followed his direction. As soon as they got horizontal, they noticed how comfortable and pleasant it felt to float here under the stars, visible above through the crystalline skin of Atlantis.

A very relaxed Athenius spoke almost in a whisper. "How nice to just breathe deeply. This feels really good."

An extended moment transpired in which everyone felt equally contented with silence.

Then a voice seemed to come out of nowhere. "I am you."

The soft tone reverberated gently throughout their beings. The visitors suddenly realized that a whole other level of reality existed beyond their sight—and always had.

Thoughts flashed through the minds of each. *We are the experiencer. I have always existed. At the core of you, look inside, there am I. We are one and the same. There is only one of us playing all roles. This is our game throughout eternity.*

Now reality changed dramatically. All the same people the visitors came in with now appeared as luminous bubbles with incredible and ever-changing internal details, floating in space.

The soft voice continued. "Consciousness can make forms appear. Those forms can be changed by consciousness. Everything is illusion and real at the same time. You get to choose which illusion you prefer to live in."

"Who are you?" Athenius asked boldly.

"I am the One Self, the same One that is inside of you. I just asked myself that question."

"Why do you do this?" Athenius asked, slightly shaken.

"What would you do—if you found yourself all alone in nothingness—and would be *alone* for *eternity*?" The One asked, this time in a strong deep voice.

"That's a fair point, sir." Athenius felt sudden empathy. Now sitting up, he resumed his earlier Thinker posture.

"You take for granted," The Great Being continued, "the *wonderfulness* of having *other beings* around you."

"Give us a sign!" Sniike blurted out. "How do we know this isn't just talk?"

"Oh, that." The One laughed. "I'm just coming to that. Hold on."

Athenius felt himself voluntarily give up motor control over his body, which now appeared to be made up of little cubes, each of which expanded into a gas. Suddenly, he could see no couch, no body, just space—exploding all around in beautiful color strokes from different angles, with galaxies being born. He suddenly remembered the many other lives he had lived and how it all started, and now he found himself back at the beginning—of himself, the Only Self.

This isn't a story. It's complete and it's undeniably real, Athenius thought to himself.

Sniike had a very similar experience but he didn't remember it that way. Instead, he remembered hearing the voice as the whining patronizing lies and deception of the backstabber. Clearly remembering all of his lives reminded him of his true identity as a Rebel, a being at a higher level of evolution than humans.

Part of him later admitted, "I'm convinced a powerful Self is within me, which I can communicate with, but I'm not sure if I approve of that Self or not."

Maitreya could read Sniike and thought to himself with a flicker of disappointment, *He's not ready for such an experience, so he didn't get much out of it except to feel more confused.*

Now back on their couches, Athenius opened his eyes. Everyone sat up and looked to him first.

"I'll carry this message," Athenius said confidently.

"Me too," Sniike echoed.

12

Thus began the diaspora of human messengers to the ends of the Earth, spreading the message that the most powerful being in the Universe is living through us. Athenius returned to Hellas to a warm reception, as the populace largely believed his stories of Atlantis, and what he had learned there.

Word spread and a group of Rebels accosted him on a side street and searched him thoroughly, dealing a blow to his dignity. Agents appearing as a pack of feral dogs gave chase to the Rebels, who retreated only after assuring themselves that Athenius carried no treasure from Atlantis. The Rebel grapevine had somehow led them to believe he would be carrying some advanced weaponry given to him by the Atlanteans.

Athenius already had a solid backing in Polis, being widely seen to be nothing if not the One Honest Man among them with his reputation for speaking only the truth. So, the idea that he of all people would make up such a story seemed incongruous and people laughed at the notion, despite Rebel efforts to paint him as an ambitious liar. He thus rose swiftly to great influence and his philosophical ideas spread like wildfire throughout the land and beyond.

Athenius had become the first of the Agent emissaries. Once the process started to deliver positive results, the Agents dispatched more and more Atlantean expeditions to the farthest reaches of the Earth to find exceptional leaders, inviting them to visit Atlantis and bring new learning back to their people.

By popping up in unexpected places and with considerable evanescence, the Agents largely evaded Rebel efforts to thwart the program. Their ability to mask telepathic signals without being detected gave Agent forces an enormous advantage over most Rebels. Moreover, Agents had much more control over their own consciousness because they had unity and peace within themselves, whereas Rebels, living a nightmare of their own imaginations, thus had more internal division within their consciousness—a state not conducive to advanced telepathic techniques.

Sniike had remained in Atlantis, and not by choice.

"What do you mean?!" he said defiantly when first told of his fate.

"Let's face it, Sniike, old buddy," Adam said affectionately, "deep down inside, you know you're a Rebel. You know it, and we all know it."

"Is that what you call it?" Sniike snorted furiously. "You're the dupes of a traitor who stabbed the rest of his brethren in the back. His *coup d'état* started it all, we're just counterattacking."

Adam merely smiled, a tad sadly. He wished he had greater power to help Sniike. So did everybody in Atlantis. Sniike, the only permanent guest—still staying at the palatial pad they gave him—became somewhat of a celebrity on the island. Everyone wanted to meet him to see if they could be the one to talk sense into him, in what came to be a pleasant and well-intended competition.

The Agents had Sniike under constant surveillance by microscopic flying gold rings—Atlantis's eyes and ears, noses, tongues, and fingers as needed—able to bring back whatever the five human senses and beyond could detect.

"He's doing what?" Melchizedek asked incredulously upon hearing a briefing from Atlantis on Sniike's activities. Mel and Layla had returned to Atlantis after escorting Athenius back to Hellas, and would soon be off again on another recruiting expedition.

It came as no surprise when they heard Sniike had tried to telepathically contact other Rebels back home; the Agents expected and routinely blocked such efforts while allowing Sniike to fantasize that he'd made contact. But another odd habit surveillance had picked up on perplexed them: Sniike would set about capturing a certain type of bug in his garden, and then grind the bugs into a paste—with unknown intent, at least to the four Agents.

"A love potion," Maitreya informed them, "except it actually irritates human females in their G-spot, and more often turns them off than on."

"Interesting!" Layla remarked, with a hint of incredulity.

They all turned to look at her. Then everyone laughed.

In the weeks that followed, Sniike dated women and tried out his love potion on them. Although appearing to be beautiful human women, many of them—actually being conscious artificial intelligence parts of Atlantis—played their assigned role of counterspies. Much bedding ensued. The AIs could read Sniike like a book, and the beetle paste had zero effect on their bubble bodies—though Sniike saw and felt only their ersatz flesh-and-blood bodies.

One day, Sniike had dropped by to visit Adam and Eve—probably knowing Adam wouldn't be home—and she detected him sneaking off to inject some of his love potion into a fruit hanging on a large tree. Sure enough, a little while later, while strolling casually together in the Eden Garden, Sniike reached up and took a certain apple off the tree, bit and ate of it enthusiastically, and then offered the apple to Eve.

To be cordial she took a dainty bite, and as he encouraged her to take more, she took a great gulp. Moments later, she imagined having sensations in her genitals; of course, knowing it to be metaphysically impossible, she'd feigned having them, just for fun. Sniike, shortly thereafter, tried to sit closer to her, but she pretended to already be in motion and unaware of his actions. A few tries later, being pretty smart, he got it and gave up, even though he'd wanted her since he first saw her.

Eve or Layla, he reminded himself.

Sniike remained a rake, trying to bed every quasi-woman on Atlantis, but he also embarked upon what he imagined could be a lifelong study of natural cures, testing each on himself. This became a sort of hobby that gave meaning or at least content to his life.

He saw himself as a determined, loyal, courageous spy for the Rebels, doing his best to get telepathic messages through, reporting his endless spying on Atlantis. Often, he would learn something he considered valuable from his conversations with the Agents or with Atlantis, or with one of the Angels or Cherubs impersonating humans in Atlantis, but especially when he met new guests from around the world. He valued these freedoms the Atlanteans gave him, and even their friendship.

One day, as he approached Eden, the kids came running to greet him.

"Uncle Sniike!" both PlayAllDay and ThinkAllNight called gaily as they came up to hug him.

Clearly, they liked him very much. And on this one day, he realized he felt just as attached to them, as he hugged and kissed them both with utter sincerity.

Eve and Adam came up to join them. "Say, friend," Adam asked, "do you have any more of that tree-bark stuff?"

The Atlanteans made sure Sniike knew they took his practice seriously and considered it a valuable contribution to their society. Sniike opened a pouch at his waist and handed over a few pinches of pycnogenol to Adam, who licked it off his own hand.

"Yum!" Adam said. "Good stuff."

φ

Playing in the pool with the kids, Sniike imagined Adam and Eve making out in the house.

Dirty old man, ThinkAllNight pathed to PlayAllDay, and they both giggled intensely in Sniike's delighted and clueless face.

"Daddy says you believe in many gods, and not in the One Self," ThinkAllNight said to Sniike, with no particular emotion, just curiosity.

"That's what my parents taught me," Sniike explained. "I'm sure they would have told me what they believed to be the truth about such an important subject."

"But you—you're not sure which way it all is?" PlayAllDay guessed.

"I don't really know any more." Sniike's realization dawned on him as he spoke. "It could as easily be one way as the other. I don't remember what my parents taught me in any kind of detail. I used to know, and then I lost it. My mind once had a sharp clarity, but it's been a long time since I felt that way."

"It's these brains you know," ThinkAllNight said, pointing to her own head— which did not actually contain a human brain, she and her brother being Cherubs.

Sniike stared at her, not understanding.

"The Rebels altered the new human brain so that it's too helpful, it actually takes over," she said matter-of-factly.

"I seem to remember something about that. It has a ring of truth, but I can't say why," Sniike said, somewhat foggily.

A stubborn streak in him said he'd never give up his loyalty to...whatever...or whoever... He couldn't quite remember that either.

These kind beloved people are my enemies. I'm living among my enemies. I don't wish to live in constant enmity and it feels like the proper role of a spy is to pretend to be friendly, even if it means actually being friendly, he mused silently.

That much he remembered, the enemy part. He walked this razor's edge and avoided being cut.

"I don't think it could be as easily one way as the other," PlayAllDay returned to the conversation. "I can't explain it, but the idea of there being just one thing in the beginning seems somehow more logical, more probable—I can't say why."

Sniike waved his arm, alluding to the profusion of the world around them, splashing them both and causing them to giggle and splash him back lightly. "And yet, all around us we always see multiplicity, and almost never do we apprehend oneness."

"You did feel it once, though," ThinkAllNight said, revealing that Adam and Eve must have told the kids about the visit to the capstone and the experience of being one with The Great Being.

"Yes," Sniike admitted, "I did feel it, but I've been fooled by illusions before. Since I couldn't recapture the experience, it became less credible. Sometimes, taking one of my potions will cause me to hallucinate. Maybe I hallucinated the experience in the capstone."

"There's another reason I find it hard to believe the rendition your parents taught you," PlayAllDay said. "If a multiplicity of Gods always existed, how come today all we know about are two Gods, one of which says HeShe is inside all of us, and the other that says there's a multiplicity—but where is everybody else who's a God? Shouldn't we be seeing a big free-for-all of Gods, if multiple Gods really exist?"

"There's a reason for that," Sniike replied. "I wish I could remember it."

φ

Dozens of emissaries had visited Atlantis and received the key message. The Agents had trained them in writing and code, given them tools with which to subdue their overpowering brains, along with other necessary tradecraft, and then sent them back to their homelands. Yet the Rebels still had no idea what took place in Atlantis.

On a day like this, I could destroy them all, Perse ruminated. A long league above his followers, he often saw them being as much of a hindrance as a help—today being one of those times. But he would never diminish his forces out of sheer disappointment, since they could at least keep his adversary busy.

Perse sat alone on the bridge of his ship, the same planetbuster that many years ago had destroyed the fifth planet, Phaeton, creating the asteroid belt between Mars and Jupiter. He accounted to no one for his movements, and although his followers believed him to be traveling outside of the Sol system, his ship actually hovered over Earth—invisible to Agents and Rebels, and even to Atlantis.

Thus undetected, Perse dove from his ship down to Earth's surface, where he took on the appearance of a pigeon and flew toward a nearby island with a large pointy mountain. Flying onto the first beach in sight, he blended in easily with the gulls, who ignored him. Walking toward the water, he spied his amnesic follower, Sniike, whom he knew had come to drown himself. He called out.

Sniike turned suddenly and his eyes landed on a pigeon staring at him from a few feet away. He almost spoke to the bird but then realized how ridiculous that would be, and started toward the water again. Perse then flew past his face, much closer than would an ordinary bird. Sniike stopped ankle-deep in the sea and watched the bird circle back and then land on the water, bobbing gently and staring at him. Sniike watched and waited—for what, he did not know.

Giving up? he heard in his head.

Yes, I guess I am, Sniike said mentally to the pigeon but mostly to himself. *Unless my messages have gotten through and you're here to reinforce me,* he thought with ironic resignation at the dubiousness of it all.

I can fly your message out, the pigeon said in his mind.

φ

The pigeon flew into the occasional home of General Ares, the planetary Shaitan, who had recently arrived on one of his frequent trips planetside to keep a personal eye on things. The bird strode directly up to the General as he sat by the fire contemplating his next political moves. Ares understood immediately that to be able to appear as such, the bird must be a Rebel of at least the status of Prince, and so he stood deferentially.

The pigeon spit out a folded piece of paper-like bark on the floor. Ares knelt and carefully opened it, flattened it with his palm, and took it closer to the fire to sit and look at it, glancing occasionally at the tight-beaked bird.

He saw what appeared to be a map. The "X" surely marked Ares' current position, amidst an archipelago of islands. The left side of the map depicted rough outlines of continents and two prominent objects.

This one has to be the Pillars of Heracles, but the one farther out in the ocean, what is that? Ares wondered.

The pigeon stood up, morphing into a giant man, about ten feet tall, bowing over slightly to avoid hitting the high ceiling. Handsome, dignified, and impeccably dressed down to his ebon hooves—highly polished as always, perfectly gleaming without a speck of dust or hangnail—he appeared to be deeply saddened.

General Ares stood at high attention before his supreme commander, who now preferred to be called Perse.

"Sir?" the General asked.

"You'll recall the ship we destroyed some time ago on the other ocean," Perse began.

The General suddenly realized that the other object on the map, located very close to his position, looked like another colossally powerful ship like the one Perse invoked—which had proved formidably difficult to destroy. Ultimately, Perse's own ship had to come down to Earth to finish her off. The General became acutely aware of the danger looming, not only from the enemy, but from his boss.

"Wool gathering is I guess your explanation for being asleep at the switch?" Perse spoke with apparent even temper. "Brooding over some political move?"

The General knew Perse could read everything in his mind and had caught him with a smoking mental gun—derelict from his duty, thinking only of his petty schemes, and thereby not having detected the enemy nearby before someone had to point it out to him as if to a child.

"Guilty, sir." Ares threw himself on the mercy of arguably the most merciless being in the universe.

"Now that I've made you aware of the situation, General, what are your plans?" Perse asked coolly.

"If it please you, sir, we will destroy the vessel," Ares returned, standing tall now.

"Have fun." Sounding bored, Perse scoffed and then disappeared.

Ares sprang into action, calling his general staff together and giving them their orders. Many of his staff, out in space somewhere, attended the meeting virtually, including the most powerful battlecraft, which had purposely kept its distance so as to present less of a tempting target. Now they all streaked toward Atlantis.

φ

"What now?" Athenius yelled from his bed. Well-accustomed to being called upon at all hours to solve difficult problems, make decisions, provide advice, and sometimes just to commiserate, Athenius took this as his duty and the role he'd always worked toward—the unofficial sage of Polis—supported by donations from those who wanted "free" access to him. Of course, he tended to welcome everyone with kindness, even those unable to make a donation. However, he'd worked himself to a frazzle this way, the current late caller being one of many, and Athenius longed for at least a nap.

He tied his toga and walked toward the front door just as General Ares—in full battle armor—barged in, followed by a squad of his toughest men. Athenius stopped in his tracks, his mind moving swiftly.

"Where are we going?" he asked.

"All our ground forces in Ereba and Aethiopia, as heavily armed as possible, are now marching to the west," Ares told him, using the names the Greeks then called Europe and Africa.

"What do you mean *our?*" Athenius asked. "Hellenes have armies everywhere and no one has told me about their movements?"

Of course, Athenius had no way of knowing Ares meant the Rebels, not the Hellenes.

The General got annoyed at being questioned but reminded himself of Athenius's nature, which Ares saw as a doggedly obsessive need for complete information. Any other man foolish enough to press him like that would normally be quickly dead, by Ares' own hand.

"Athenius, you ask too many questions for your own good. This much I'll tell you: we've formed a secret alliance with tribes in all directions, reaching farther than your own expert knowledge of geography." Ares revealed this in a whisper, not wanting to be overheard by his own men.

Ares, an awake Rebel in a human body, had mostly conquered the overly-helpful human brain that wanted to run the show, and thus had become one of the strongest-minded Rebels in the zone. Nonetheless, he had to follow Perse's orders not to divulge full knowledge of the Rebels to mere humans like his men and Athenius—though he made occasional exceptions.

For this situation, Perse had ordered Ares to let Athenius in on a small piece of the truth, filling in the rest with lies. Ares himself preferred not to lie because it took too much mental effort. Having learned to counteract the human brain by constant inner attention to its machinations, he avoided any distraction from that task. Like lies.

So, he planned to tell as little as possible to Athenius, without distracting himself by having to make up and maintain lies. He knew Perse would yell at him for this, since Perse could read everyone's mind at once it seemed, but he also knew his value to Perse and thus he wouldn't be punished any more than he could handle.

"I'll fill you in en route," the General said, loudly enough for all to hear. "Right now, these men will help you into the battle armor we brought and will quickly familiarize you with weapons and procedure. Then we'll be off to lead the attack."

"What city are we attacking and why?" Athenius asked insistently, waiting for an answer before moving into action.

"It's the city you found for us," Ares whispered.

Athenius's eyes opened wide.

φ

Four weeks had passed by the time the Hellenes arrived at their ships in Morocco, joining a much larger Rebel force. Athenius asked, "Are we boarding now?"

Ares hesitated, not wanting to say they'd be launching the boats when the spaceships arrived. Instead, he simply barked, "I don't know!"

An hour later the orders came through to start the attack.

Atlantis's klaxon horn rang out like temple bells in the middle of the night, waking the entire population of Angels, Cherubs, Agents, and visiting humans, including some Rebel spies. All but the humans could hear Atlantis's broadcast warning:

"A huge fleet of Rebel warships is heading this way from across the galaxy and beyond. Please move indoors, away from the surface of the ship."

Their hosts guided the visiting humans into the interior parts of Atlantis while the outer surface returned to her original diamond-textured appearance.

An enormous Rebel army had assembled on the beaches of what is today known as Gibraltar and Morocco, and now launched hordes of boats, bringing assault troops to attack Atlantis. In the boat leading the sea fleet, standing at the bow and taking the full blast of the sea spray, Ares affected a heroic posture, though felt a little foolish for it.

Athenius held on and observed everything from his position on deck. He had seen moving stars in the night sky but kept this to himself. Ares had told him that Atlanteans had subjugated most of Ereba and Aethiopia and would be coming for the Hellenes and Parsans next.

"This Rebel attack is preemptive and it's our only hope of success. If we lose, the Hellenes will become the slaves of the Atlanteans, like everyone else." Ares implied further that his men could as easily die in this battle, but duty bound them to make this attack and they would be hailed as heroes.

Athenius took it all in with a grain of salt, knowing that even when people as sincere as Ares said something, he didn't necessarily have to believe it. Whoever had aligned all the tribes—a mysterious entity about whom Ares wouldn't say another word—could have told Ares a fiction, a guess, a cover story.

So, he felt unsure about what action he'd take when the moment came. Would he kill the first Atlantean he saw, or would he interrogate him or her, or would he be in a position to do anything but kill or be killed? He intended to stay alert internally and externally, and not prejudge anything.

Ares sensed this ambiguity in Athenius but had no time to think about it. He knew the first blows would come soon, and they would be horrific and devastating.

φ

Thousands of Rebel warships, now directly overhead, coordinated their bombardment of Atlantis on a single point: the capstone. They hoped such an attack would break through the immensely powerful shields of energy protecting the vessel and its city-state within.

The combining streams of destructive radiation, pouring down in a single ray, became diffused due to slight errors in calculation by computers aboard the attacking craft. The sloping sides of Atlantis withstood the blows, casting them off at angles.

This boomerang of destruction rained down as far away as the beaches where the Rebel boats had launched off from. To the soldiers still massed on the beaches, the shoreline appeared to be cracking apart as in a natural earthquake, while the ocean flooded in with tsunami-size waves, killing thousands of soldiers. Most of the survivors ran away and trekked back to their homelands, giving up the fight. Only the Hellenes remained. The Rebels in space noticed this, but since they hadn't given the human ground forces much chance of being helpful or of surviving, it didn't occupy their minds for long.

Out at sea the waves grew mightily, roiled by the fast heavy particles raining down from space. Many of the attacking boats had turned back or sank, with hundreds of men lost. Atlantis transported thousands of men who would have otherwise drowned, and cared for them aboard the vessel. She also reached out to save others—a muddy lot—from the disaster-ridden shoreline across the way.

Meanwhile, Atlantis herself remained unhurt by the torrent of energy from space, which again slid down her sides and ricocheted in all directions—causing yet more damage to the army remnants and the populations on the two continents to the east.

Knowing it would be safer for the planet and its inhabitants if she left, Atlantis suddenly shot upward into the sky and on into space. Without Atlantis there to protect her, the Rebel-directed energy weapons quickly razed the island itself to a submerged mound of rubble.

Atlantis considered abandoning the solar system entirely at this point, but Perse himself cut off that option.

φ

Atlantis began her broadcast: "Perse is in the attacking force in his planetbuster—" seconds before the shock of an enormous power ray brought Atlantis to a near stop while pummeling her over and over. Everyone grabbed on to something as the huge ship shook like a maraca.

"It's holding," Maitreya reported. "The shield is not letting Atlantis be destroyed."

"Yes," Atlantis wheezed, "the shields can withstand even Perse's planetbuster. But it does make it hard to move out of this system rapidly."

Atlantis continued moving below light speed—a petty pace relative to her full capacity—while a swarm of Rebel ships closed around her and shot off their own firepower. Still, Atlantis held together and swam slowly toward the periphery of the solar system and up out of the plane of the ecliptic.

"Look!" Templegard shouted and pointed at a viewscreen. "Perse has taken his fire off of Atlantis and is turning his aim toward Earth."

They looked at each other, knowing what they had to do. Atlantis dropped her shields and laid the vessel open to be instantly vaporized.

Perse stopped firing at Earth. He had already, in the first second or two, created a huge slice, which today is known as the Grand Canyon and is visible from space. In just a few more seconds, he would have split the Earth in two, like an apple, which he hadn't really wanted to do— he wanted Earth and had invested a lot of time and trouble in getting it. Now that he had it, more or less, he wanted to preserve it. But he would have sacrificed Earth had Atlantis called his bluff and not sacrificed herself to save Earth. He knew his game would go on forever, sadly, bitterly, so he had all the time in the world, and if he had to start all over on some other planet, it would just be another predictable annoyance.

Down on the ground, Athenius, with the help of other still able-bodied men, had rescued Ares and whomever else they could from the sea, and then from the horror of the land of death and mud. Now, in a small band, they set out to trudge back to Hellas.

The men carried and attended to the still unconscious General, along with several others. The journey would be difficult but the ubiquitous Athenius supported people, gave orders, and did a lot of the hardest work himself, setting the best possible example. Some died but he saved as many as he could.

A hero's welcome awaited them at Polis. The Rebels had leaked their own version of the story to the Hellenes and Parsans, extolling Ares and Athenius as the heroes who had destroyed Atlantis. The story went something like this:

"They fought with valor and overcame impossible odds. They literally freed all of the tribes from a powerful invader. Then something—perhaps some last cruel trick of the Atlanteans, some secret weapon though too late to save Atlantis—exploded, creating earthquakes and floods, and almost all of our warriors sank into the earth. Only these few, Ares, Athenius and the others, survived. Their names will be known down through the generations as the heroes who saved the world."

Later, the name of the city of Polis would be changed to Athens, in honor of Athenius. Ares would live on in legend as an Olympian god, the god of war.

Many great and wonderful deeds are recorded of your state in our histories. But one of them exceeds all the rest in greatness and valour. For these histories tell of a mighty power which unprovoked made an expedition against the whole of Europe and Asia, and to which your city put an end. This power came forth out of the Atlantic Ocean, for in those days the Atlantic was navigable; and there was an island situated in front of the straits which are by you called the Pillars of Heracles; the island was larger than Libya and Asia put together, and was the way to other islands, and from these you might pass to the whole of the opposite continent which surrounded the true ocean; for this sea which is within the Straits of Heracles is only a harbour, having a narrow entrance, but that other is a real sea, and the surrounding land may be most truly called a boundless continent. Now in this island of Atlantis there was a great and wonderful empire which had rule over the whole island and several others, and over parts of the continent, and, furthermore, the men of Atlantis had subjected the parts of Libya within the columns of Heracles as far as Egypt, and of Europe as far as Tyrrhenia. This vast power, gathered into one, endeavoured to subdue at a blow our country and yours and the whole of the region within the straits; and then, Solon, your country shone forth, in the excellence of her virtue and strength, among all mankind. She was pre-eminent in courage and military skill, and was the leader of the Hellenes. And when the rest fell off from her, being compelled to stand alone, after having undergone the very extremity of danger, she defeated and triumphed over the invaders, and preserved from slavery those who were not yet subjugated, and generously liberated all the rest of us who dwell within the pillars. But afterwards there occurred violent earthquakes and floods; and in a single day and night of misfortune all your warlike men in a body sank into the earth, and the island of Atlantis in like manner disappeared in the depths of the sea. For which reason the sea in those parts is impassable and impenetrable, because there is a shoal of mud in the way; and this was caused by the subsidence of the island.

—Plato, *Timaeus*

13

Nastassia came to life in a familiar location but a strange situation. She found herself on Layla and Melchizedek's beautiful beach, on their fantasy planet with its several colorful moons in the sky, including the one with rings. Off in the distance, Atlantis shone. She recognized the beach and sensed the presence of her four friends. At the same time, she realized she somehow still wore her most recent human body—except half of her body lied in one place on the beach and half in another, as if cut in half at the waist.

As the scene clarified, she identified it as an elaborate joke, which she knew Maitreya often played to lighten even the saddest moments. Superimposed on the beach scene she saw a theater, and herself onstage with Maitreya, and the others in the entourage seated in the audience. Dressed as a stage magician, with her as his assistant, Maitreya held a magic wand. He had just sawed her in half, and had spread apart the two boxes containing her body halves, to the amazement of the audience—still stunned from having been vaporized. It took a moment for them to reorient, the way it had for Nastassia.

"And now, for my next trick..." Maitreya announced, referring to the failure down on Earth—the demise of Atlantis—and taking full responsibility for it in his humorous way.

The theater faded and the Agents found themselves lying on the beach in their bubble bodies, recovering. First to take on a human form, Melchizedek appeared in his favorite male body, and Layla followed a moment later, appearing in her favorite female body. They enjoyed appearing this way in their vacation reality. They rolled over and embraced.

Templegard, thus inspired to take on his own human form, appeared as a youngish tough guy with a stubbly face and hair casually falling on his forehead. He smiled engagingly at Nastassia, who materialized in a bodily form looking a lot like Neva. He reached over and drew her closer, kissing her gently.

Layla whistled and then called, "Hey, Atlantis, is that you?" but no answer came. From her viewpoint, Atlantis looked like one of those trees that some northern Earth human tribes liked to decorate at the winter solstice.

Maitreya shared his ponderings about Atlantis. "I still have never found out what happens with artificial intelligences. I wonder, do they reincarnate the way we do, or need to be repaired, or what?"

"I guess The Great Being put the image of Atlantis over there to cheer us up," Melchizedek intuited. "So then, what do we do now?"

Maitreya followed suit with the others and donned a human body, if only to be polite. He reappeared as himself but dressed as the King of Atlantis, covered in a magnificent outfit made mostly out of colorful feathers.

"Well, that last episode ties the game," he declared. "The straight-out warfare option is now closed off forever. Perse knows that we know he will destroy the Earth rather than give it up in battle. He's laid it out for us: we'll have to sacrifice ourselves in any future battle so as to save the Earth. Kind of a stalemate."

"Then, what's left for us to do next?" Templegard asked.

Maitreya seemed to be thinking, which meant he didn't know. They all wondered if they'd be shown a sign. But rather than thinking, Maitreya prayed for an answer.

Vamping for his mentor, Melchizedek summed up the situation. "Earth humans are being systematically enslaved by their Rebel masters, who train them as warriors by means of incessant war. They're further enslaved by their Rebel-altered, overly-helpful and meddling brains, which act as automatic dog collars to keep them distracted from—and eager to run away from—whatever is going on inside themselves. So, they focus outwardly on their senses, material things, and pleasures. They have no sense of connection with each other or with The One, and so they're naturally competitive."

"Easy to manipulate," Layla added.

The answer to Maitreya's prayer came—as usual, through someone. His star pupil, Melchizedek, had helped midwife the answer, which arose from the place in his gut that channeled the most realistic intuitions.

Maitreya read Melchizedek's mind and gave voice to the solution. "The only possible strategy left to us is to educate a few of the most able people to lead the others out of this dual enslavement."

"Like the emissaries we sent out in our last two missions," Layla suggested.

Maitreya nodded. "Yes, that's the only approach left to us. The only question is whether The Great Being will back off on miracles or not—whether Earth will remain a mystery planet, whereby we're back to the original rules of the Lost Lamb Game, no miracles, no interventions."

That left them all musing.

Alone among them, Maitreya had visited many alternate futures on other Missions, although he didn't talk about his experiences. He had yet to visit a future in which they won. Still, in his heart he knew victory would ultimately prevail. As he reminded himself often, *one's toe cannot take over the whole of a being, and one's own Self sent out on a journey could not in the end come back and destroy oneself.*

Or could it? he asked himself. He'd have to think long and hard on that question.

"This approach is going to take a very long time to really work," Templegard said evenly. Maitreya and Melchizedek nodded in unison.

"It's a race between education and enslavement," Nastassia posited.

φ

Circa 2100 BCE

The Rebels had seized control everywhere, which made Agent operations far more difficult than ever before. Only Melchizedek would be risked for this particular Mission; the other Agents would remain in their spirit bodies.

Melchizedek had a humble birth in a small desert oasis, far from the big cities. From a very early age, he began a lifetime of conquering and reconquering the brain that came with the human body. As planned, no one noticed him as anyone of importance.

Tragically, a very high being on his way to Earth to play a central role in the new strategy wouldn't be as fortunate. Rebel spies had positioned themselves everywhere in Earth's solar system and little escaped their notice.

But now Templegard and Nastassia, in their bubble bodies, played the role of spies in the great palace of Ur. They operated in stealth mode to avoid detection by the disembodied Rebels guarding their human puppet and beneficiary, Nimrod—the most powerful man on Earth, ruler of Ur in Chaldea, later to be known as Iraq.

Nimrod, completely unaware of the Rebels manipulating him, believed his size, strength, and iron will alone had brought him to the position he held. And indeed, those qualities did help him stand out as the one the Rebels chose to give such power.

The Agents had never seen anything as lavish and ornate as the palace of Ur—not on any planet, nor in any other plane of existence save Heaven itself. Fine artists had wrought splendor all over the beautiful city, reaching an apex in the palace and in the ziggurat temple. Equally opulent, Nimrod clad himself in fur-trimmed purple robes and much priceless jewelry, though the cut of what he wore still bore the look of a warrior, his fundamental core.

De Agostini Picture Library

The Great Ziggurat of Ur

A third of the human race at that time specialized in war, ruling over the other two thirds, which joined in fighting whenever needed. Most of the people on the enslaved planet, being ignorant of their slave status, thus served the Rebel cause well.

φ

"I don't like that news!" Nimrod roared.

His seers cringed. They'd seen messengers and viziers who brought bad tidings often killed. The three who prostrated before him now—the bravest of the magi—had divined the coming occurrence. Actually, while the astrologers watched the stars, Rebels had planted the news in their minds of the impending birth of his follower Terah's son, who would become even greater than Nimrod. Other sages had refused to say a word to Nimrod about what they saw, but these three felt their duty required them to bring this important news to the King—even if they might be slain for uttering it.

Nimrod stood up and paced around the magi on the marble floor. They waited to be smitten by his huge jeweled rod, but he didn't strike them. His manner became cunning.

"Have my good friend Terah bring me this new son as soon as he's born, and I'll kill him with my own hands," Nimrod decreed.

φ

Layla had planted the idea in Terah's mind, and he ran with it. He brought a newborn baby boy to his master, who rewarded him with even more wealth and power than he'd ever before given his loyal supporter. Terah didn't have to pretend tears; they gushed as he tore his robe and pulled hair from his head watching Nimrod slay the baby with his bare hands. The heartless ruler then threw the lifeless carcass, splattering blood across the tiled marble floor.

The child of one of Terah's most faithful servants did not even scream, as Layla protected it from fear and pain during the awful event, and then took special loving care of the baby's departing soul.

Maitreya hovered nearby as servants secretly carried the intended son, Abram, to a cave where he would spend the first ten years of his life.

The infant had a generally serene nature, but when left alone hungry in the cave, he would cry interminably for food and company. The Agents never left Abram really alone, spending much time communicating with him telepathically, though he never became specifically aware of them. They helped set his mind on a course of meditation and contemplation, and he would gradually grow to use his mind with great logic.

As soon as he could crawl, Abram began to spend time just outside the cave, looking up at the stars and the daytime sky. He worshipped the stars, sensing their greatness; but when they went away in the morning, he realized—wordlessly, of course—there must be something even more powerful that overshadowed them. At first, he thought it must be Sol, the local star, which appeared so much larger and couldn't be looked at directly. But then Sol went away at night, so it couldn't be the most powerful either.

From these early thoughts and feelings, Abram derived the certainty that one most powerful thing must be supporting and behind everything else, and he dedicated his existence to this one thing.

The years rolled by, with infrequent visits from Terah and Amsalai, Abram's parents, being ever-conscious of the King's pervasive spies. Terah and Amsalai loved the boy, and Abram himself bestowed his abundant love on the servants who fed him as well as on the animals outside the cave, who didn't fear or attack him. Abram's wider explorations—often in the dark, for he had come to intuit that his parents had kept him hidden from something—made him strong in body and courageous.

When it appeared that Nimrod had forgotten the specific incident of slaying the baby—for many such ghastly events had gone down before and since—the Agents guided Abram to the tent of relatives far from the city, as The First Son had directed. Meanwhile, the Great Being informed Abram's parents of this move. Terah and Amsalai believed in the existence of many gods and so, when they heard the voice of a higher being in their minds—though astonished—they took it to be one of the gods they knew. But the event changed them: they had never realized the gods would ever communicate directly with them.

Still in his bubble body, Maitreya took human form temporarily to introduce Abram to his kin. He asked for their help in teaching the boy to speak, read, and write Hebrew (then called The Holy Language), Aramaic, and Akkadian, to which they agreed with no reservation. They sheltered and fed the boy for several years before bringing him to his parents' home in the dead of night, and then slipping unseen out of the city themselves.

Terah and Amsalai, along with Abram's brothers Haran and Nahor, his sister Sarai, and Lot—Haran's son and thereby Abram's nephew though about his same age—took him in with great love. His homecoming became the greatest joy any of them had ever experienced. They couldn't believe their good fortune that Nimrod and his spies apparently took no notice of these goings-on. In reality, the Agents had worked hard to cloud the minds of many Rebel-backed humans who might have otherwise discovered Abram's return.

φ

A quart of camel spit, about a yard long, whipped around and splattered Abram's face as he came up alongside Lot, mounted on his camel, Meherah—the front-runner who loved to set the early pace so that none could catch him. Abram felt sure that God had guided his hands to bring his camel, Ruach, up on the left, the rail—the way nobody ever tried to pass because the leader could easily slam them against the rail, which could break the rider's left leg. This time, however, Abram and Ruach managed to pass before Lot could even realize what had happened. If they'd come up and passed on the right, both knew Lot would have whacked Ruach in the face with his switch, which camels do not appreciate.

Abram used the name God to describe The One Self inhabiting all beings and all things. He'd heard the word "God" in his mind long before his move from the cave and the beginning of his human education. His relatives Noam, Ham, and Shem had found it curious that Abram, having grown up in virtual isolation, seemed to already know so many of the things they set out to teach him.

Lot punched Abram in the upper arm as his way of congratulating him for having won again. With Abram riding her, Ruach won races regularly against the fastest male camels. Abram credited God with guiding them to victory.

"Which god?" people would ask and Abram would just smile. Most people, it seemed, thought in terms of endless gods, and he didn't have the slightest idea how he could ever explain it to them. *There is only one God.*

The boys washed down their steeds and fed them before leaving the great race track of Ur, which they had the privilege of using as a family under Nimrod's personal protection. Nimrod hadn't made any connection in his mind between the new teenager from Terah's larger family, who moved in from the desert, and the infant he'd killed with his bare hands.

The camels seemed to be smiling. They loved to run, and they found cooperating with humans in a game to be intriguing, at least at their young camel age. So, they pranced with a lively step back to the shop where Abram would greet and serve customers today.

As they passed the great ziggurat, Abram got the same amazing feeling he always had near the huge pyramid temple. He dreamed about mounting its steps to see God at the top. In his dreams, as he neared the top, the bright light from above became so blinding that he had to look away—like the sun but much brighter.

Abram had overheard in the market that the top of the towering ziggurat stayed dry even in the last Great Flood. He'd learned that the Euphrates and Tigris had often flooded together—though so long ago that nobody knew the last time it had happened—causing widespread extinctions in centuries past. Hailed as the most amazing work of architecture in the known world, Rebels had secretly helped in the design and construction of the Ziggurat of Ur.

Abram became fascinated by what little he knew factually of such things while somehow feeling a direct connection with them—a native sensing of his oneness with The Great Being. Unbeknownst to him, he experienced more of that sensing than any previous human on Earth.

φ

As Lot and Abram passed the harbor, a breeze off the Gulf of Perse cooled the camels' windward sides, and they preened their coats and nuzzled each other in sheer enjoyment. Abram smelled spices from the Greek and Phoenician ships and wondered about the exotic places they'd traveled to, far off to the east, to bring back such cargo. The wind bore the sounds of sailors' voices, calling instructions to one another as they unloaded onto the docks. With his knowledge of languages, Abram could make out a few words here and there.

Near the shop, they ran into Abram's five-year-old sister, Sarai, perched confidently on her own young camel. The camels greeted each other, and Ruach held her face up for Sarai to pet. Camels could be affectionate with Sarai and so could people—she'd been so charming and bright since birth that she seemed to be an adult already, temporarily masquerading as a little girl. Her natural beauty also played its part. Abram loved her from the day he met her back in the cave, when his parents had briefly showed him his infant sister before slipping away.

"He won again, huh?" she teased Lot.

"How did you know?" Lot asked, slightly irked.

"When you win, I can see, even from far away—your face shines like the sun." They all laughed.

Sarai had raced with them but so far had never won. She rode with them a bit further and then she and Lot went off to play on their camels. Abram waved and then turned off to head up the lane leading to the shop, his turn to play shopkeeper being today. Not his favorite pastime.

He hitched Ruach, then carefully opened the wooden lock with the wooden key he kept close so as not to lose it. No one else in Ur had such a contraption; having it allowed his father to sleep at home rather than having to guard the shop at night, which had been the case years ago. The last time Terah visited Egypt, his friend, the Pharaoh, gave him the wooden lock to protect the valuable statuary in the idol shop from thieves. Nimrod's well-known protection of Terah, however, actually afforded even more safety for the shop's contents than the lock.

Abram sat on a somewhat comfortable high stool as he waited for the first patrons. His first customer, an older man who smiled and said hello as he entered, spent time reverently relating to each idol in the first room. Taking his time, he made his way into the next room and did the same ritual. Following Terah's guidelines, Abram checked in on the gentleman after a while, mostly to make sure all the idols still perched in their places and none had found their way under the man's fringed linen garment. The fact that the man wore linen indicated wealth, so this customer would likely purchase something.

Eventually, the man picked out a very expensive piece, and indicated his choice to Abram, still not daring to touch the idol—a statue of Nimrod, considered God incarnate by most including himself. The shop's collection featured many Nimrods, though the man had selected the most expensive statue in the shop. No one knew how inexpensively Terah manufactured or otherwise came by the idols; he always told stories of the high cost of tracking them down in his far-flung travels and the dangers he faced to bring them back to Ur for sale in his shop.

"Are you sure you need this?" Abram asked.

This shocked the man, being unaccustomed to shopkeepers talking customers out of buying.

"You know this is just a piece of carved stone, don't you? There is no god or magic in it," Abram went on.

The man couldn't speak, his face ashen. This sounded like treasonous talk, and he didn't want to be implicated in anything like that. Nimrod had informers everywhere, and even this child might be trying to trick him—had he said anything recently that sounded anti-establishment? Could this be a trap being laid for him? He rushed out of the store without a further word.

Abram smiled and went back to his stool, contented with his way of keeping shop in the idol store. Terah knew that Abram didn't believe in idols, but he never suspected Abram would handle the task of shop keeping in this way. The day went on in like manner, as they always did when Abram had to take his turn at the shop.

Late in the day, a poor woman came in to look at the idols. Abram recognized her as a regular customer, though she could never afford to buy anything. He always permitted her to visit anyway. Her eyes widened with awe as she studied each idol, seemingly praying to them, which made Abram slightly nauseous. He knew that a real God existed, but not in these idols.

"Do you know that these figurines can't help you?" Abram asked gently. "They're not the real God."

The woman didn't seem to understand Aramaic. Abram tried a few other languages but she simply stared at him.

Perhaps she's deaf, he thought to himself.

A short while later, he noticed she'd left. He looked around to make sure she hadn't stolen anything. She hadn't. Then he noticed the woman had left a small piece of bread next to one of the idols in the inner room, which stunned him. This woman, probably starving, had taken bread she could have eaten and instead placed it as a tribute next to a counterfeit god. Something snapped that had built up in Abram for a long time.

He found a hammer among the tools used to repair damaged statues, and then began destroying the idols in a frenzied dance that left him breathless. The largest Nimrod statue had a hand held out palm up, and he placed the hammer there. He sat back down on his stool and caught his breath. He hadn't broken all of the idols in the shop, but he couldn't begin to estimate the monetary value he had obliterated. He felt bad for Terah, whom he loved. But at the same time, he felt he'd done what he needed to do.

When Terah arrived and saw the scene, his knees went weak. In his mind, he counted up the cost, thinking about how long it would take to create substitute inventory, and how much of a loss he'd claim. In his heart, he felt hurt that Abram would have done this to him after Terah had risked his own life and everyone else's in the family to protect Abram.

"What have you done?!" he wailed to Abram.

Abram felt Terah's pain, but with the toughness of a fifteen-year-old young man—and the strength of his convictions—he stood and faced his father.

"An old, very poor, woman came in and gave a piece of bread to the idols. Then the idols began to argue about which one had the right to take the first bite. The big Nimrod next door insisted that the first bite rightfully belonged to him, and a horrible quarrel ensued, in which the big Nimrod grabbed a hammer and broke the others that dared to argue with him."

Terah stared blankly at Abram.

"What are you trying to pull?" Terah implored. "These idols cannot think, move, or eat!"

"Do your ears hear what your mouth speaks?" Abram challenged Terah. "If they have no power, then why do you worship them?"

φ

"What did you say?!" Nimrod demanded.

The officer trembled as he fought to contain his panic, fearing he'd be yet another messenger bearing bad news who Nimrod threw into the fire pit.

"Lord, the teenage son of Terah went mad and destroyed gods, including several statues of you. He blamed it on the largest idol of you, and had placed the hammer in its hand." The officer now had himself under control, which he achieved by accepting his fate that he would be the next to die by fire.

"Bring Terah and his guilty son to me at once," Nimrod ordered, sitting back down on his resplendent throne and emanating his fervent zeal for violence.

"There is more, Lord," the officer said bravely, knowing this would be the worst part.

"What is it?" Nimrod roared.

"The Chief Vizier has admitted he made a grievous error. He now acknowledges that the guilty boy is actually the one we all thought you killed in this room fifteen years ago." The officer struggled to maintain his dignity. "He said he now sees it clearly in the stars. Or saw it. The Vizier poisoned himself and is dead."

Lucky man, the officer thought. *Poison by one's own hand is far preferable to being thrown in the fire pit.*

But the officer remained among the living for that day. Nimrod saved up his vengeance for the pleasure of seeing Terah watch, hear, and smell his son burn slowly to death, screaming and begging as his skin crisped, losing all control as all burning men did.

φ

Nimrod noticed that the child didn't even bow as he entered, despite his father's pleadings. He bade them forward. Terah knew where to stop, and Abram followed his father's actions. The teenager's face lacked any sign of fear, which inwardly scared Nimrod for a fleeting instant; then he decided that the boy had no idea what awaited him, and his pleasure heightened.

"What's your name, boy?" Nimrod's voice boomed out despite his tenuous attempt at restraint.

"Abram," the boy replied simply. Though expected to call this man "Lord," meaning God, he had no intention to do so. As always, his fate would be entirely up to God.

Abram had never heard of the Free Will Zone, so he couldn't know that God plays by His own rules; and that since God also plays all roles, He wouldn't necessarily intercede.

Humans, Angels, Agents, and all creatures are wise to admit they can't predict what God will do. Abram didn't know either, but he assured himself by thinking, *Whatever is good enough for God is good enough for me.*

"Terah, I know you lied to me and deceived me. After all I've done to make you the wealthiest man in Chaldea, to protect you from thieves, this is how you show your gratitude," Nimrod said harshly.

Terah trembled with fear of being tortured, and couldn't speak.

"What do you worship?" Abram asked Nimrod.

Nimrod's eyes narrowed at the boy's effrontery.

"I worship myself, and fire," he hissed, salivating for the burning soon to come.

"But since water puts out fire, wouldn't it make more sense to worship water?" Abram asked.

"Sure," Nimrod quipped, half-listening. "Worship water then."

"But then water evaporates into air," Abram continued.

This confused Nimrod and got his attention, evaporation being little known at the time. But Abram had seen mist rising from water and knew what it had to mean. He spoke little about it, since he took it to be obvious.

"So, we should worship air then, shouldn't we?" Abram suggested, almost playfully.

"Worship *me* and you might live another few minutes, or even longer. You're interesting," Nimrod admitted.

Then he remembered his sages auguring that this harmless-looking yet strapping boy is destined for greatness beyond imagination. He couldn't afford to keep Abram around just for amusement. *The boy is a danger and must be killed at once,* he told himself.

"The point is, it's not any one thing we can see that we should worship," Abram said. "Clearly something greater stands behind all these things, is causing them, and so is the sole proper object of worship."

Nimrod had no appreciation for logic and these words meant nothing to him. He gave the order. His guards seized Terah and Abram and dragged them out to the fire pit, followed first by Nimrod and then, in a funeral-like procession that lengthened in the short walk from the throne room to the fire pit, hundreds of onlookers.

The fire, already blazing, sent up a dark cloud that the light wind whipped into a spiraling dance.

God, do with me as you wish, Abram prayed with equanimity.

φ

The guards threw him so strongly that he did the only thing he could do: he rolled like a ball down into the flaming pyre. The heat amazed him, and he envisioned all the hair on his body burning up immediately. He stood up in the leaping flames but felt nothing.

Hold real still, a female voice said in his mind, and he obeyed.

This isn't going to be easy, Layla signaled to Maitreya, Templegard, and Nastassia.

The four had arrayed themselves at the cardinal compass points around Abram in their invisible bubble bodies. They held the fire away from Abram with precision telekinetics, by interposing a forcefield that shielded him from the heat—a touch-and-go challenge even for the four of them combined. Though unsure whether or not they should be doing this—given the possible abandonment of miraculous intervention as a strategy after Atlantis—they followed their intuitions nonetheless.

Relax, a motherly voice said to them, and they felt The Great Being irradiating them from within. Their realization of Oneness with The Original Self felt almost palpable. Relaxing naturally, they felt buoyed up by sublime bliss, and their telekinetics effortlessly jumped many quantum levels—with The Great Being doing it all.

You can move as you like now, Abram, the voice said lovingly.

Thank you, God. Abram heard the voice and calmly responded with equal love. *And please protect my father, if it pleases you.*

Just outside the fire pit, the crowd avoided mobbing Nimrod, giving him respectful distance. But all around the fire, men elbowed their way to a better view, with some climbing onto others. The women drew back, crying instinctively.

"Now that your son is dead, Terah, you will be next," Nimrod said, playing master of the obvious.

Terah still had no control of his vocal cords, but the yells from the men closest to the fire saved him from further elongation of the bodeful conversation.

"He's alive!" one man proclaimed incredulously.

"He's walking around in there!" shouted another.

Abram waved as the guards hauled Terah forward, just behind Nimrod, whose approach parted the crowd—with one man almost falling into the fire. Nimrod saw Abram with his own eyes, wandering around complacently, seeming to be looking at the fuel under the fire in idle curiosity.

What if there is a God? Nimrod thought, shaken but already scheming. *I have to be prepared to win no matter what the truth is. Perhaps I should meet this God and charm him with my evident leadership skills, get closer to him, find his weaknesses, and exploit them to take his kingdoms too.*

Nimrod ordered his soldiers to drown the fire and then pull Abram up. This took quite a while. Eventually, Abram stood outside of the fire pit, dripping water but with all his hair intact, and looking none the worse for wear. The big smile on his face even cheered Terah, who cried with happiness and flung himself in Abram's arms. Abram kissed and hugged him tightly.

"You may return to your home in safety and we'll speak more of this later." Nimrod addressed them both, while presenting the façade to the gathered crowd of still being in charge.

Abram took Terah home, and the family celebrated that night, awed by the realization that Abram's God really existed.

On the way home, The Great Being had proposed a Covenant with Abram and his people, which included the contingency that they all had to move at once to a land The One would show Abram. This Abram announced at dinner.

φ

Abram set out for the desert and his family came along. They trusted him to know which way to go but felt relieved when they got to Haran, and didn't want to move again for a while. The One Self told Abram to go on alone, which he did, though Sarai and Lot joined him. He thought they'd never leave him.

But Lot did leave after a period of time. Abram had become embroiled in Egyptian ambitions and captained mercenary armies in their service on many military adventures—all of which he had fought on the side of justice, and all of which succeeded, making Abram very rich.

The whole scenario held no appeal for Lot. Sensing that Abram would be going on many more military adventures, whereas Lot wanted a peaceful life in a business or on a farm, he left Abram and went to live in Sodom.

Abram moved on, guided by The One Self, this time to a place called Salem. As if expecting their arrival, King Melchizedek welcomed Abram and Sarai, and treated them royally. With them invisibly, Maitreya, Layla, Templegard, and Nastassia formed a potent honor guard. They had never left Abram's side.

Not long after they arrived, the King took Abram off alone, up a long hill, almost to the top of an olive tree-covered mountain. Far from any human habitation—a wild country left to nature—they could look back the long way down to the city of Salem.

Melchizedek placed his strong hands firmly on Abram's broad shoulders. "I've been looking forward to this moment for a very long time."

Abram replied humbly, "I'm honored to be here with you, King Melchizedek."

Having incarnated about twenty years earlier than Abram, King Melchizedek had established himself throughout the Mediterranean and surrounding lands as a priest-philosopher, proclaiming there is only One God, that He/She is All-Inclusive, and that we're all part of Him/Her.

He had an uncanny knack for making friends and not making enemies, a trait most uncommon to the times. Many cities had asked him to be their King, but he had for some reason chosen Salem rather than Babylon, Ur, or the other much larger cities whose people had reached out to him. Melchizedek had become known as the most trusted man in the world by the time Abram and Sarai arrived.

Now Melchizedek and Abram stood and looked out at the vast panoramas from their position high up the mountain.

"There's so much to see in every direction from right here," Abram observed.

"This is where your people will erect a great temple of worship for all peoples," Melchizedek revealed.

Abram stared at him and felt icy fingers up his spine.

Semi-transparent walls resolved into existence around them, with beautiful colors favoring variations of yellow, orange, gold, and light blue. Seen in a transparent view, the enormous structure included fortresses, temples, courts, and a built-in city, all surrounded by walls far away down the hill, even beyond the outskirts of Salem.

Abram had never seen an apparition before. Stunned by the life-changing experience, he knew he could never again rely solely on his senses. His assumption of materialism now broken; he stood speechless beside Melchizedek.

"This is the way it will look at one point in time. It will keep changing with the times. It will always be a place of worship for all peoples. Not just for your descendants, but for everyone," Melchizedek went on.

"Your people will build this temple," he repeated. "Then you, yourself, along with your sons, will repair another temple, far from here, which will become the holiest place on Earth to over a thousand-thousand-thousand people."

To be continued in

THE FIRST SON

There is never an End

ABOUT THE AUTHOR

Emmy® Award winner and media research industry leader, Bill Harvey has been lauded as a visionary and technological pioneer of the changing mediascape over the last 35 years.

With an imaginative, unorthodox mind for research, innovation and invention, Bill started his career in the media business. He predicted today's media reality with his *MediaWorld 1990* report to the industry and in his widely-read *Media Science Newsletter*, and he invented media research tools and measurement systems, including some now written into FCC regulations.

Bill became a leader in the field as media morphed into being more interactive, putting the viewer in charge. In 2022, Bill received an Emmy® Award for the pioneering development of technology. In practical terms, his invention helps diverse audiences with a wide range of interests to get all the types of programs they enjoy the most.

Considered the dean of living media scientists, Bill in 2008 received the Advertising Research Foundation's Great Mind Award, and in 2014 he became the first recipient of the ARF's Erwin Ephron Demystification Award. He holds four issued US patents and has consulted for over a hundred Fortune 500 companies.

Bill first experienced the Zone—that space where innovative and successful ideas and actions flow out of you effortlessly— as a young child. The son of legendary orchestra leader/emcee Ned Harvey and former Ziegfeld Follies showgirl Sandra Harvey, Bill started performing on stage at age four, dancing with showgirls and exchanging lines with comedic greats like Jack E. Leonard. He liked this feeling of being "on" and wanted to learn how to be "on" more often—and so began his lifelong quest to understand how to bring on higher states of consciousness and to help others do the same.

Earning his degree in philosophy, the first school subject he ever loved, Bill founded the Human Effectiveness Institute, with the goal of sharing the consciousness techniques he had learned and developed. Bill's ideas didn't all come from the inside, as he was inspired by something that Milton Berle once told him: "Always steal from the best, kid." His ideas were further inspired by Alan Watts, Buddhism, and Zen, and by his parents and his adopted older brother, the multitalented Bill Heyer, second trumpet in Ned's band.

Bill's first book, ***Mind Magic: The Science of Microcosmology*** (1976), was praised by thousands of readers who wrote saying their lives were changed by it. Fans included John Lennon, Ram Dass, Norman Cousins, Daniel Goleman, and Jimmy Carter. The book is now available in its 6th edition, ***Mind Magic: Doorways into Higher Consciousness*** (2012).

In his second book, ***You Are The Universe: Imagine That*** (2014), Bill speculates about the true nature of reality, in which all that exists is a single divine consciousness made of information. In this view, religion is not at odds with science. His latest book, ***A Theory of Everything including Consciousness and "God"*** draws extensively on Albert Einstein and John Wheeler to make this case.

Turning to fiction, Bill conceived an epic series of novels entitled *Agents of Cosmic Intelligence*. ***The First Son*** (2018) was the first to be released as Episode 2, covering the ancient world and its great prophets—some of whom Bill casts as cosmically-inspired Agents. ***The Message***, Episode 11, and ***Pandemonium: Live to All Devices***, Episodes 12 and 13, were published in 2022.

Bill lives with his wife Lalita in New York's beautiful Hudson Valley. He has a daughter Nicole; four grandchildren, Nicholas, Gabrielle, Jessica and Alexander; and a great-grandchild, Zara.

AGENTS OF COSMIC INTELLIGENCE
the epic adventure chronicle of the universe

Agents of Cosmic Intelligence emerges from a viewpoint in which science and religion meld into a singular explanation that makes each person a vital part of the greatest real-life adventure ever. The series is a sweeping saga that unfolds forward and backward in time to become a story of the universe, how it might have "started" and where it might be "going."

Other Books in the Series

THE FIRST SON
Episode 2 | 3067 BCE—27 AD | Published October 2018

Rebel groups form nation-states to continue the endless wars they have propagated to make Earth people the toughest fighters in the Universe, to eventually storm the gates of Heaven and take over the Multiverse entirely. The First Son and the Agents quietly build up the character of Earth humans by incarnating as great Teachers, beginning and spreading that tradition across the planet.

I love the way Harvey uses science fiction to express the deep truth of the unity of all things, and the common theme of all wisdom literature. An engaging story line and beautiful prose.

—Jim Spaeth, NY

THE MESSAGE
Episode 11 | Ca. 2035 | Published December 2022

The five Agents have all fallen asleep to their true identities. Four of them lead the U.S. Army's top-secret psychic Theta Force. Nastassia is in a rival unit in Russia. The Agents suddenly become uplifted to the highest state of consciousness they ever remember experiencing, as a result of a Message apparently from outer space that is heard by every psychic on Earth, though each one hears something slightly different.

Bold, brisk, conspiratorial psychic thriller imagines humanity's secret history. Harvey takes wild narrative risks readers will not see coming... it's the ideas that drive this series: Harvey spins a secret history of all of us, urging us to be more.

—BookLife Reviews by Publishers Weekly

PANDEMONIUM: LIVE TO ALL DEVICES
Episodes 12 & 13 | Ca. 2037 | Published June 2022

In this fast-moving thriller, a heady amalgam of hidden war, psychics, Nazis, aliens, artificial intelligence, virtual reality, and transcendental love takes place against a backdrop wherein the latest media/technology revolution triggers sudden unprecedented changes in world politics.

Harvey continually upends reader expectations…daring to go bigger and stranger, the in-the-moment suspense connected to the mind-blowingly cosmic. Pandemonium *gets wilder as it goes, with international romance and a savvy sense of how media shapes minds, nations, and history.*
>—BookLife Reviews by *Publishers Weekly*

Pandemonium is a masterful piece of cautionary fiction that will likely ring with relevance for years to come.
>—Independent Review of Books

Controlling outcomes and confronting evil has never felt so multifaceted and thoroughly engrossing.
>—Midwest Book Review

Other Books by Bill Harvey

A THEORY OF EVERYTHING
INCLUDING CONSCIOUSNESS AND "GOD"
Published June 2023

*It is long past time to discuss the ultimate questions such as
"why are we here?"*

Scientists can do much to help humanity simply by acknowledging that there is no scientific basis for ruling out the possibility that the universe is intelligent. This simple and eminently justifiable act of open-mindedness can permeate world culture, causing personal reconsideration of everything by everyone. Because it is a more positive view than materialistic accidentalism, an increase in hope and courage is a logical outcome.

In his third work of non-fiction, the author draws extensively on well-sourced quotes by Albert Einstein and John Wheeler, as well as on his own unorthodox imagination, to make his case.

I wrote this book mainly for physicists but also for everyone. I'd like physicists to accept the scientific possibility of something very much like "God", and to prioritize the subject.

—Bill Harvey

MIND MAGIC:
DOORWAYS INTO HIGHER CONSCIOUSNESS
6th Edition | Published 2012

Mind Magic: Doorways into Higher Consciousness is a guide to discovering who you really are beneath all the influences of other people and things in your life. What do you really want to do with your life? What will make you most effective and bring out your creativity in meeting life's challenges?

Reading ***Mind Magic*** is a unique experience. You glide along effortlessly, stimulated in light, sometimes humorous and often unexpected ways. It is designed to evoke your ideas, and get you thinking and acting in new ways.

There is no fixed formula for how to use ***Mind Magic***. Some people enjoy opening it to random pages, finding they get just what they need at that moment. Others read it all the way through, going back to it again and again.

Highly recommended…will loosen your moorings and open you to creative vistas.

      —Daniel Goleman, author of *Emotional Intelligence*

YOU ARE THE UNIVERSE: IMAGINE THAT
Published 2014

A theory of what the universe is, reconciling science with religion, this book shows you a way of looking at reality that changes the way you look at yourself. You see the highest use of your life. Your own life becomes more exciting and inspiring. You have new understanding of individuals and your love flows easily.

Bill shows that the precepts of the major religions find support in this theory, but in the modern age have been obstructed from communicating their true wisdom as a result of outdated language, spiritual materialism, and the forgotten ability to reach into one's own essence feelings. Unlike the unified field theories of Albert Einstein and modern unified field theorists, Bill's picture of the universe can be visualized by non-mathematicians. Anyone can test this theory by means of objective scientific experimentation.

Sheds light on humankind's ancient burning questions, which boil down to…"What's going on here?"

—Peter Sorensen, England

Praise for Bill Harvey's Books

THE FIRST SON

Action-packed sci-fi adventure of a supremely mind-blowing kind. A real page-turner, always surprising.
—Dennis, Amazon Review

In this stimulating novel, Bill Harvey takes what Aldous Huxley called The Perennial Philosophy to the next level of detail. Harvey offers an imaginative approach to the underlying dynamics of how this philosophy might have gradually permeated human thought from the Hebrew Bible, though the Mahabharata, Buddhist Sutras, the I Ching, Plato's Academy and even Christianity. Harvey accomplishes this task by integrating modern terms such as artificial intelligence...with classical concepts like avatars...bold vision.
—Mike Hess, Polymath Scientist

THE MESSAGE

Whether for its futuristic social experiments in transformation, its riveting action-packed world, or the changes characters experience in the redefinition of their perceptions and purposes—the story is complex, inviting, and hard to put down.
—Midwest Book Review

It's a pleasure to suspend your disbelief in the face of this semi-dystopian premise with a wide cast of colorful characters. Harvey isn't afraid to dig deep into a particular type of tech, an ideology, or a military procedure, and that storytelling flair for flowing in and out of detail keeps the rhythm enticing and the read addictive...A riveting addition to Harvey's enigmatic Agents of Cosmic Intelligence series.
—Independent Review of Books

Thoughtful and provocative...[Isaac] Asimov would be proud and [Neal] Stephenson will be overjoyed to have Harvey as a contemporary. —BookTrib

PANDEMONIUM: LIVE TO ALL DEVICES

A science fiction spy thriller with deep metaphysical undertones where the future of humankind is at stake. Fueled by brilliantly insightful scientific speculation...meticulously described science fiction backdrop...full of big ideas...mind-bending and thought-provoking. —BlueInk Review

The depth of psychological examination of individuals, organizations, country leaders, and worldviews makes for an outstanding enhancement of the usual sci-fi attention to action and confrontation...Gives Pandemonium *a transformative feel and quality that makes it as much an intellectual pursuit as an action-packed adventure. Bill Harvey leads readers on a satisfyingly unpredictable romp through a future world in which special interests have humanity's future in thrall...Controlling outcomes and confronting evil has never felt so multifaceted and thoroughly engrossing.* —Midwest Book Review

Plentiful and accurate projections for the future...each element is conceivable both in terms of technology and the sociology behind the ways in which it has evolved...will have readers thinking long after they close the book. With the scope of Asimov and the prescience of Bradbury, Bill Harvey makes the greats proud. —BookTrib

A THEORY OF EVERYTHING including CONSCIOUSNESS AND "GOD"

Harvey creates a thought-provoking dialogue that encourages scientists and readers alike to adopt bigger-picture perceptions of the universe's possibilities...The breadth and scope of this inquiry is unprecedented. —Midwest Book Review

MIND MAGIC

Mind Magic *is a delight. Sets forth with neat precision just how to do it [think].* —Ram Dass, author of *Be Here Now*

What sets your book apart from all others in this field...is that it is a rare combination of frontier knowledge, wisdom, and plain old-fashioned warmth...in your debt for the insights it provides. —Norman Cousins, founding editor of *Saturday Review*

Mind Magic *is an exquisite example of "transformational software'"...A practical guide for developing the power of mindfulness. The most striking thing to me about* Mind Magic *is its incredible clarity. It is a brilliant condensation of wisdom that resonates with the higher aspects of our beings and is experienced as truth...And it really works. Experience this book and share it."* —Rick Ingrasci, *New Age Journal*

[I] have given away countless copies of Mind Magic *over the years, finding used copies in bookstores when it was out of print...your book was instrumental in my own journey, and it has influenced my life and my teaching. When I first read it, it felt like I was being reminded of what I already knew but had not been able to articulate clearly. It affirmed a sense of deep truth.* —Selene Kumin Vega, Faculty, Saybrook University

YOU ARE THE UNIVERSE: IMAGINE THAT

How great it is that your book came along at this time. It's just what I asked for... a way of understanding the true nature of my self. —Richard Fusco, Music Industry Executive

Bill Harvey's writing is courageous... not just with his words but with the ideas he asks his readers to explore, which can benefit their lives. —Bob DeSena, Marketing Executive

ACKNOWLEDGMENTS

My Deepest Thanks...

To my parents Ned and Sandy, my role models for being openminded, compassionate, and generous, and for their "noble experiment" of letting me make up my own mind after hearing their inputs, from my earliest days throughout their lives.

To Bill Heyer for telling me at age 4 when I wrote my first story that I'm destined to be a writer.

To F. Scott Fitzgerald, Ernest Hemingway, Fyodor Dostoevsky, Robert A. Heinlein, and all the other writers whose work inspires me.

To my guru for showing me how an awake being behaves.

To my wife Lalita and my daughter Nicole for believing in me and helping me in every way they can at every moment, including as editors.

To my main editor Yana Lambert, and to George and Christine Niver, Nicole David and Karen Kennedy for their unstinting devotion as editors, art creators and curators, social media implementers, and in every other role bringing my work to its audience.

To my assistant Kristin Dragos for making it possible to juggle so much and still get through each day with a smile.

To Endre Balogh, who channels the enchantment of The One into multiple art forms from art to music, for his incredible cover art and his stunning visual of the city-ship Atlantis. And to fellow cosmic artist Bruce Rolff for his early inspiration.

To Harvey Kraft for teaching me the derivation of the word "Aryans".

To the world's religions for allowing me to fictionalize their work in service to making their wisdom more accessible in the present turbulent age. I set out to show that it is possible to imagine a plausible scenario in which religion is not at odds with science, and one which perhaps makes the world's present difficulties easier to understand. I feel intuitively certain that the real truth is far stranger than my story, though there are similarities.